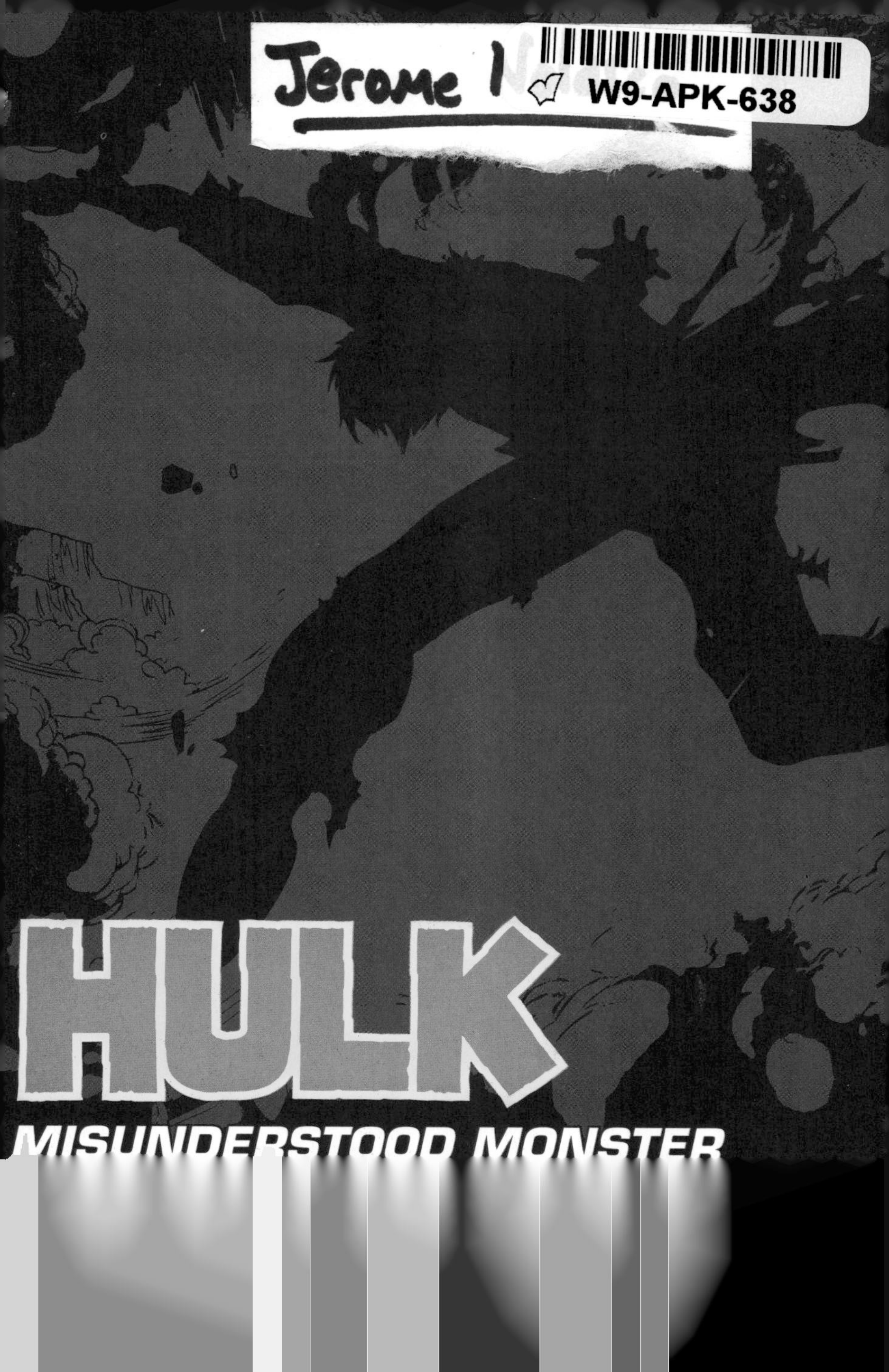

HULK

MISUNDERSTOOD MONSTER

HULK
MISUNDERSTOOD MONSTER

WRITER: PAUL BENJAMIN
PENCILERS: DAVID NAKAYAMA WITH JUAN SANTACRUZ (ISSUE #2)
INKERS: GARY MARTIN WITH RAUL FERNANDEZ (ISSUE #2)

COLORISTS: WIL QUINTANA, MICHELLE MADSEN & SOTOCOLOR'S A. STREET
LETTERER: DAVE SHARPE WITH CHRIS ELIOPOULOS

COVER ARTISTS: CARLO PAGULAYAN, JEFFREY HUET, DAVID WILLIAMS,
DAVID NAKAYAMA, CHRIS SOTOMAYOR & GURU EFX

ASSISTANT EDITORS: NATHAN COSBY & JORDAN D. WHITE
EDITOR: MARK PANICCIA

COLLECTION EDITOR: JENNIFER GRÜNWALD
ASSISTANT EDITORS: CORY LEVINE & JOHN DENNING
ASSOCIATE EDITOR: MARK D. BEAZLEY
SENIOR EDITOR, SPECIAL PROJECTS: JEFF YOUNGQUIST
SENIOR VICE PRESIDENT OF SALES: DAVID GABRIEL
BOOK DESIGNER: JOHN DAUGHERITY

EDITOR IN CHIEF: JOE QUESADA
PUBLISHER: DAN BUCKLEY

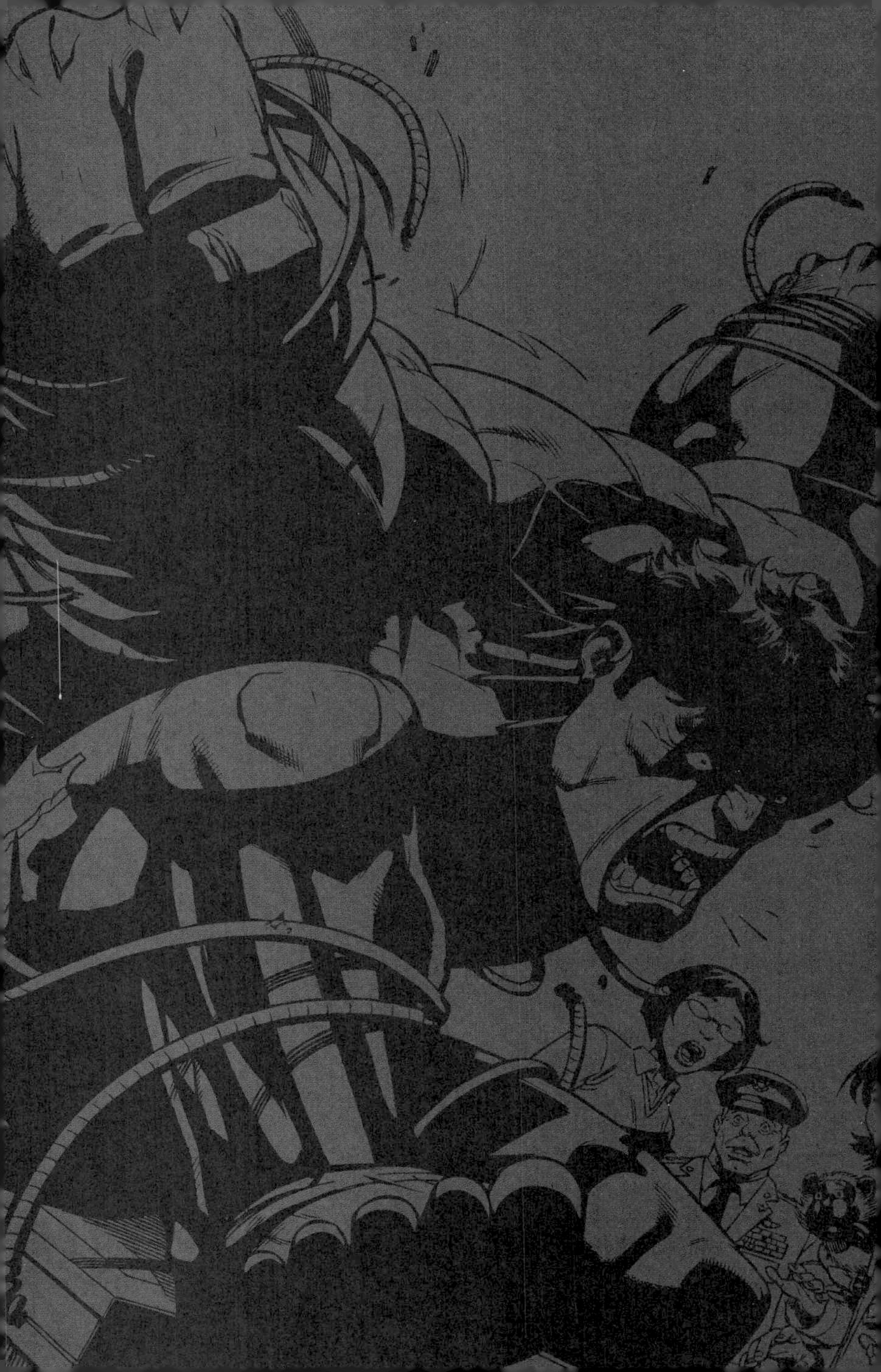

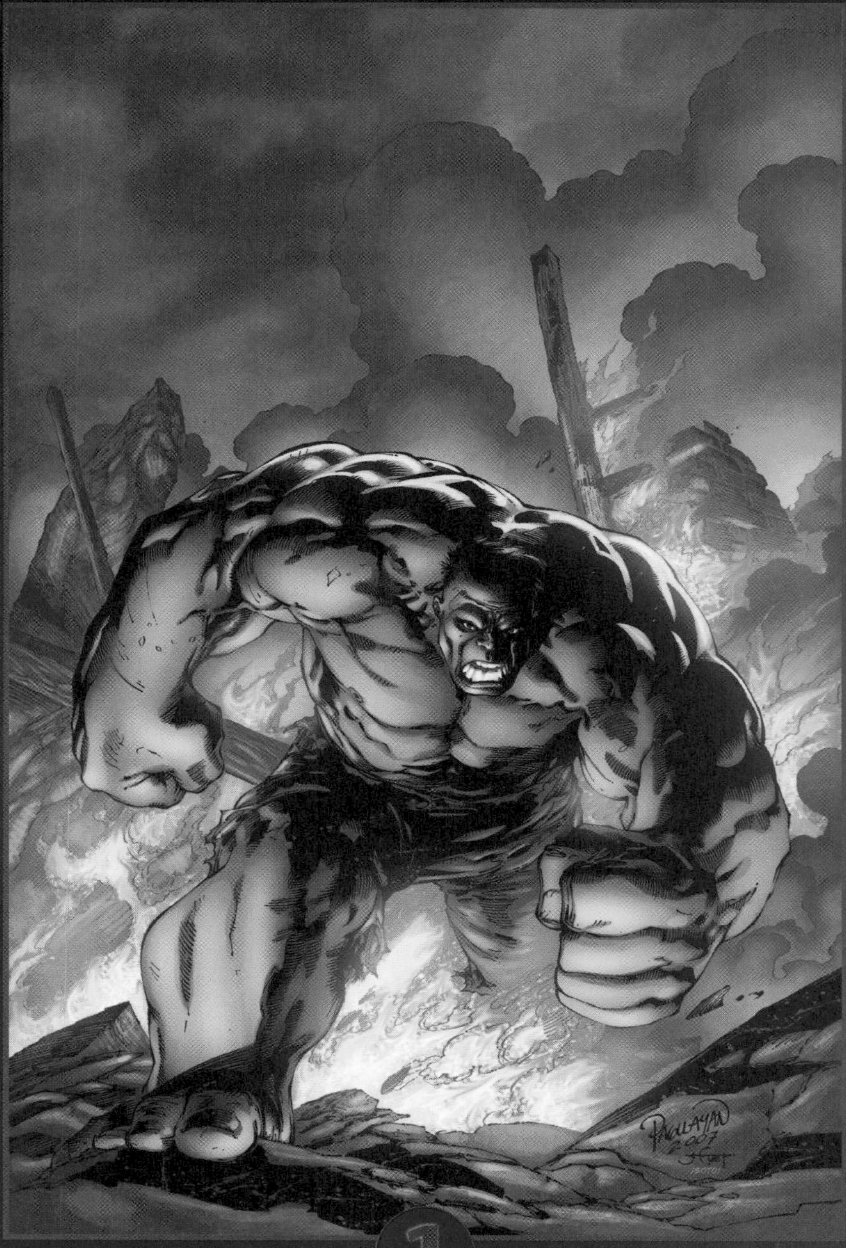

1

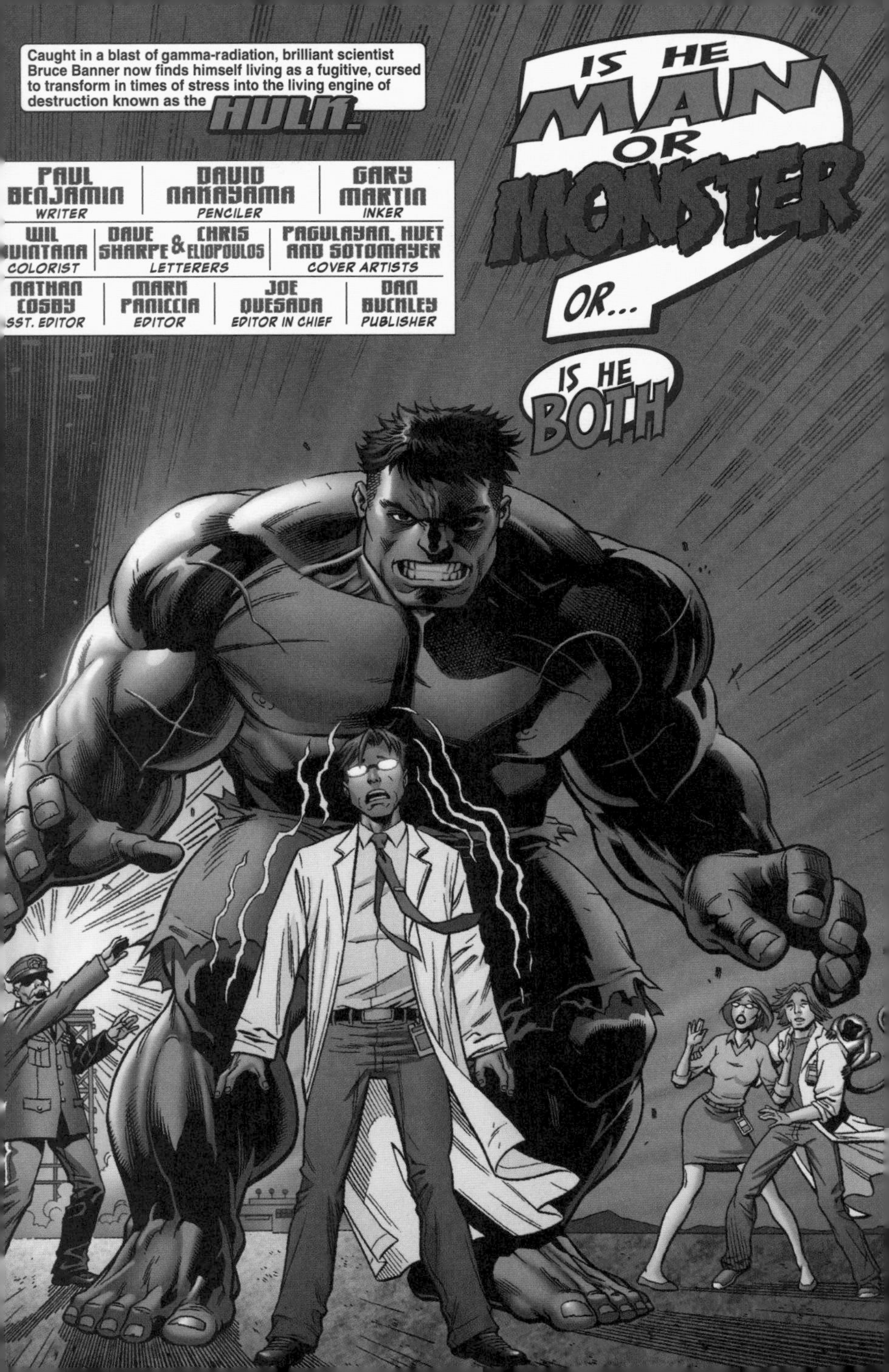
Caught in a blast of gamma-radiation, brilliant scientist Bruce Banner now finds himself living as a fugitive, cursed to transform in times of stress into the living engine of destruction known as the HULK.
IS HE MAN OR MONSTER
OR...
IS HE BOTH
PAUL BENJAMIN WRITER
DAVID NAKAYAMA PENCILER
GARY MARTIN INKER
WIL QUINTANA COLORIST
DAVE SHARPE & CHRIS ELIOPOULOS LETTERERS
PAGULAYAN, HUET AND SOTOMAYER COVER ARTISTS
NATHAN COSBY ASST. EDITOR
MARK PANICCIA EDITOR
JOE QUESADA EDITOR IN CHIEF
DAN BUCKLEY PUBLISHER

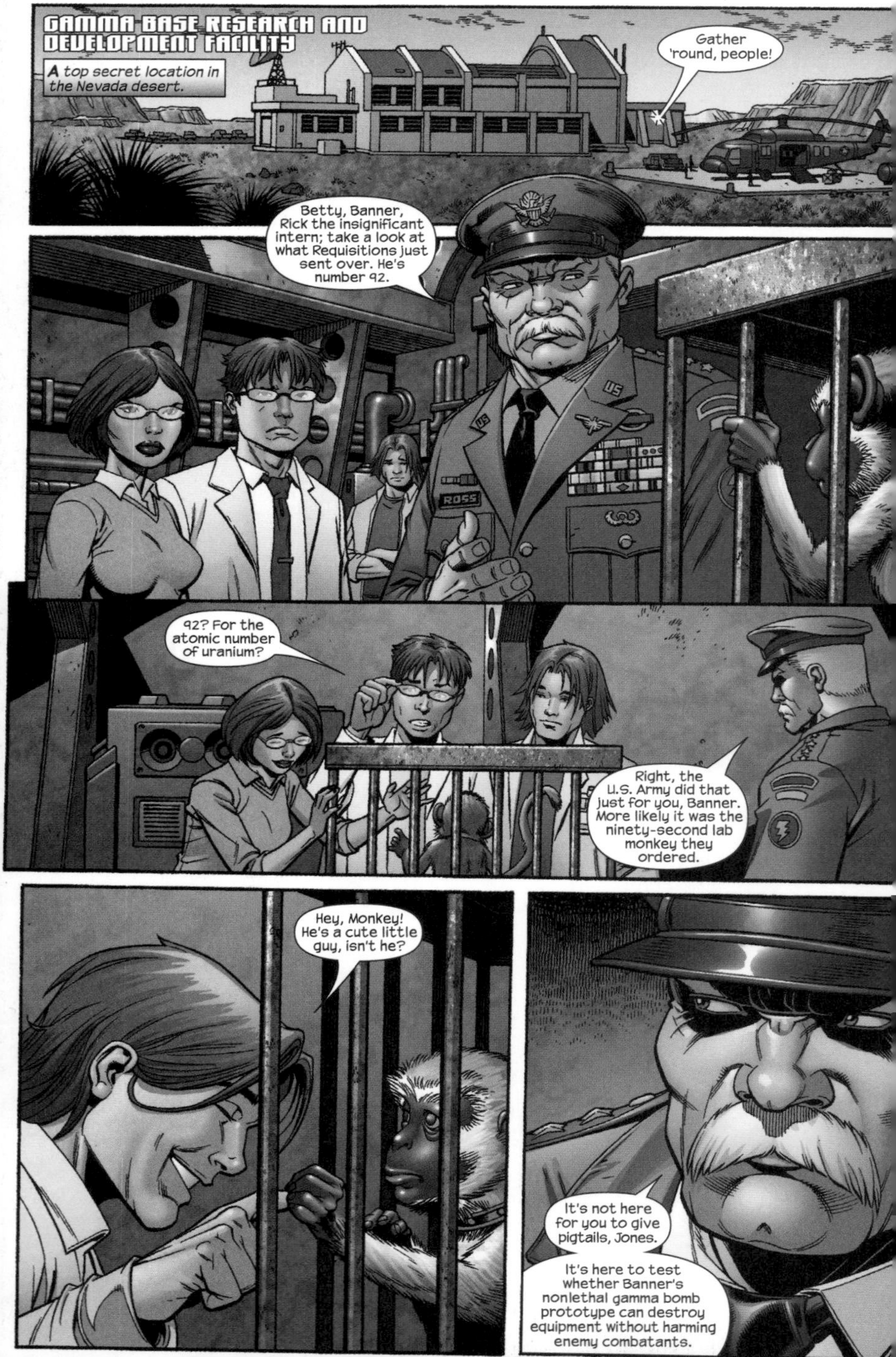
GAMMA BASE RESEARCH AND DEVELOPMENT FACILITY
A top secret location in the Nevada desert.
Gather 'round, people!
Betty, Banner, Rick the insignificant intern; take a look at what Requisitions just sent over. He's number 92.
ROSS
92? For the atomic number of uranium?
Right, the U.S. Army did that just for you, Banner. More likely it was the ninety-second lab monkey they ordered.
Hey, Monkey! He's a cute little guy, isn't he?
It's not here for you to give pigtails, Jones.
It's here to test whether Banner's nonlethal gamma bomb prototype can destroy equipment without harming enemy combatants.

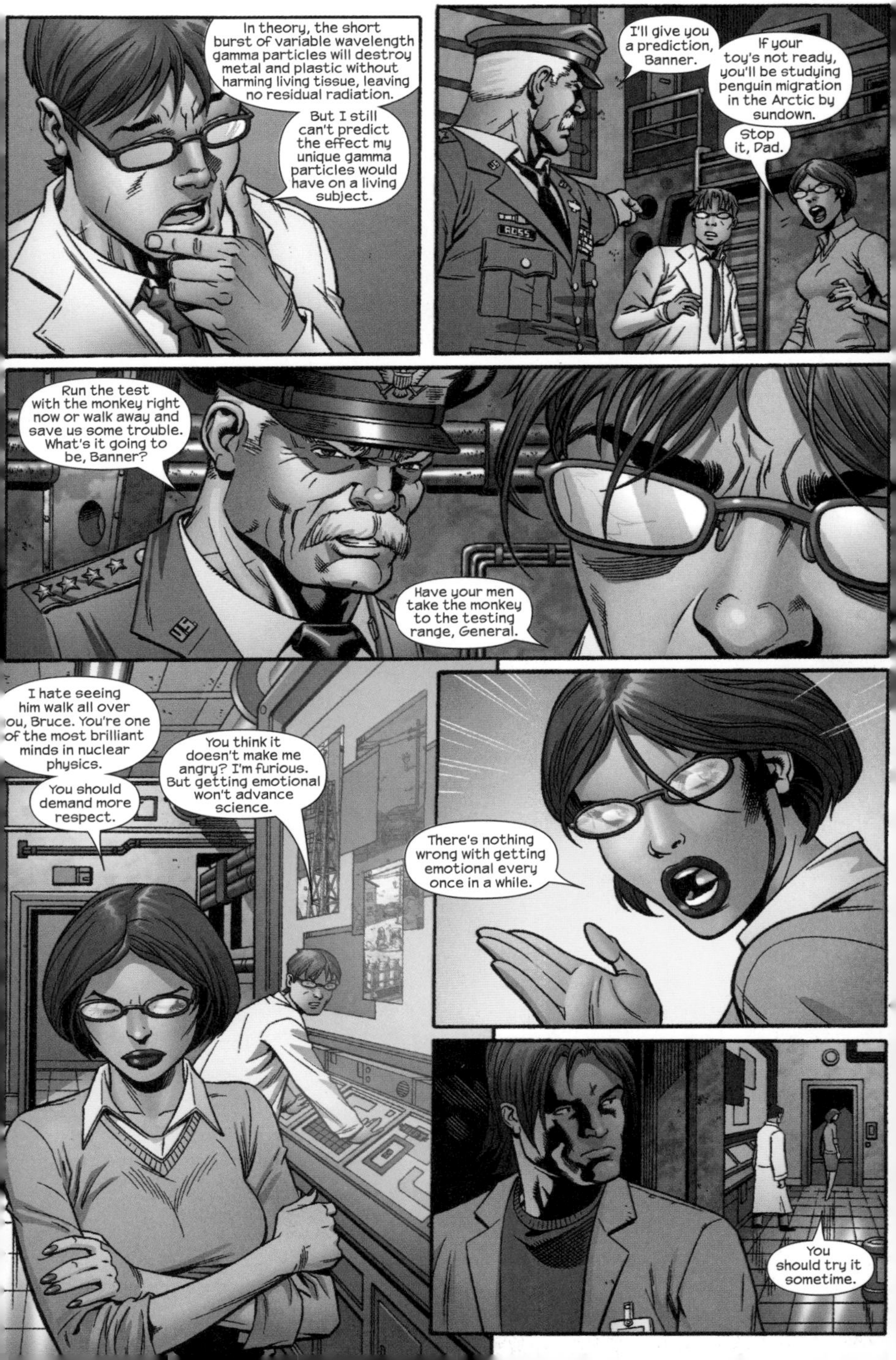
In theory, the short burst of variable wavelength gamma particles will destroy metal and plastic without harming living tissue, leaving no residual radiation.
But I still can't predict the effect my unique gamma particles would have on a living subject.
I'll give you a prediction, Banner.
If your toy's not ready, you'll be studying penguin migration in the Arctic by sundown.
Stop it, Dad.
ROSS
Run the test with the monkey right now or walk away and save us some trouble. What's it going to be, Banner?
Have your men take the monkey to the testing range, General.
I hate seeing him walk all over ou, Bruce. You're one of the most brilliant minds in nuclear physics.
You should demand more respect.
You think it doesn't make me angry? I'm furious. But getting emotional won't advance science.
There's nothing wrong with getting emotional every once in a while.
You should try it sometime.

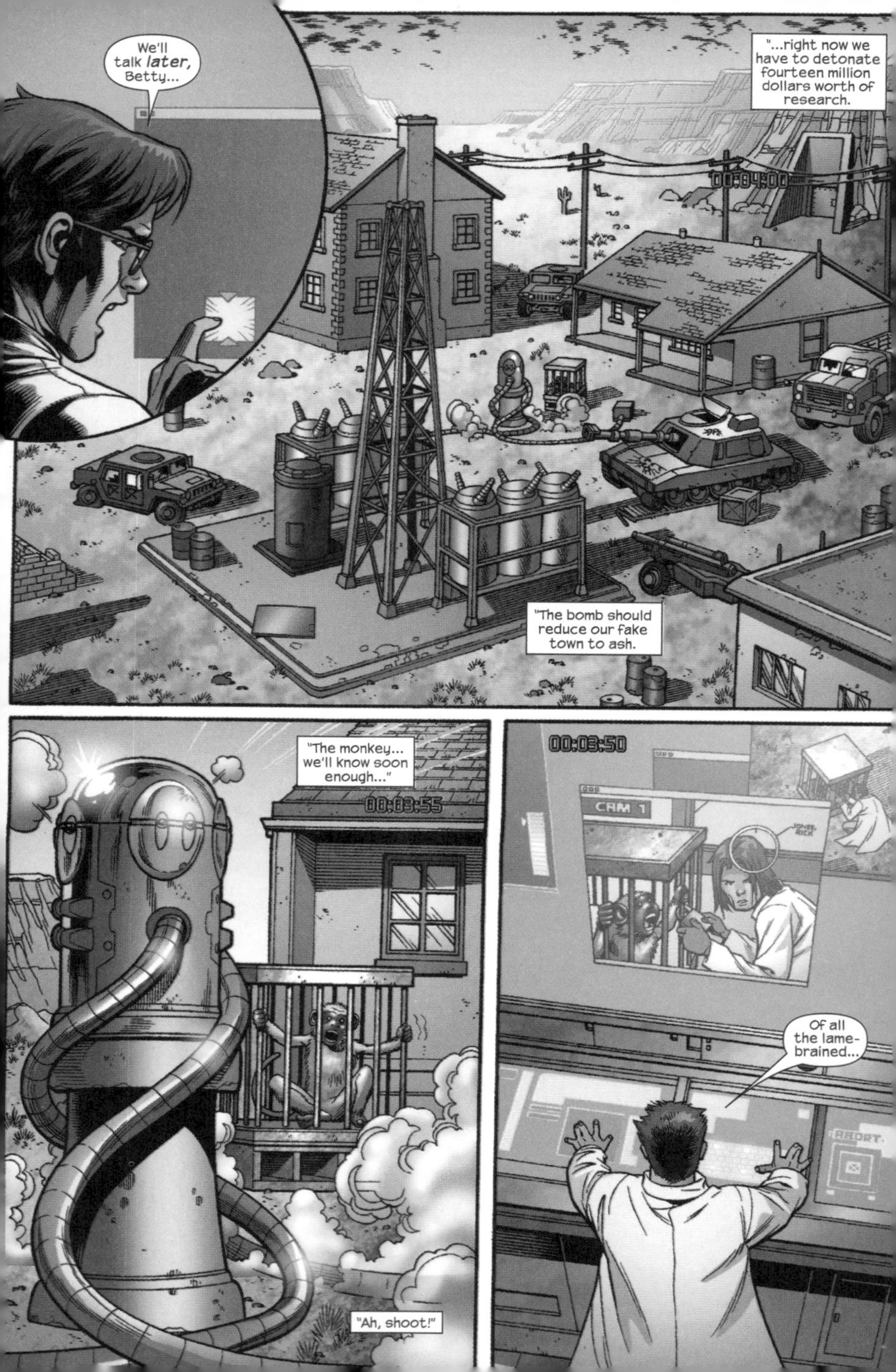

We'll talk *later,* Betty...
"...right now we have to detonate fourteen million dollars worth of research.
00:04:00
"The bomb should reduce our fake town to ash.
"The monkey... we'll know soon enough..."
00:03:55
"Ah, shoot!"
00:03:50
CAM 1
Of all the lame-brained...
ABORT

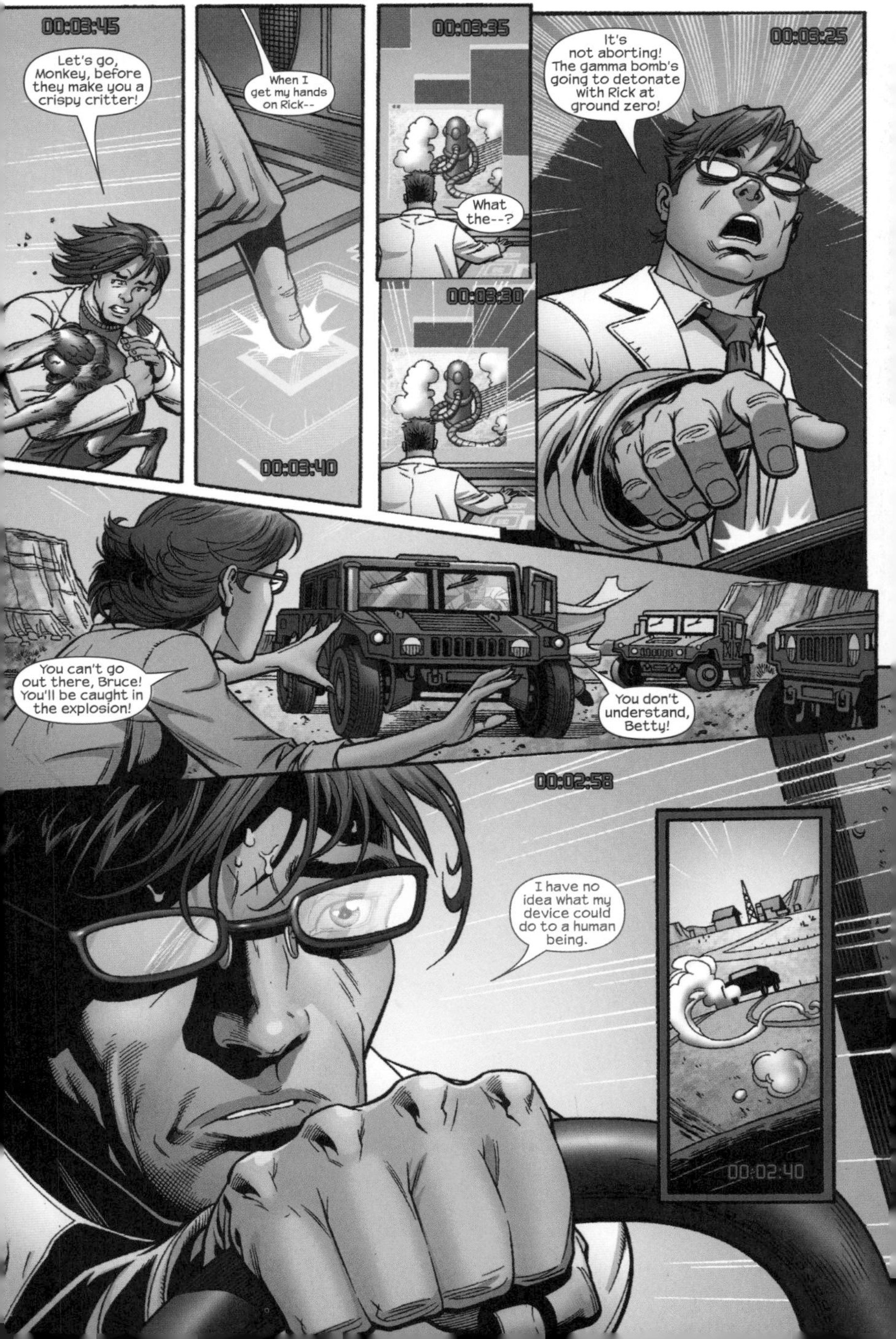
00:03:45
Let's go, Monkey, before they make you a crispy critter!
When I get my hands on Rick--
00:03:40
00:03:35
What the--?
00:03:30
00:03:25
It's not aborting! The gamma bomb's going to detonate with Rick at ground zero!
You can't go out there, Bruce! You'll be caught in the explosion!
You don't understand, Betty!
00:02:58
I have no idea what my device could do to a human being.
00:02:40

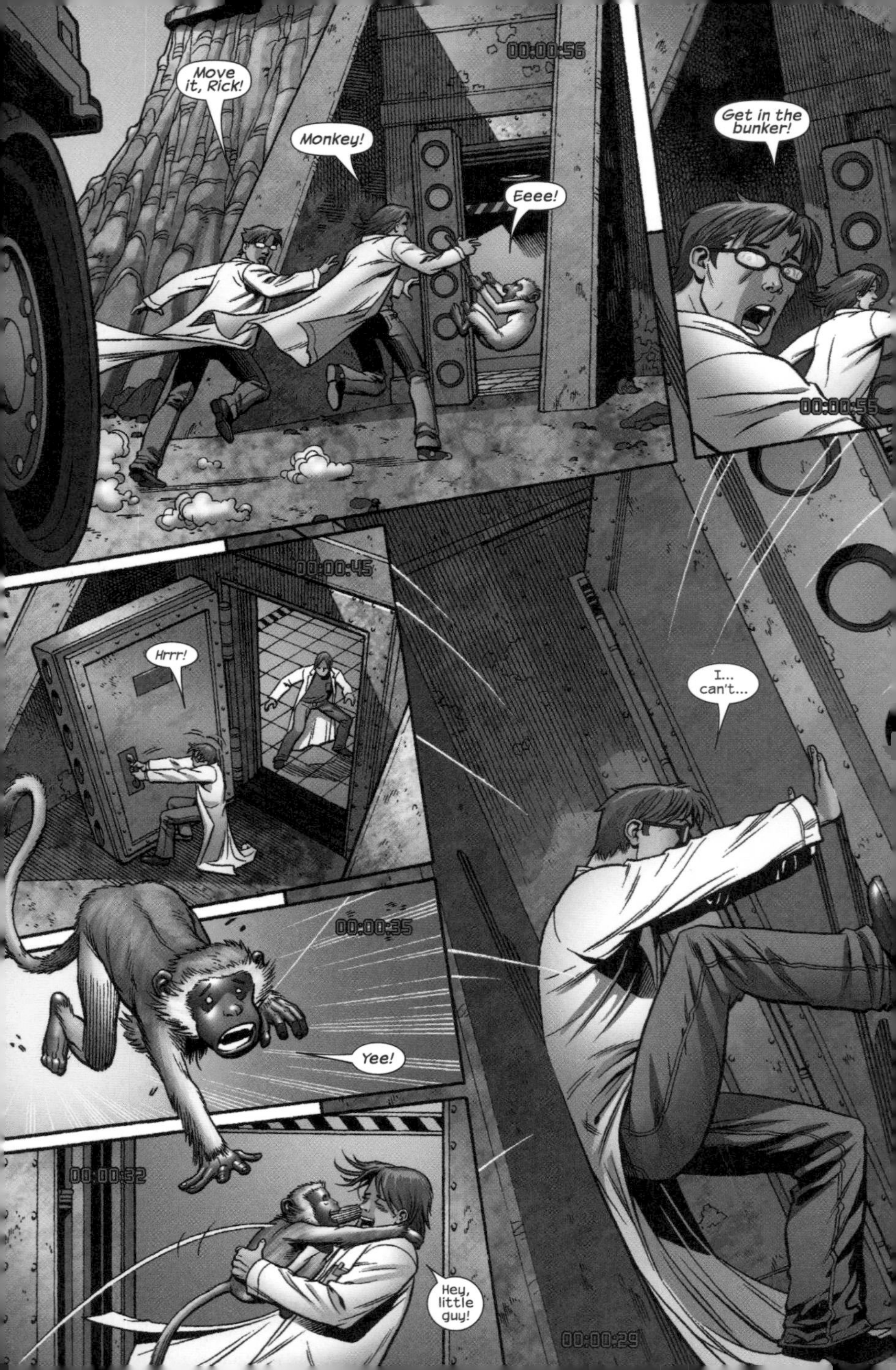
00:00:56
Move it, Rick!
Monkey!
Eeee!
Get in the bunker!
00:00:55
00:00:45
Hrrr!
I... can't...
00:00:35
Yee!
00:00:32
Hey, little guy!
00:00:29

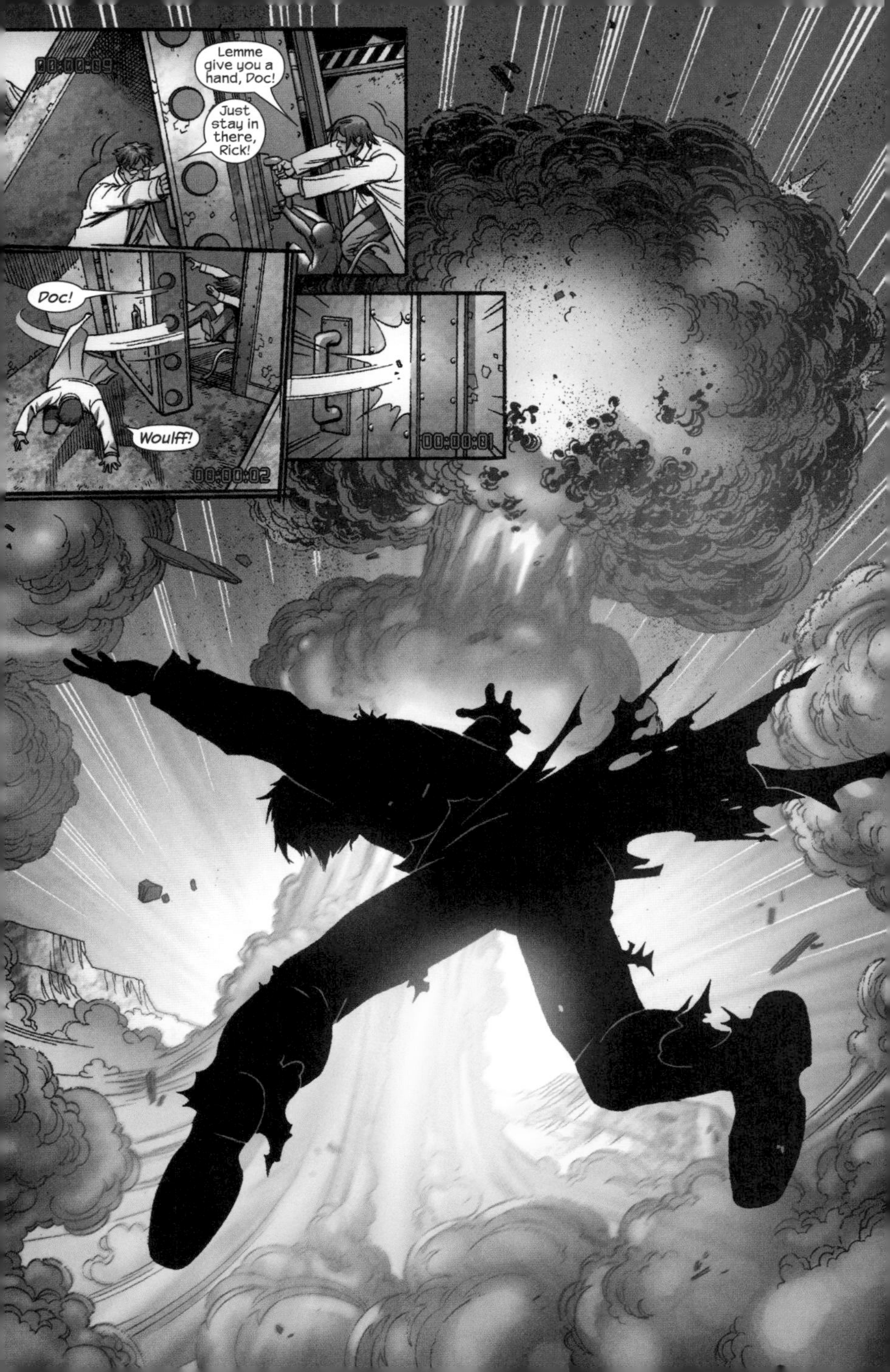
00:00:09
Lemme give you a hand, Doc!
Just stay in there, Rick!
Doc!
Woulff!
00:00:02
00:00:01

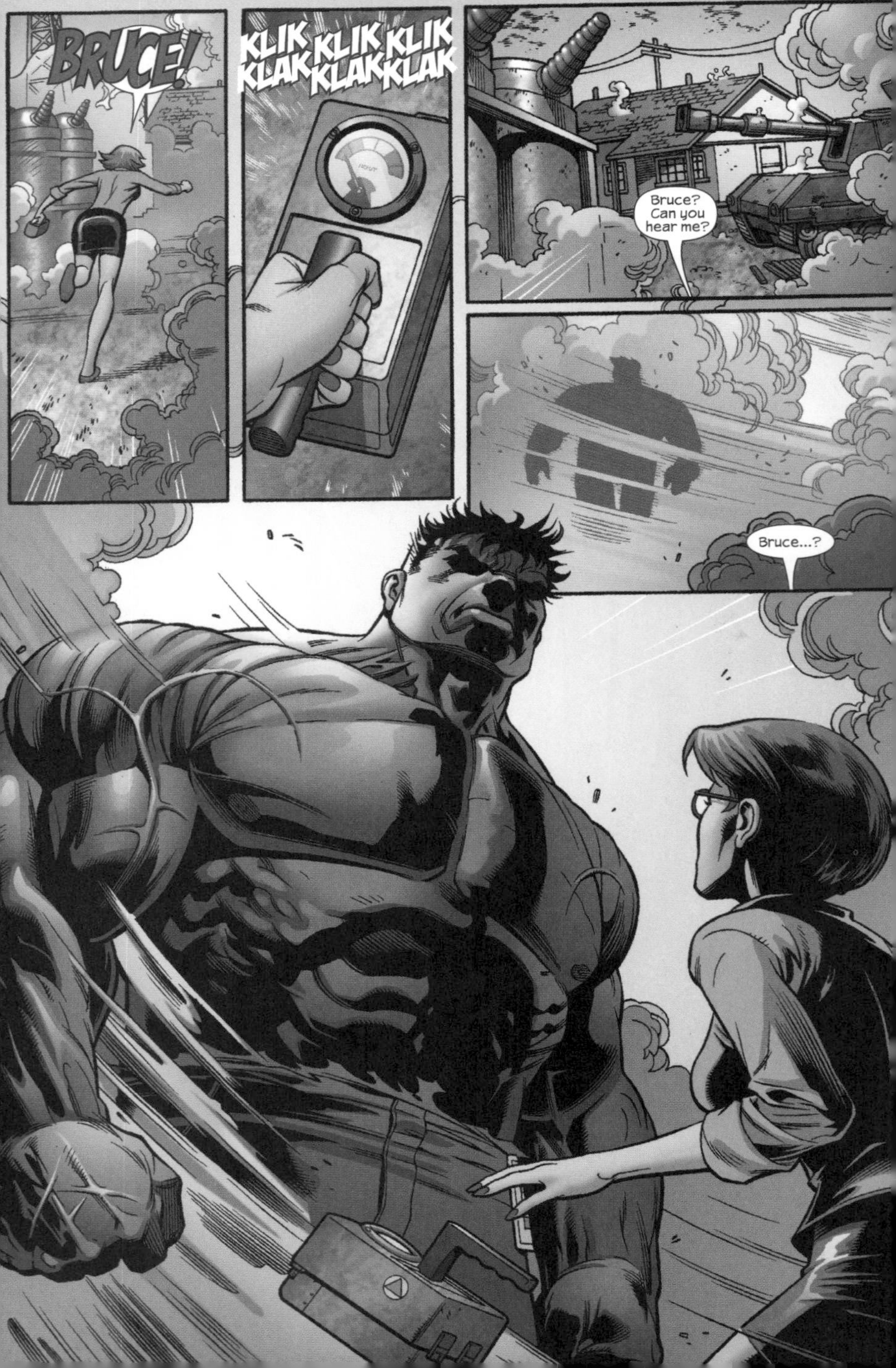
BRUCE!
KLIK KLIK KLIK
KLAK KLAK KLAK
Bruce? Can you hear me?
Bruce...?

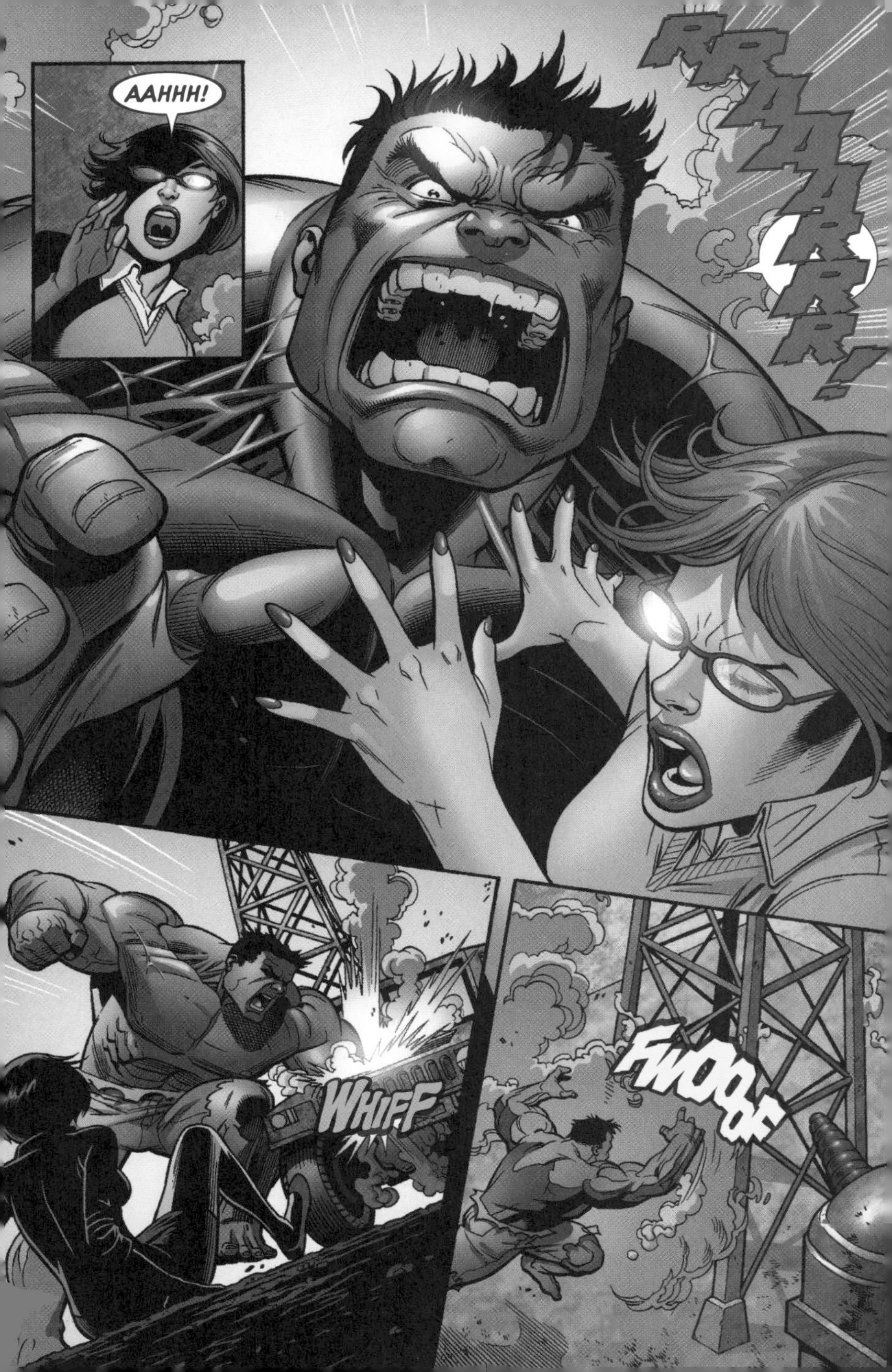
AAHHH!
RRAAARR!
WHIFF
FWOOOF

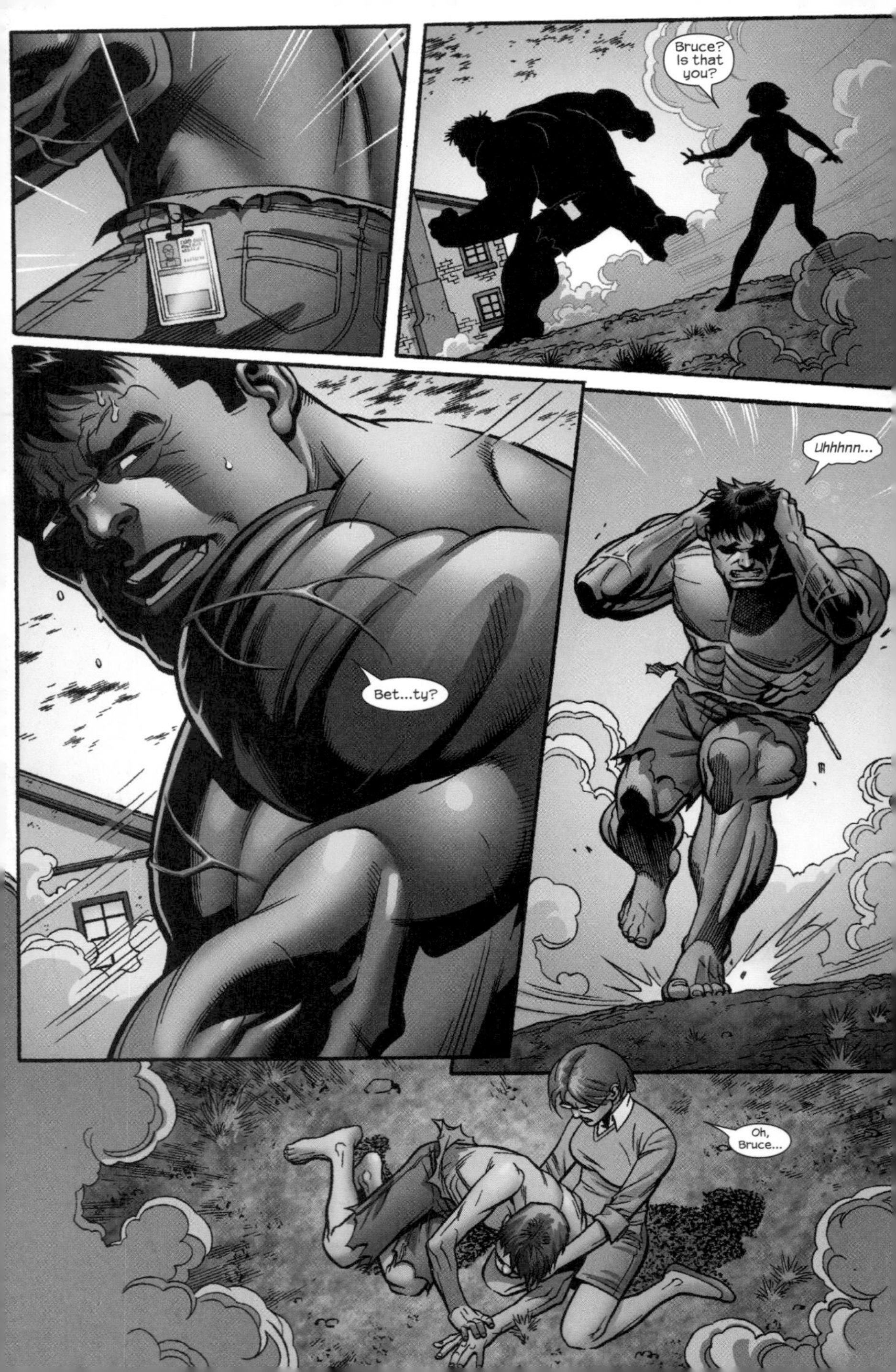
Bruce? Is that you?
Bet...ty?
Uhhhnn...
Oh, Bruce...

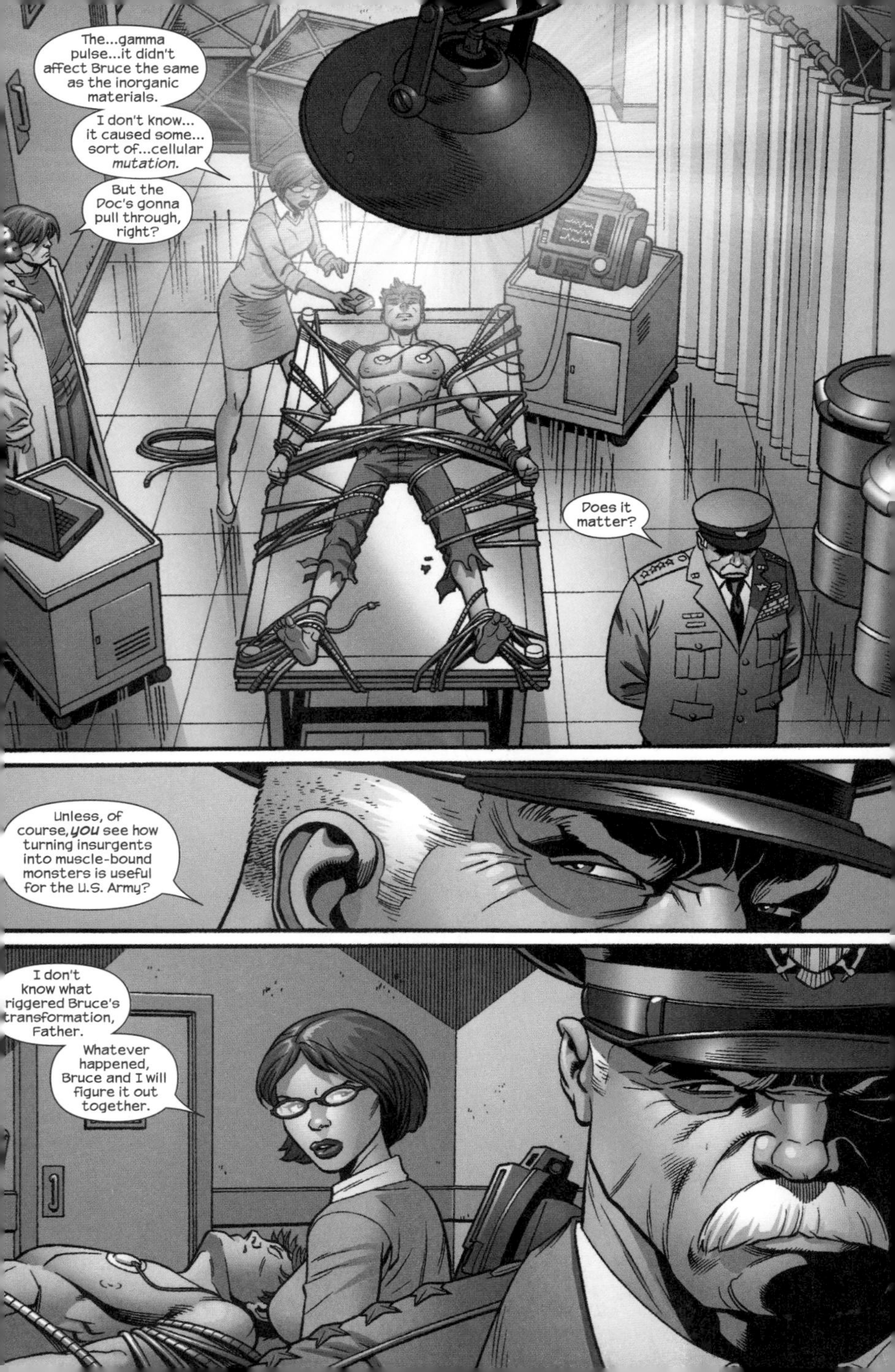
The...gamma pulse...it didn't affect Bruce the same as the inorganic materials.
I don't know... it caused some... sort of...cellular *mutation*.
But the Doc's gonna pull through, right?
Does it matter?
Unless, of course, ***you*** see how turning insurgents into muscle-bound monsters is useful for the U.S. Army?
I don't know what riggered Bruce's ransformation, Father.
Whatever happened, Bruce and I will figure it out together.

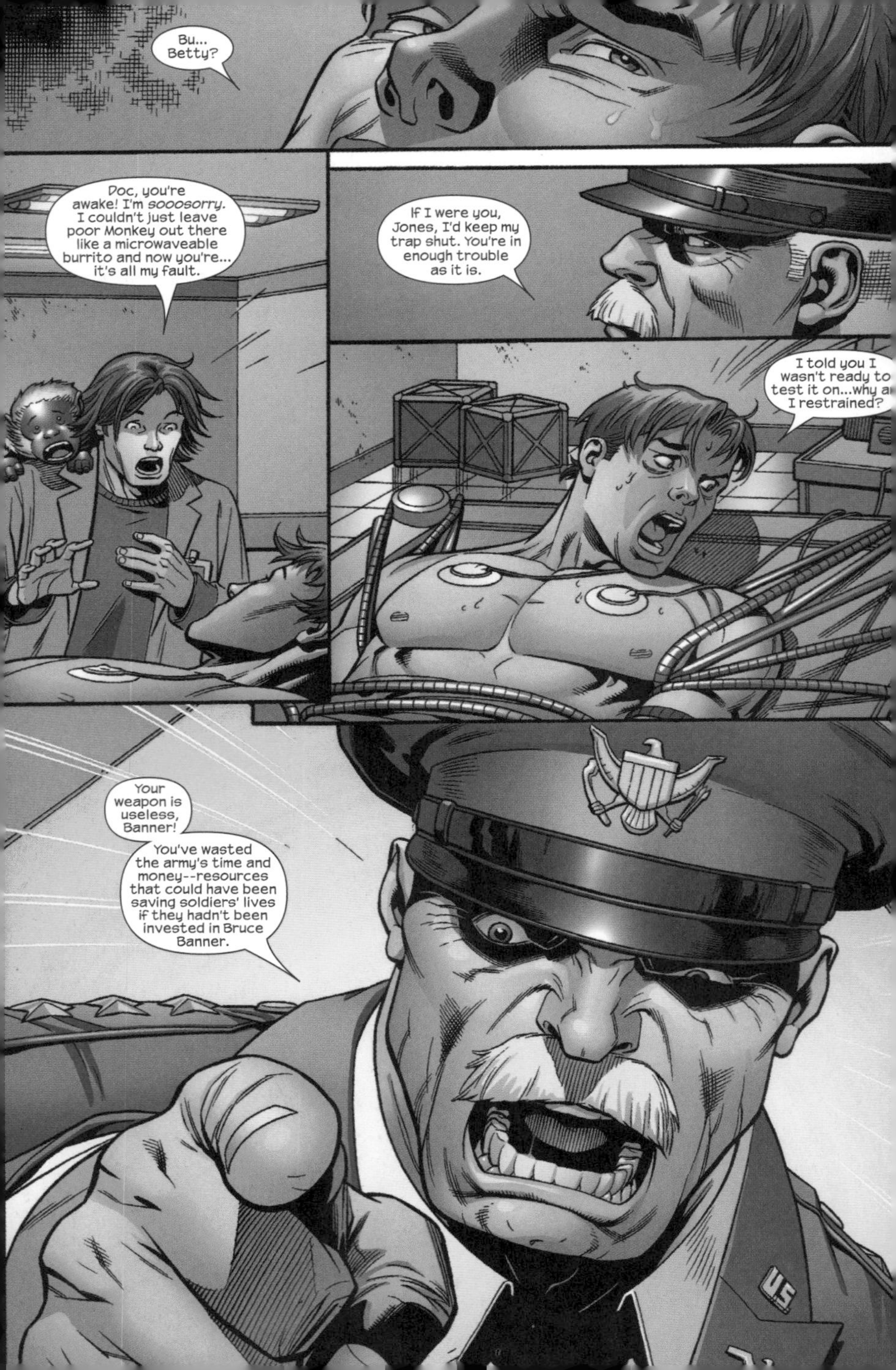
Bu... Betty?
Doc, you're awake! I'm *sooosorry.* I couldn't just leave poor Monkey out there like a microwaveable burrito and now you're... it's all my fault.
If I were you, Jones, I'd keep my trap shut. You're in enough trouble as it is.
I told you I wasn't ready to test it on...why a I restrained?
Your weapon is useless, Banner!
You've wasted the army's time and money--resources that could have been saving soldiers' lives if they hadn't been invested in Bruce Banner.
U.S.

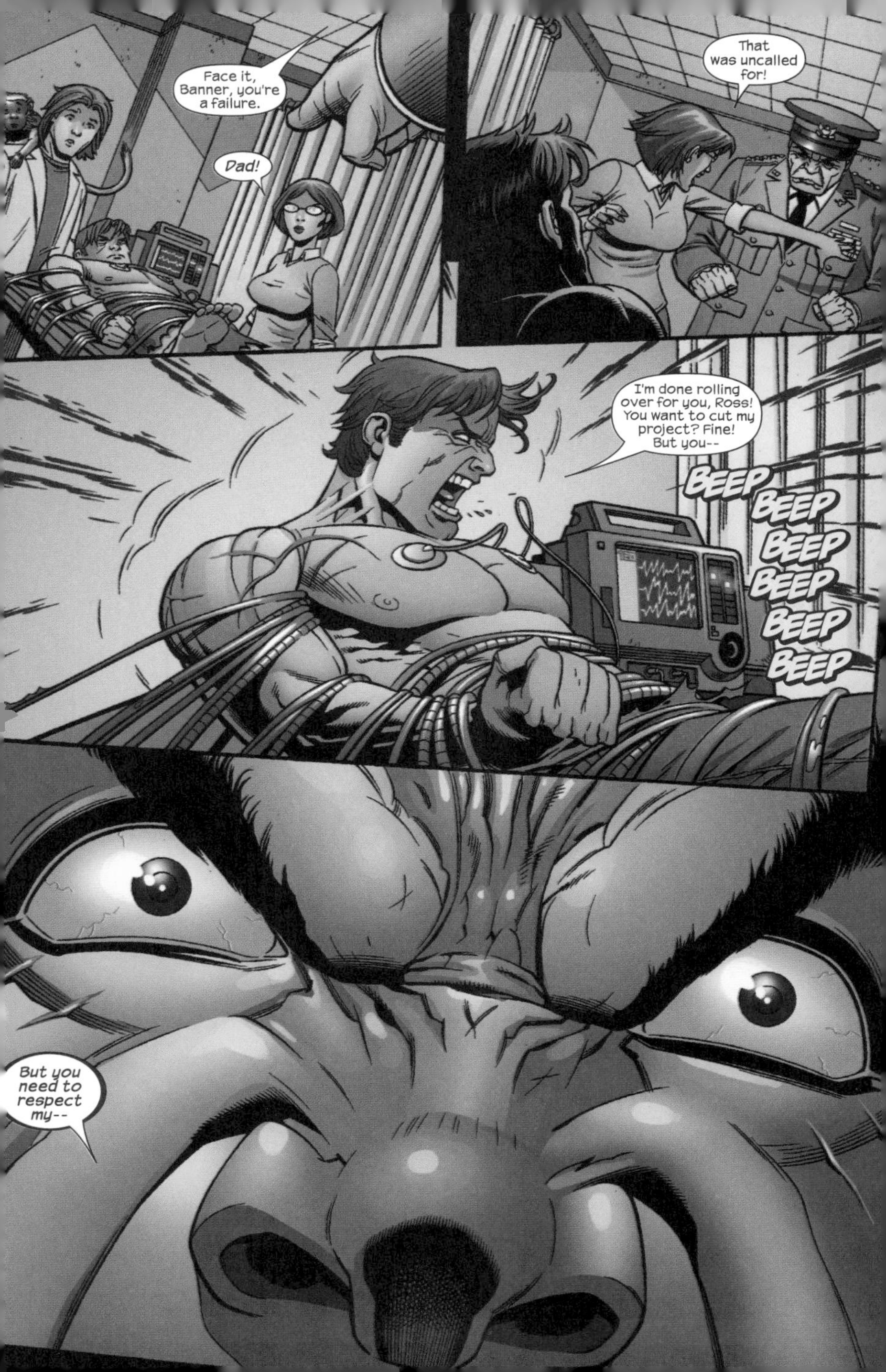
Face it, Banner, you're a failure.
Dad!
That was uncalled for!
I'm done rolling over for you, Ross! You want to cut my project? Fine! But you--
BEEP BEEP BEEP BEEP BEEP BEEP
But you need to respect my--

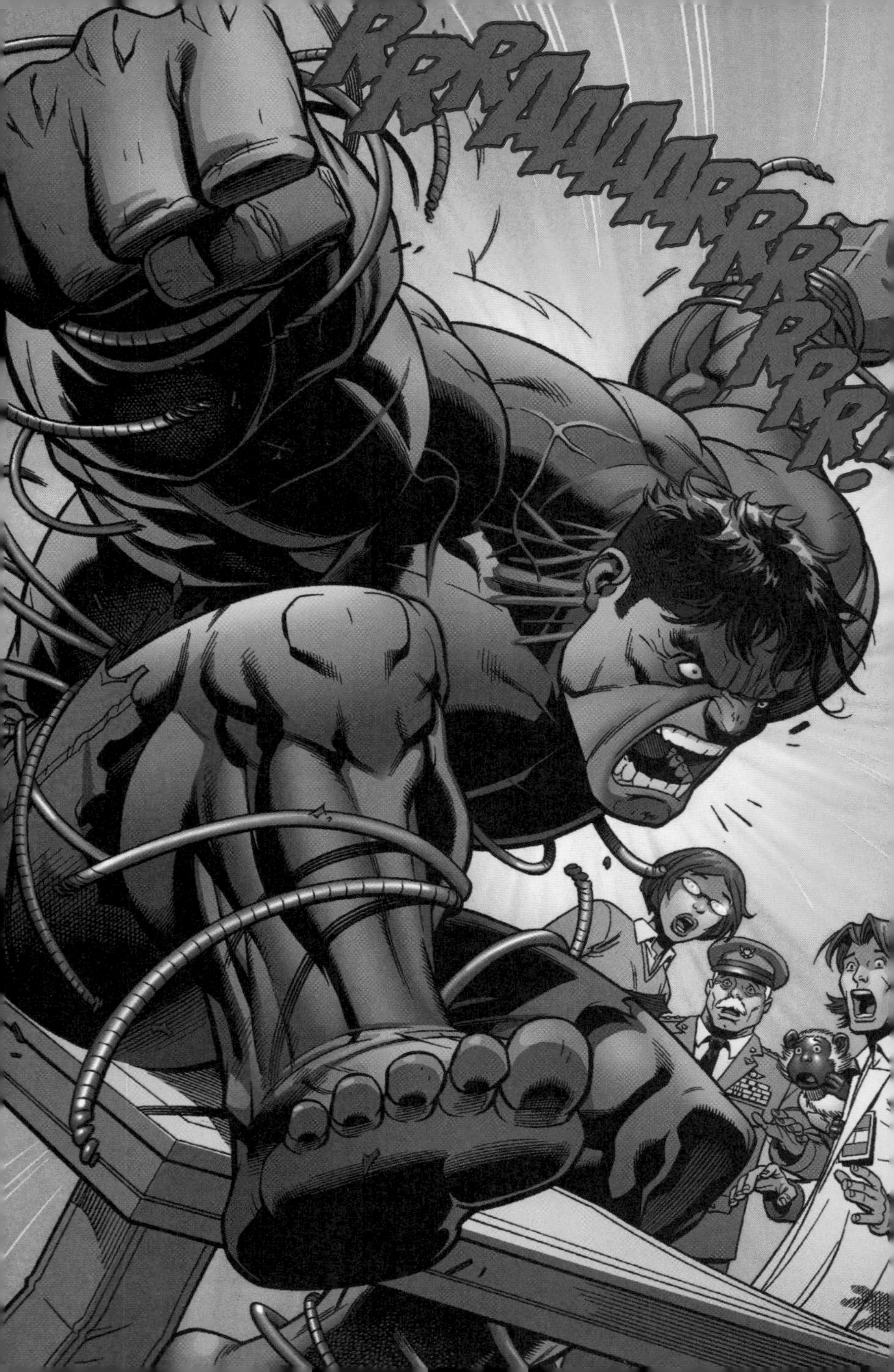
RRRAAAARRRRRR!

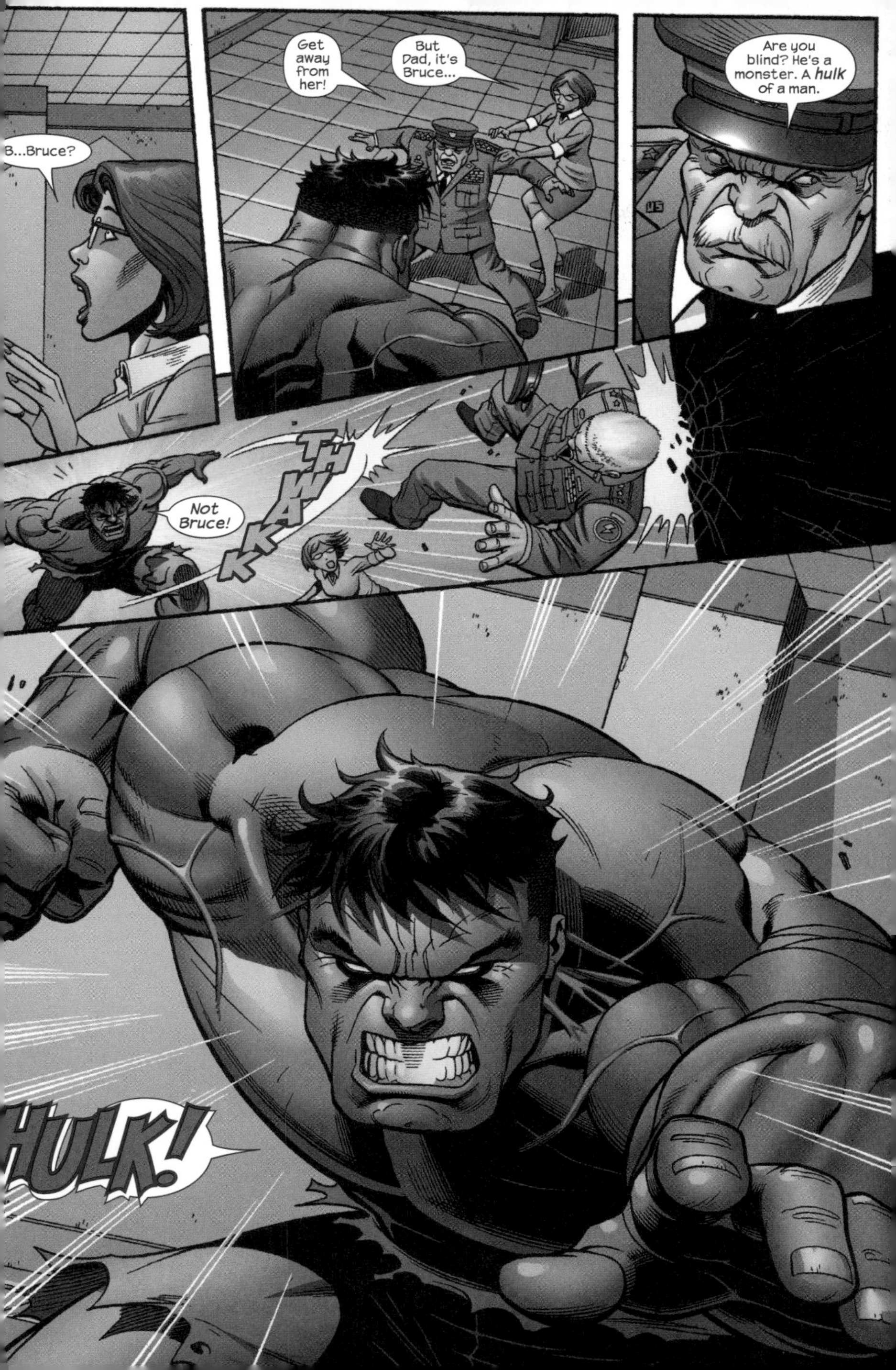
B...Bruce?
Get away from her!
But Dad, it's Bruce...
Are you blind? He's a monster. A *hulk* of a man.
Not Bruce!
THWAKKK
HULK!

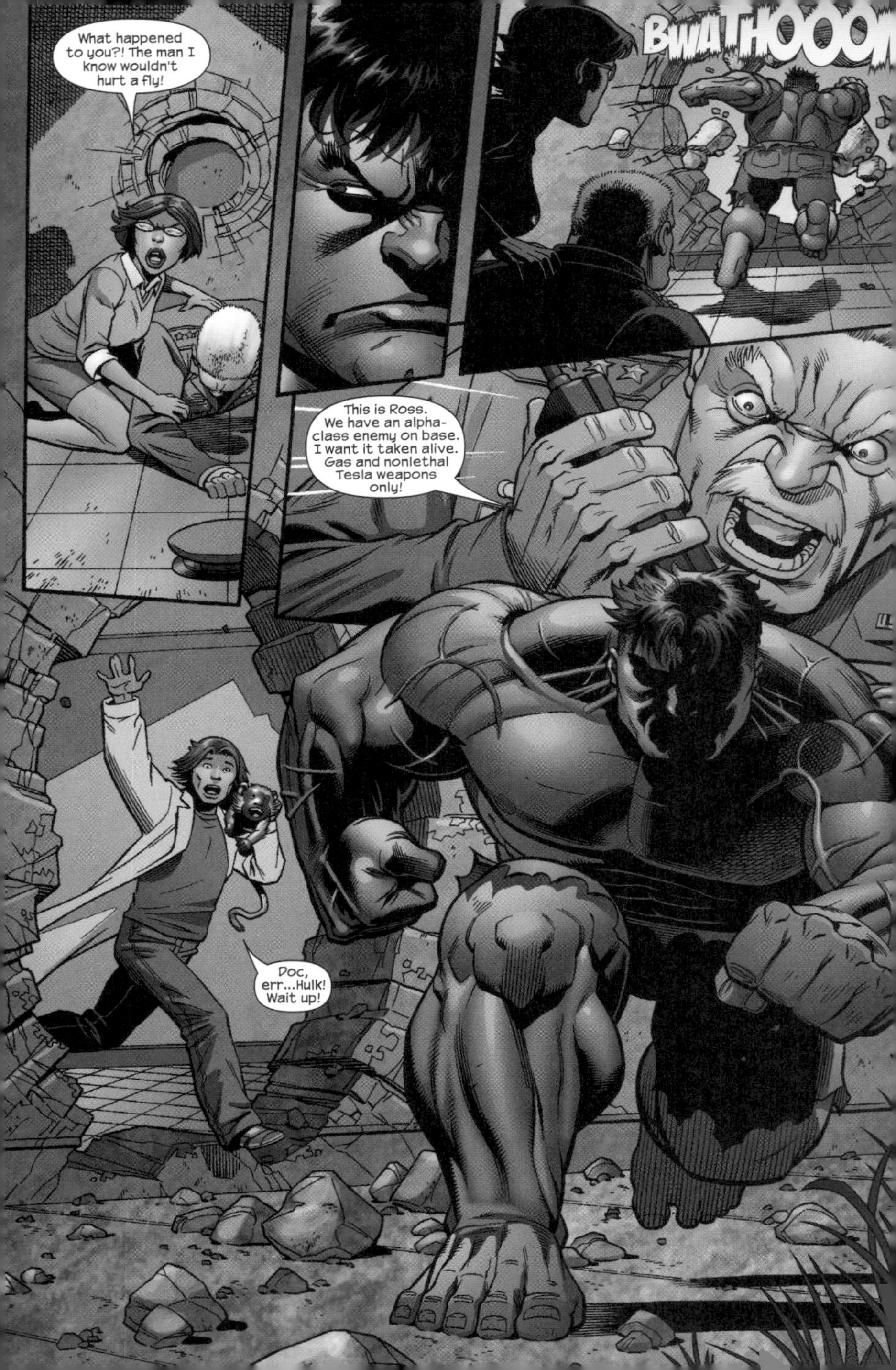
What happened to you?! The man I know wouldn't hurt a fly!
BWATHOOOM
This is Ross. We have an alpha-class enemy on base. I want it taken alive. Gas and nonlethal Tesla weapons only!
Doc, err...Hulk! Wait up!

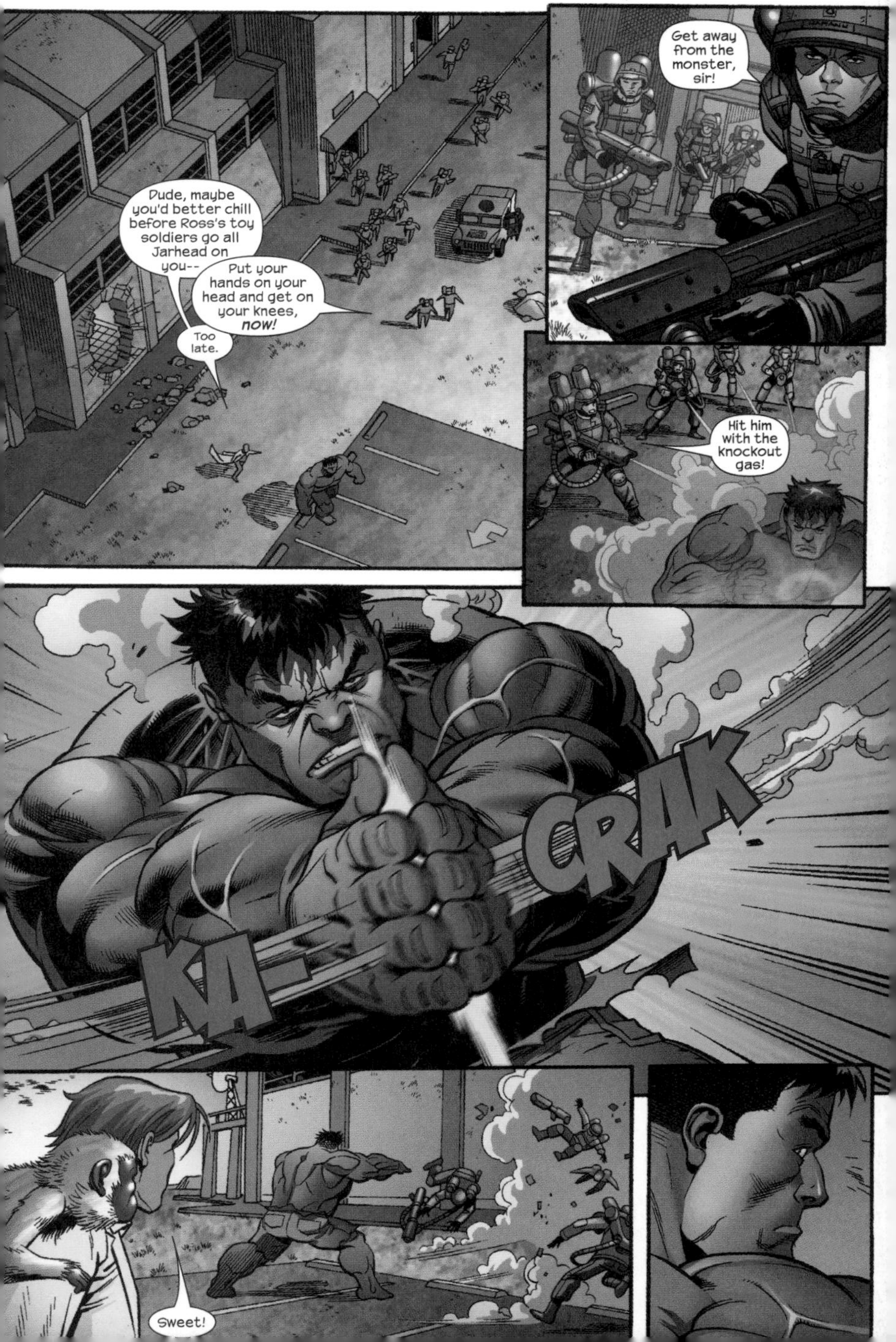

Dude, maybe you'd better chill before Ross's toy soldiers go all Jarhead on you--
Put your hands on your head and get on your knees, *now!*
Too late.
Get away from the monster, sir!
Hit him with the knockout gas!
KA-
CRAK
Sweet!

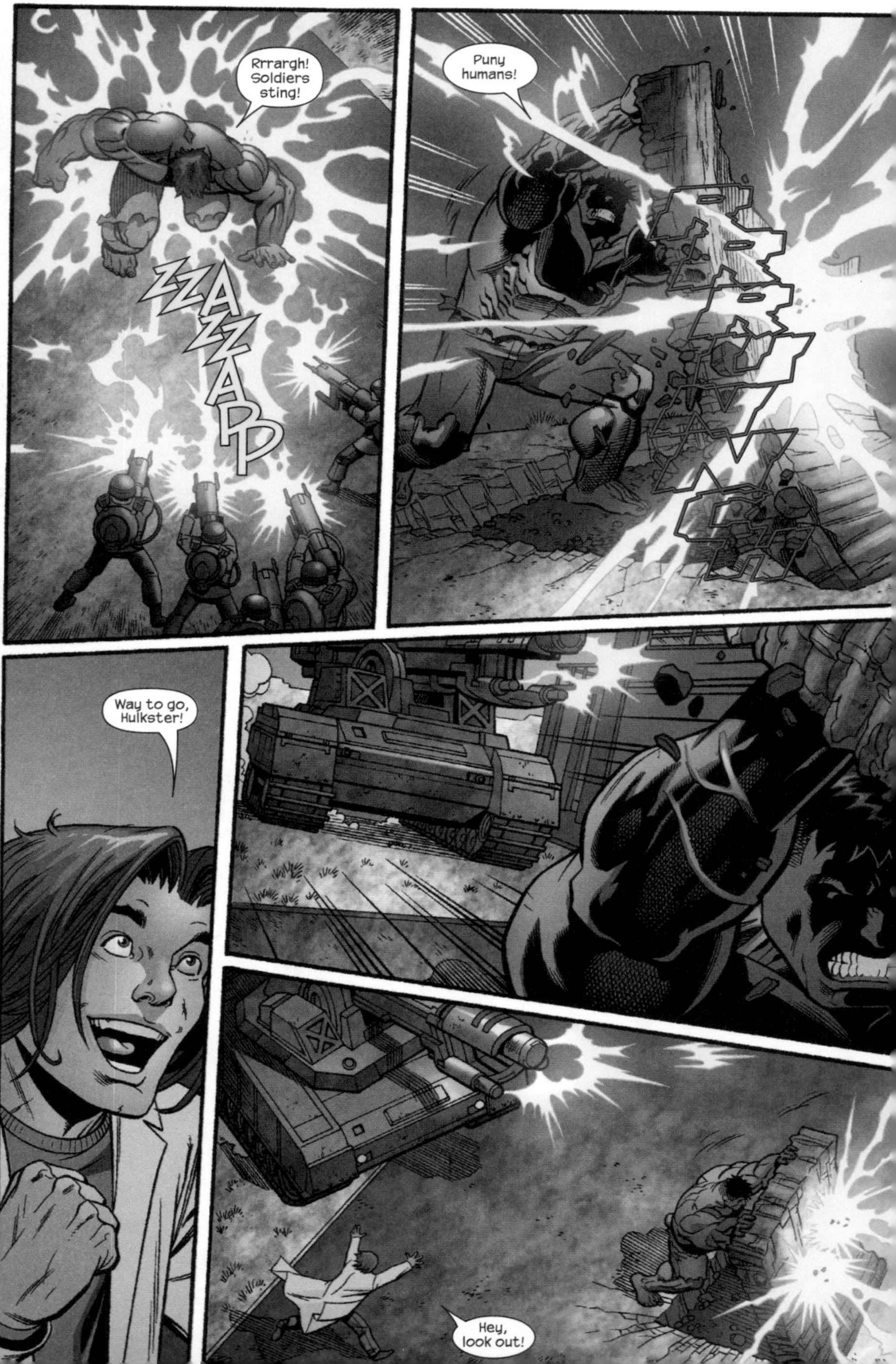
Rrrargh! Soldiers sting!
ZZAZZAPP
Puny humans!
Way to go, Hulkster!
Hey, look out!

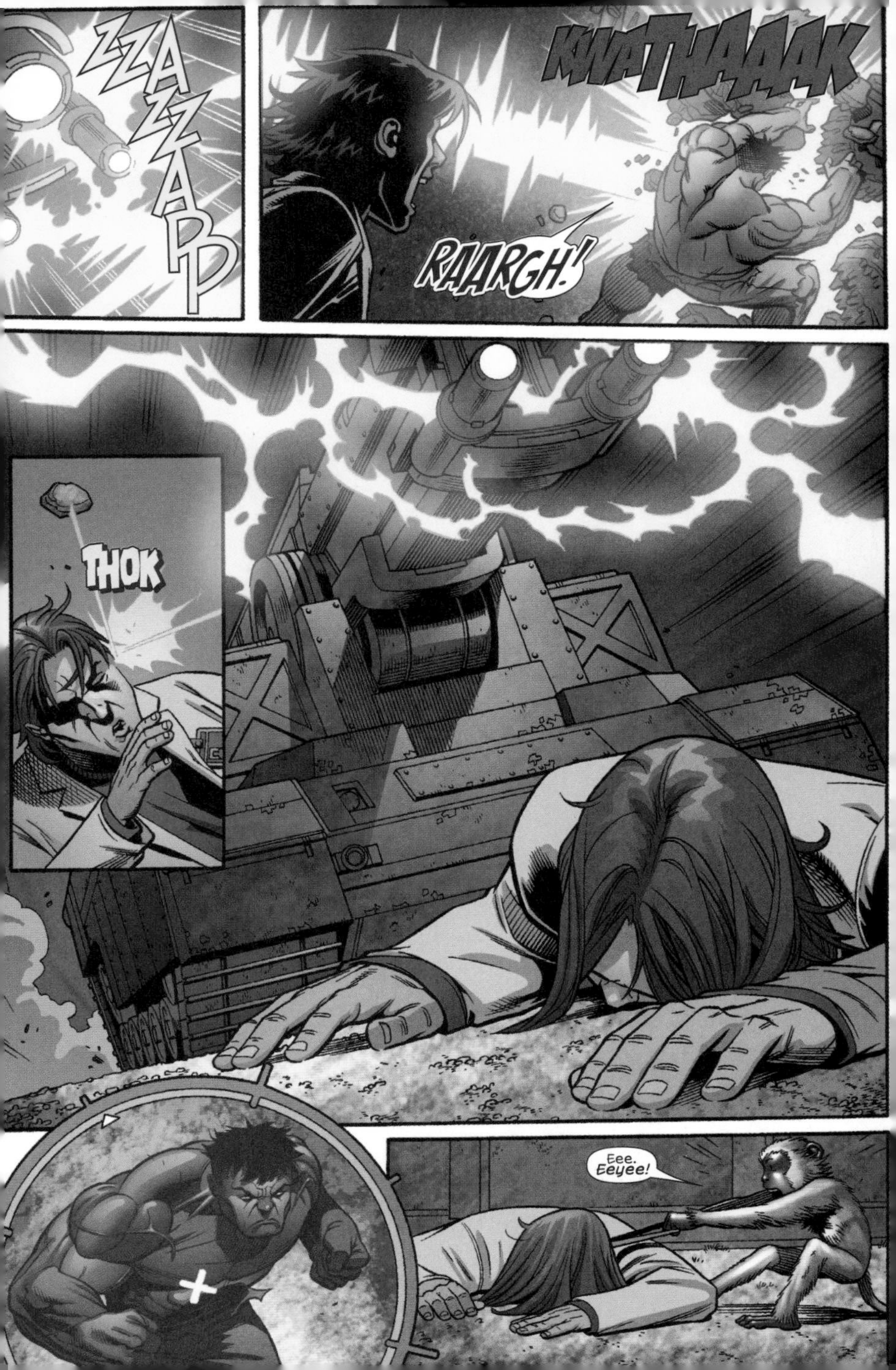
ZZAZZAP
KWATHAAAK
RAARGH!
THOK
Eee. Eeyee!

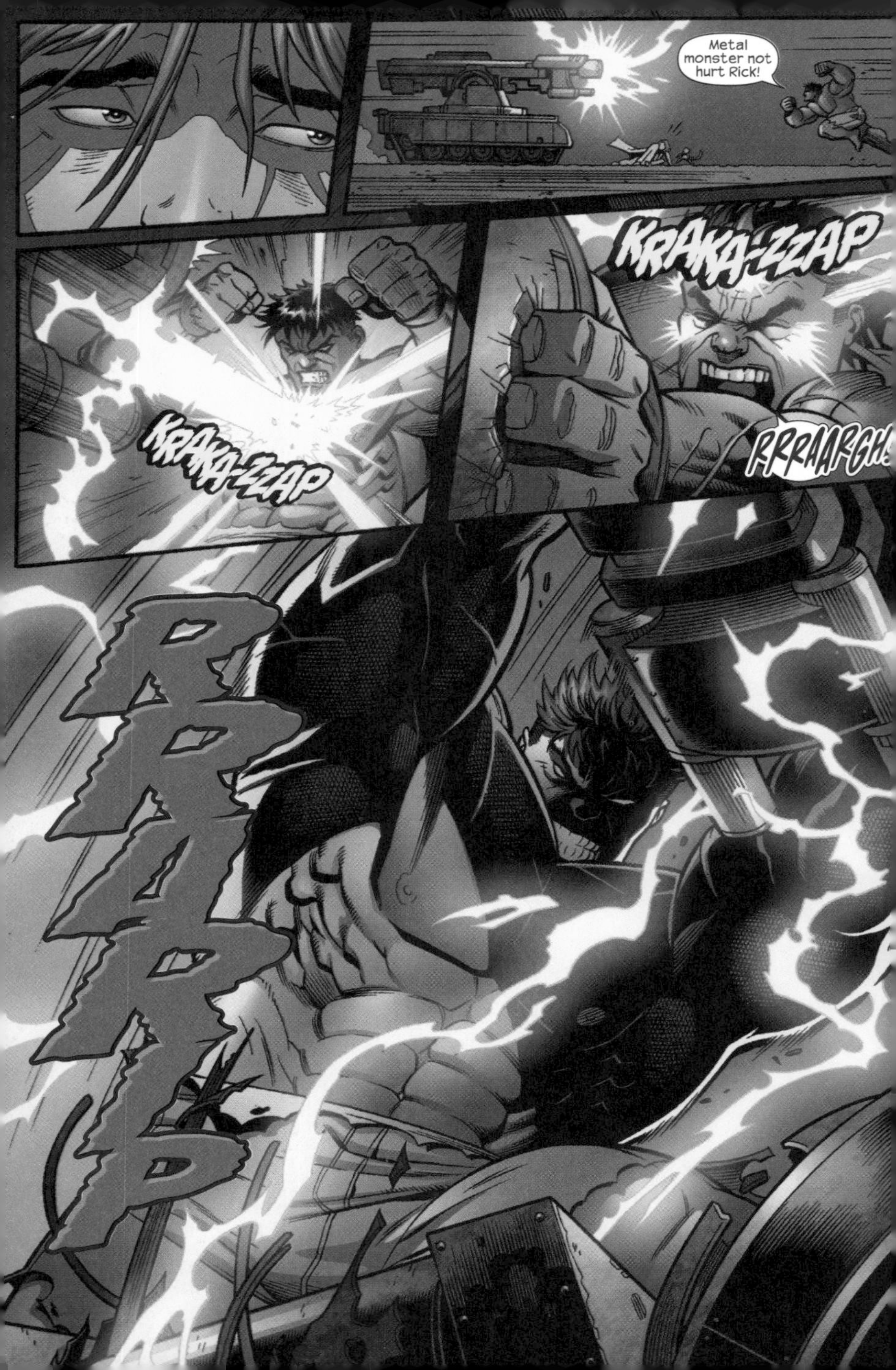
Metal monster not hurt Rick!
KRAKA-ZZAP
KRAKA-ZZAP
RRRAAARGH!

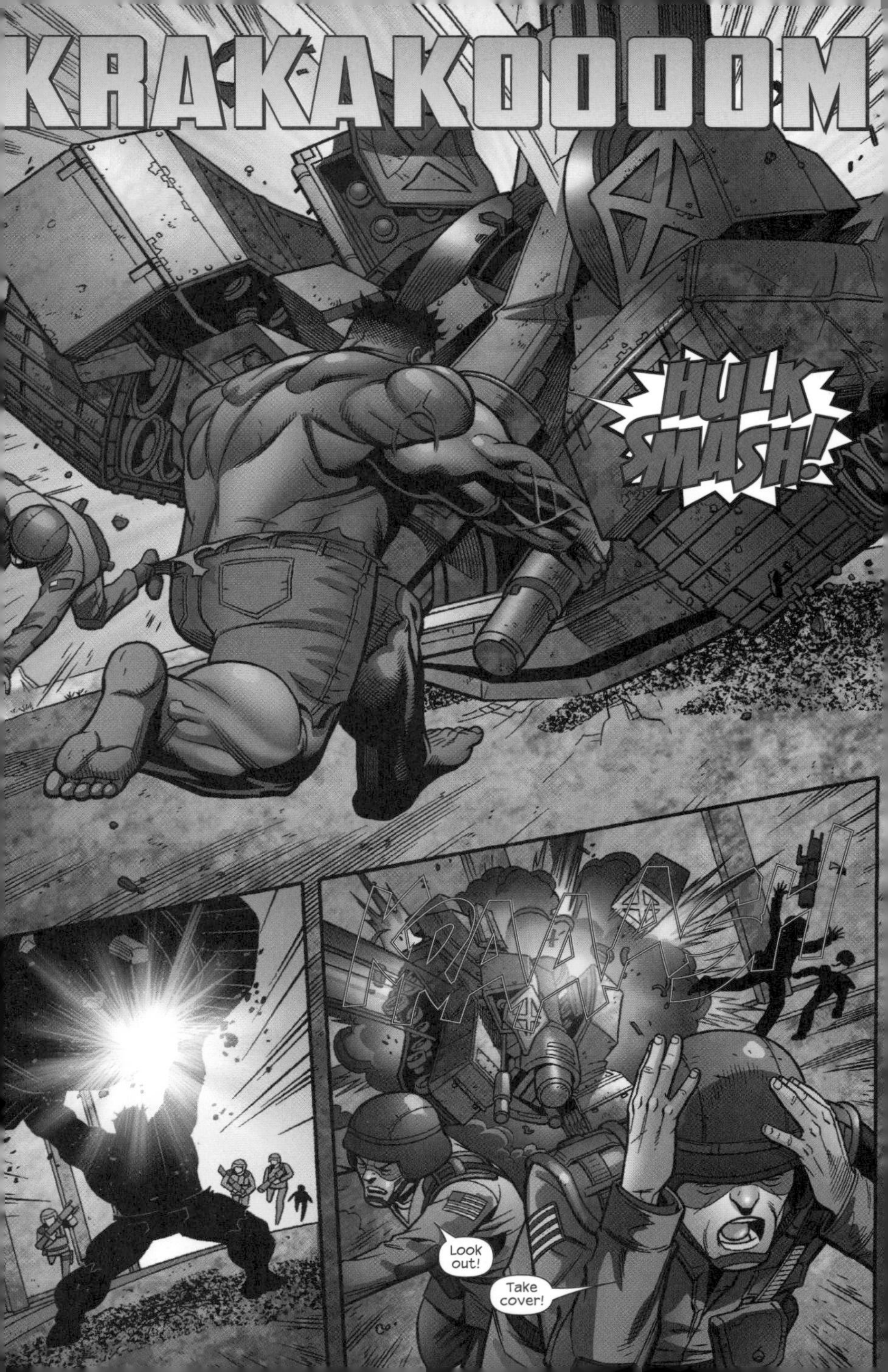
KRAKAKOOOOM
HULK SMASH!
Look out!
Take cover!

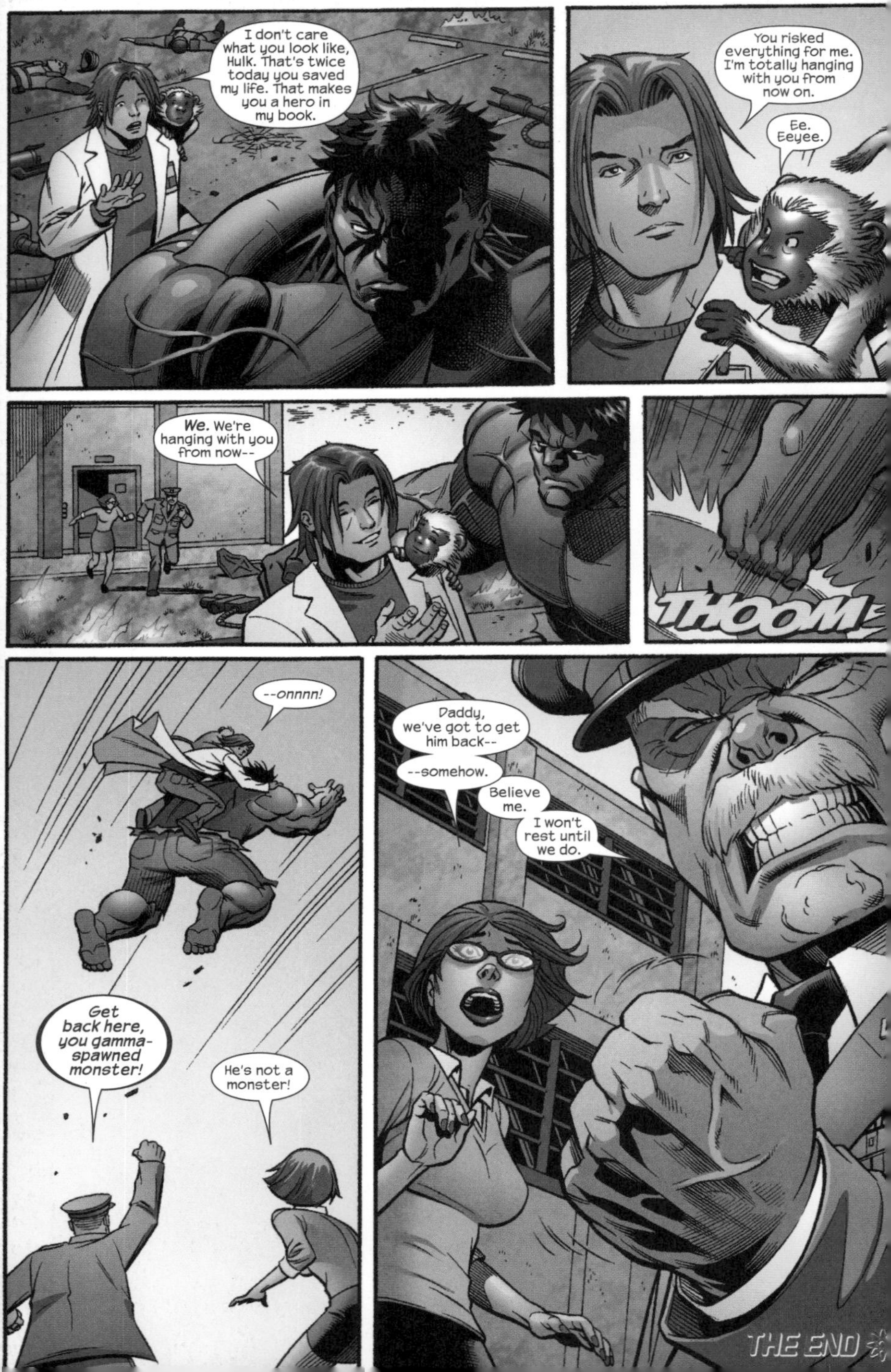
I don't care what you look like, Hulk. That's twice today you saved my life. That makes you a hero in my book.
You risked everything for me. I'm totally hanging with you from now on.
Ee. Eeyee.
We. We're hanging with you from now--
THOOM
--onnnn!
Get back here, you gamma-spawned monster!
He's not a monster!
Daddy, we've got to get him back--
--somehow.
Believe me.
I won't rest until we do.
THE END

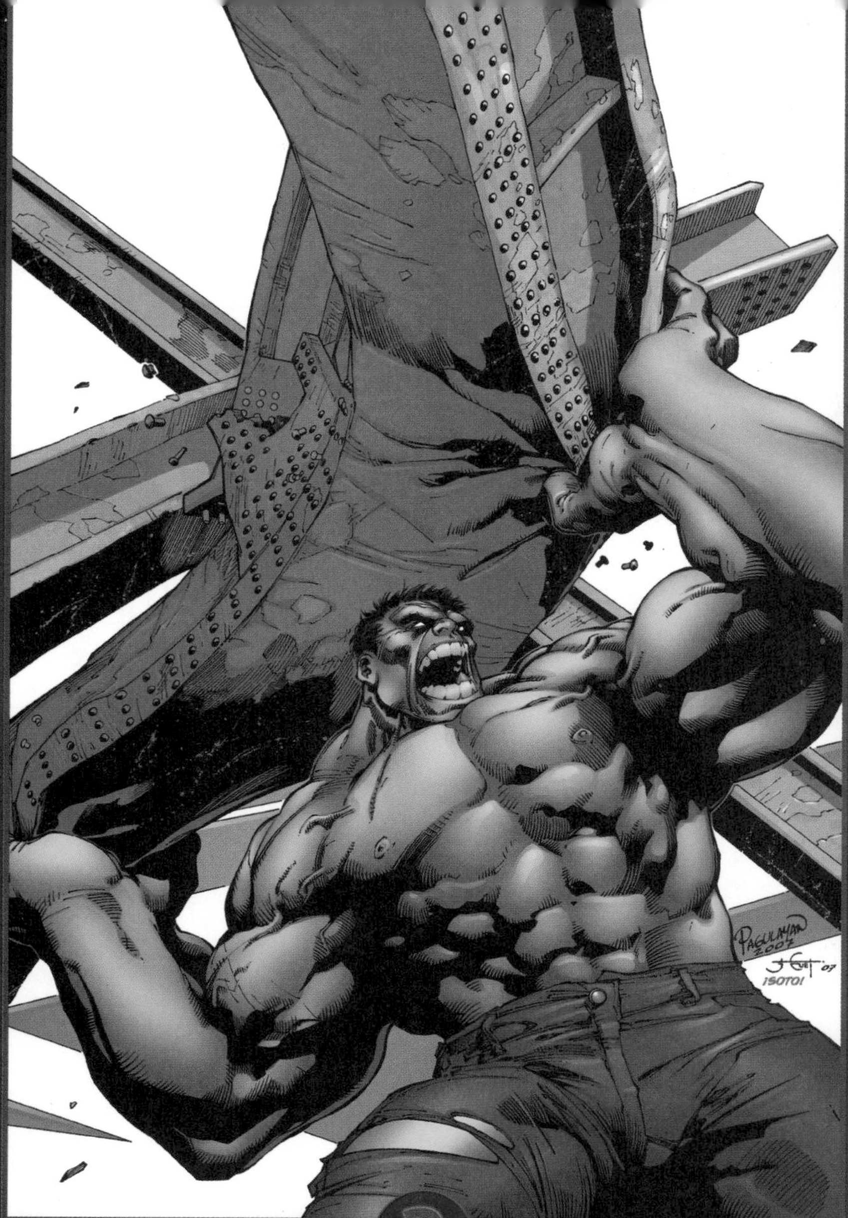
PAGULAYAN
2007

2

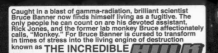

Caught in a blast of gamma-radiation, brilliant scientist Bruce Banner now finds himself living as a fugitive. The only people he can count on are his devoted assistant, Rick Jones, and the former lab monkey Bruce affectionately calls, "Monkey." For Bruce Banner is cursed to transform in times of stress into the living engine of destruction known as THE INCREDIBLE HULK.

THE HULKS TAKE MANHATTAN

PAUL BENJAMIN
WRITER

JUAN SANTACRUZ
PENCILER

RAUL FERNANDEZ
INKER

WILFREDO QUINTANA
COLORIST

DAVE SHARPE
LETTERER

PAGULAYAN, HUET AND SOTOMAYOR
COVER ARTISTS

IRENE LEE
PRODUCTION

NATHAN COSBY
ASST. EDITOR

MARK PANICCIA
EDITOR

JOE QUESADA
EDITOR IN CHIEF

DAN BUCKLEY
PUBLISHER

You gonna gimme the money or do I gotta give ya a fat lip?

P-please...

This hood didn't know it yet, but his fists were writing checks his skull couldn't cash.

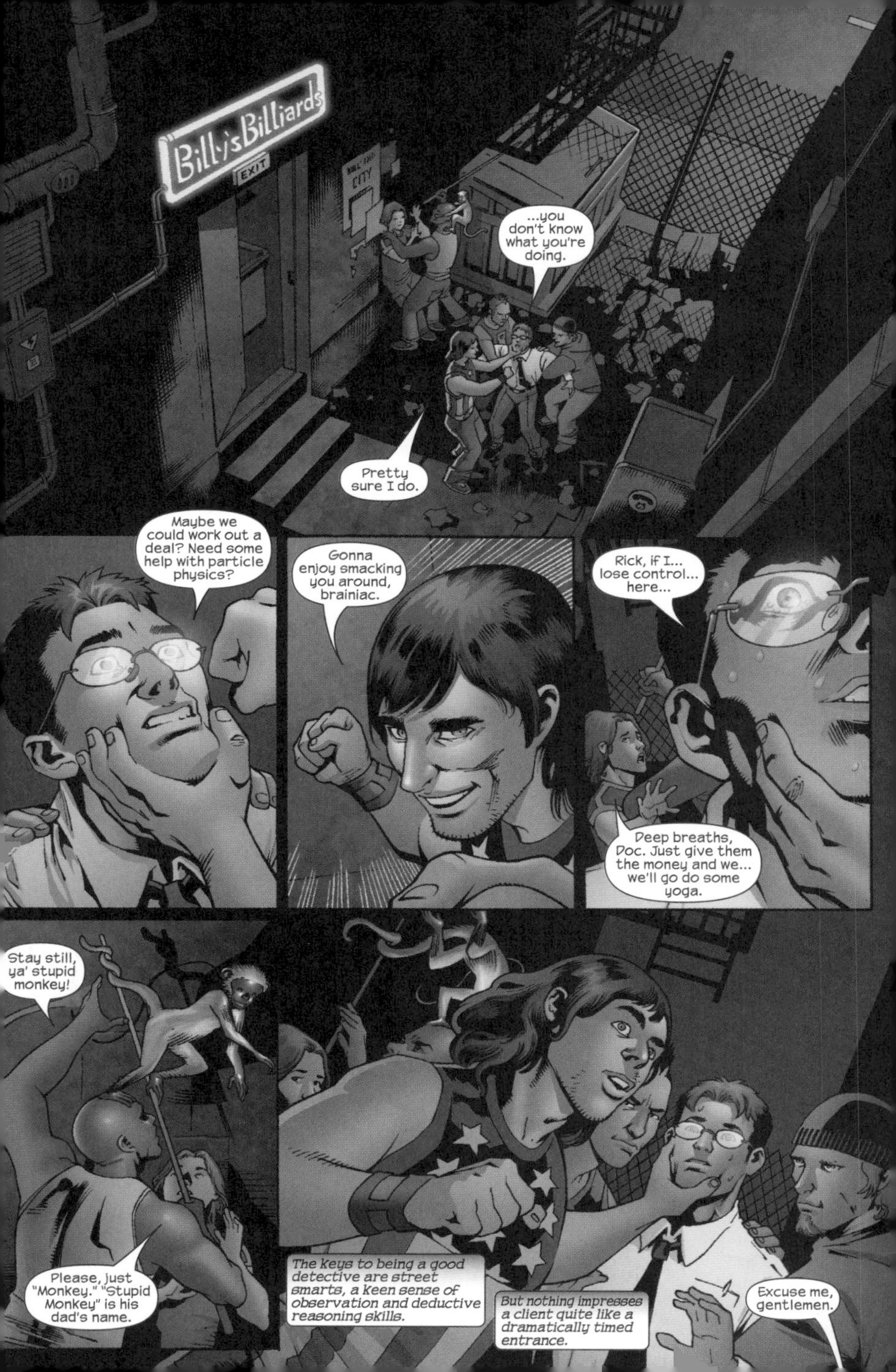
Billy's Billiards
EXIT
...you don't know what you're doing.
Pretty sure I do.
Maybe we could work out a deal? Need some help with particle physics?
Gonna enjoy smacking you around, brainiac.
Rick, if I... lose control... here...
Deep breaths, Doc. Just give them the money and we... we'll go do some yoga.
Stay still, ya' stupid monkey!
Please, just "Monkey." "Stupid Monkey" is his dad's name.
The keys to being a good detective are street smarts, a keen sense of observation and deductive reasoning skills.
But nothing impresses a client quite like a dramatically timed entrance.
Excuse me, gentlemen.

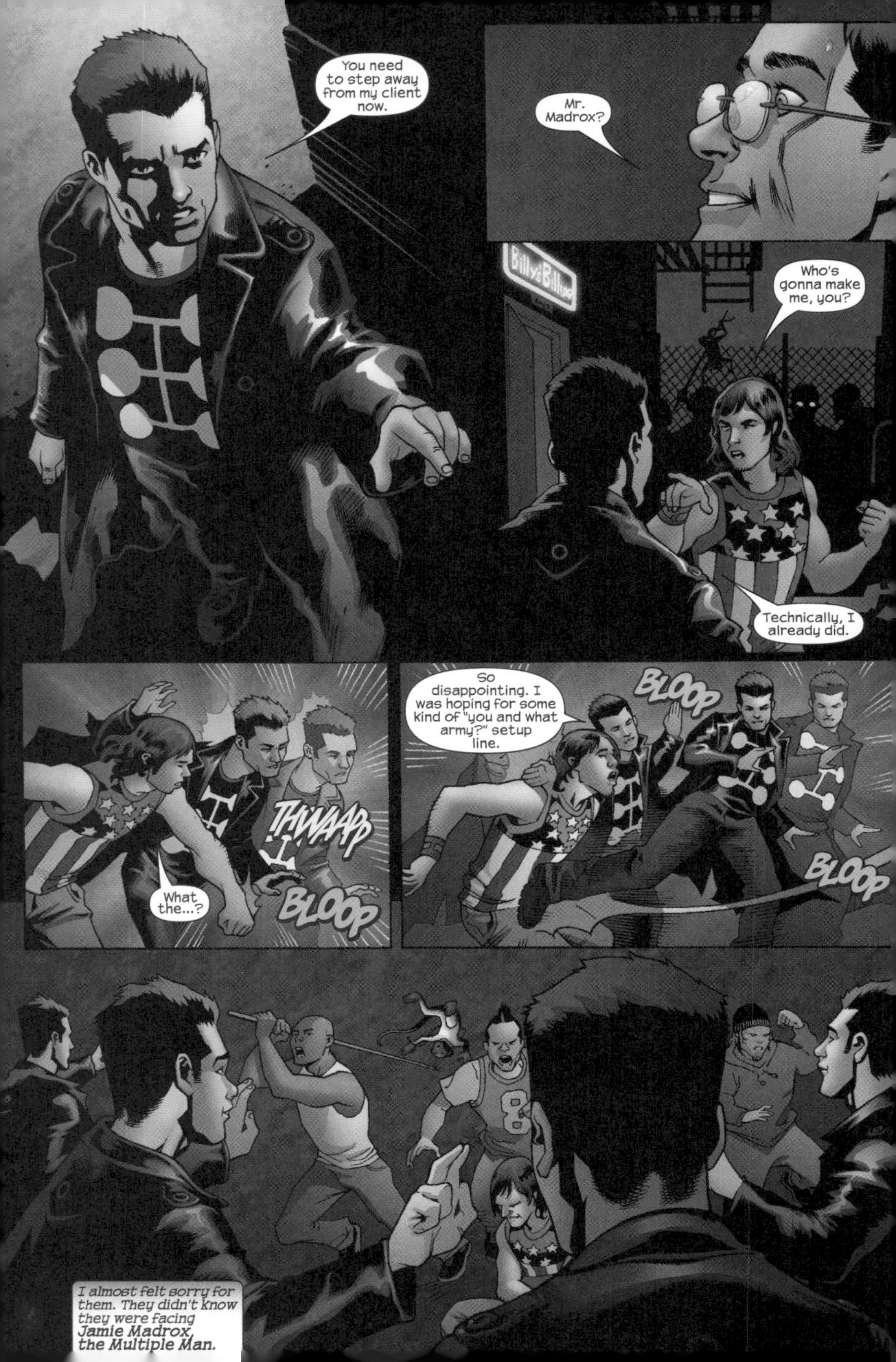
You need to step away from my client now.
Mr. Madrox?
Billy's Billiards
Who's gonna make me, you?
Technically, I already did.
THWAPP
What the...?
BLOOP
So disappointing. I was hoping for some kind of "you and what army?" setup line.
BLOOP
BLOOP
I almost felt sorry for them. They didn't know they were facing Jamie Madrox, the Multiple Man.

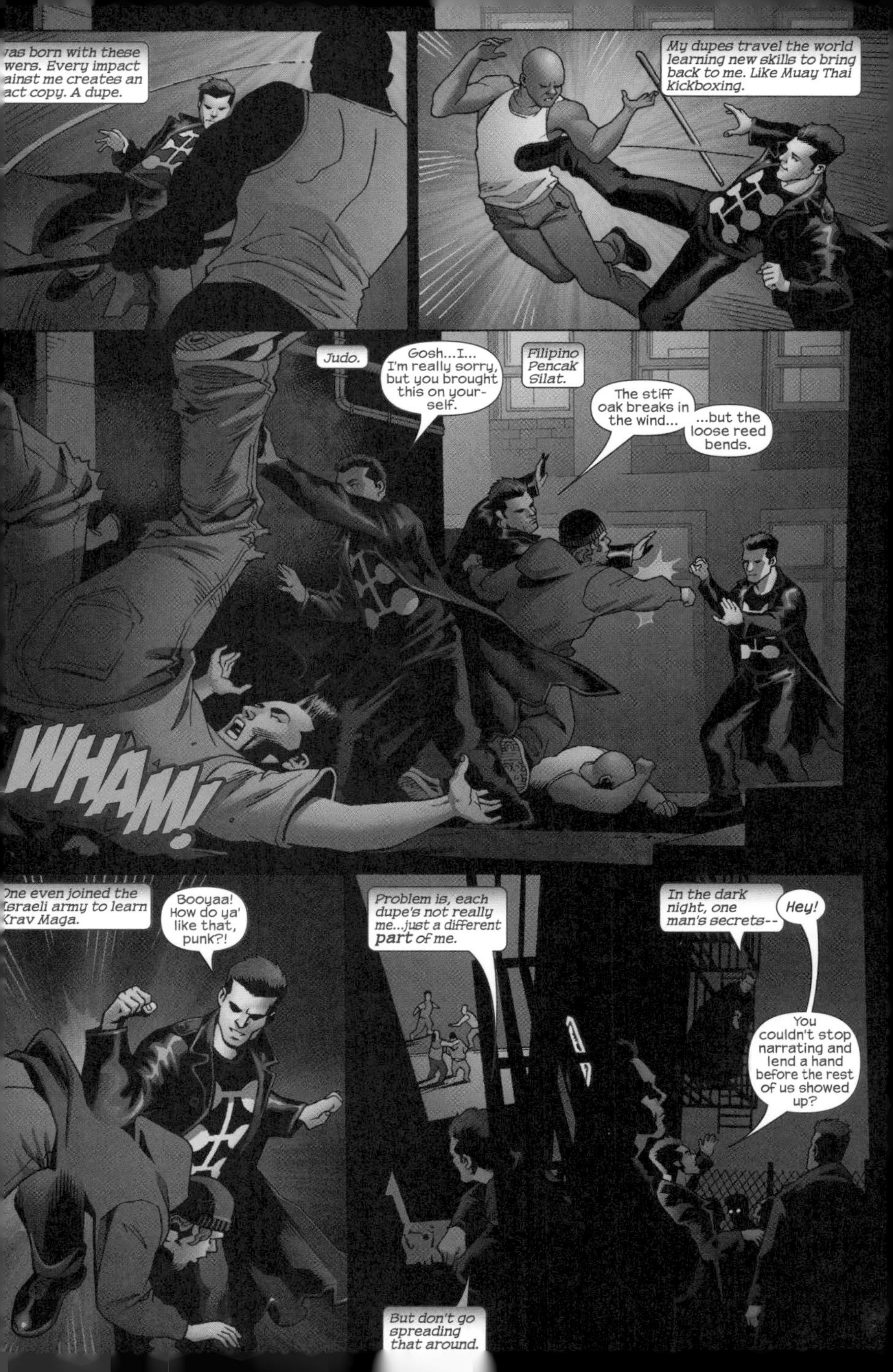

vas born with these wers. Every impact ainst me creates an act copy. A dupe.
My dupes travel the world learning new skills to bring back to me. Like Muay Thai kickboxing.
Judo.
Gosh...I... I'm really sorry, but you brought this on your-self.
Filipino Pencak Silat.
The stiff oak breaks in the wind...
...but the loose reed bends.
WHAM!
One even joined the Israeli army to learn Krav Maga.
Booyaa! How do ya' like that, punk?!
Problem is, each dupe's not really me...just a different part of me.
But don't go spreading that around.
In the dark night, one man's secrets--
Hey!
You couldn't stop narrating and lend a hand before the rest of us showed up?

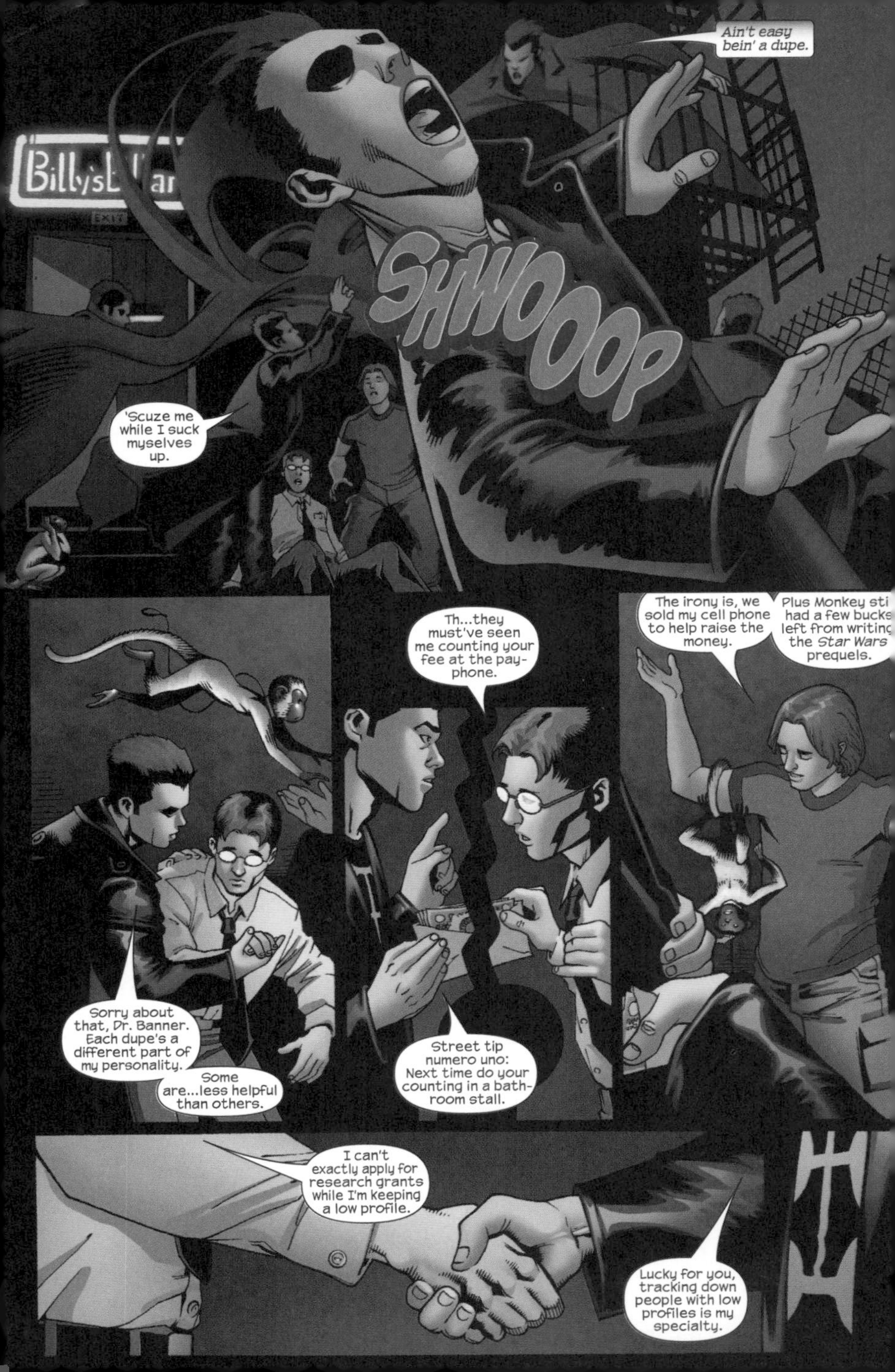
Ain't easy bein' a dupe.
Billy's B
EXIT
SHWOOOP
'Scuze me while I suck myselves up.
Sorry about that, Dr. Banner. Each dupe's a different part of my personality.
Some are...less helpful than others.
Th...they must've seen me counting your fee at the pay-phone.
Street tip numero uno: Next time do your counting in a bath-room stall.
The irony is, we sold my cell phone to help raise the money.
Plus Monkey sti had a few bucke left from writing the *Star Wars* prequels.
I can't exactly apply for research grants while I'm keeping a low profile.
Lucky for you, tracking down people with low profiles is my specialty.

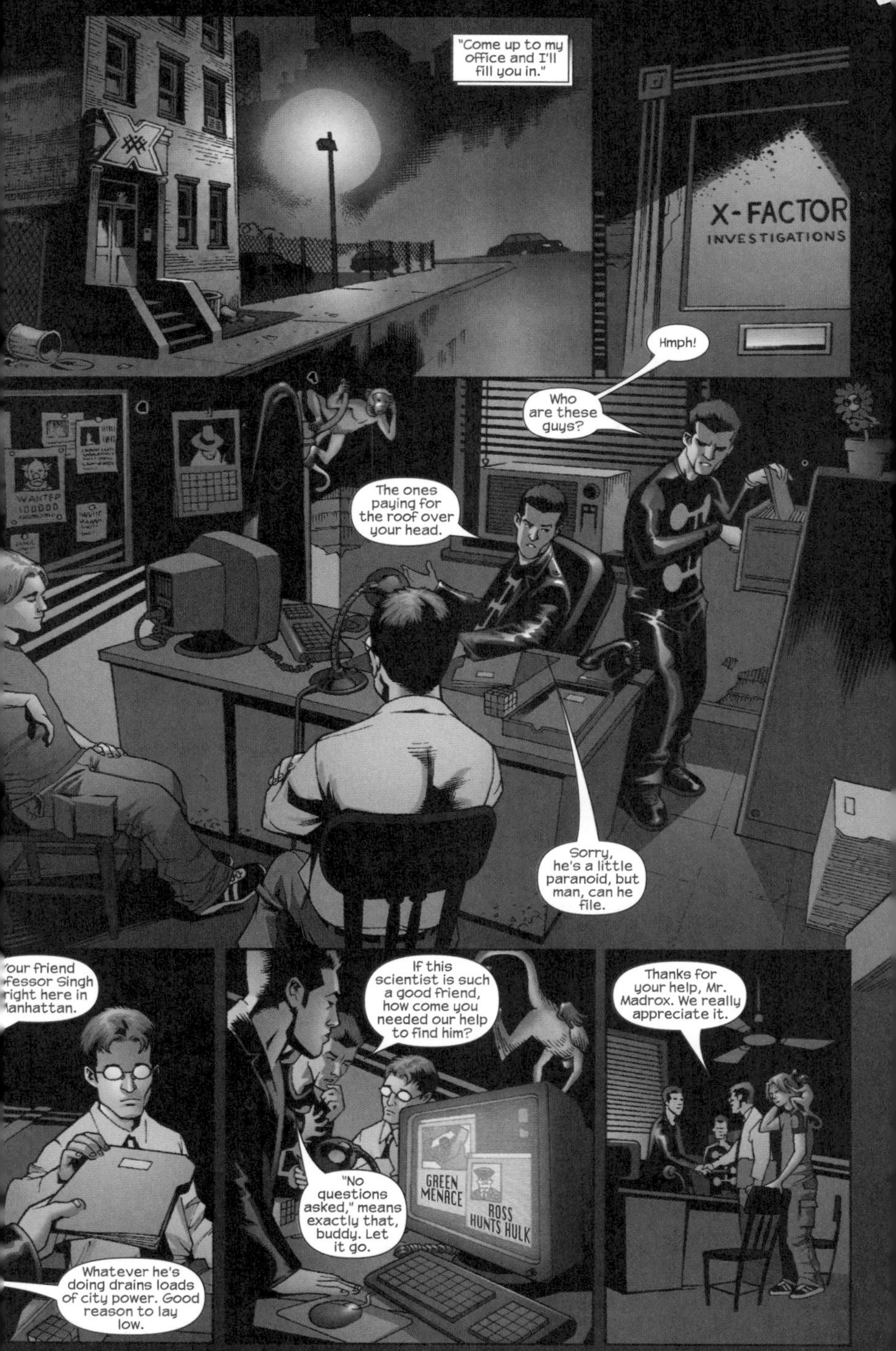
"Come up to my office and I'll fill you in."
X-FACTOR INVESTIGATIONS
Hmph!
Who are these guys?
The ones paying for the roof over your head.
Sorry, he's a little paranoid, but man, can he file.
WANTED
our friend fessor Singh right here in anhattan.
Whatever he's doing drains loads of city power. Good reason to lay low.
If this scientist is such a good friend, how come you needed our help to find him?
"No questions asked," means exactly that, buddy. Let it go.
GREEN MENACE
ROSS HUNTS HULK
Thanks for your help, Mr. Madrox. We really appreciate it.

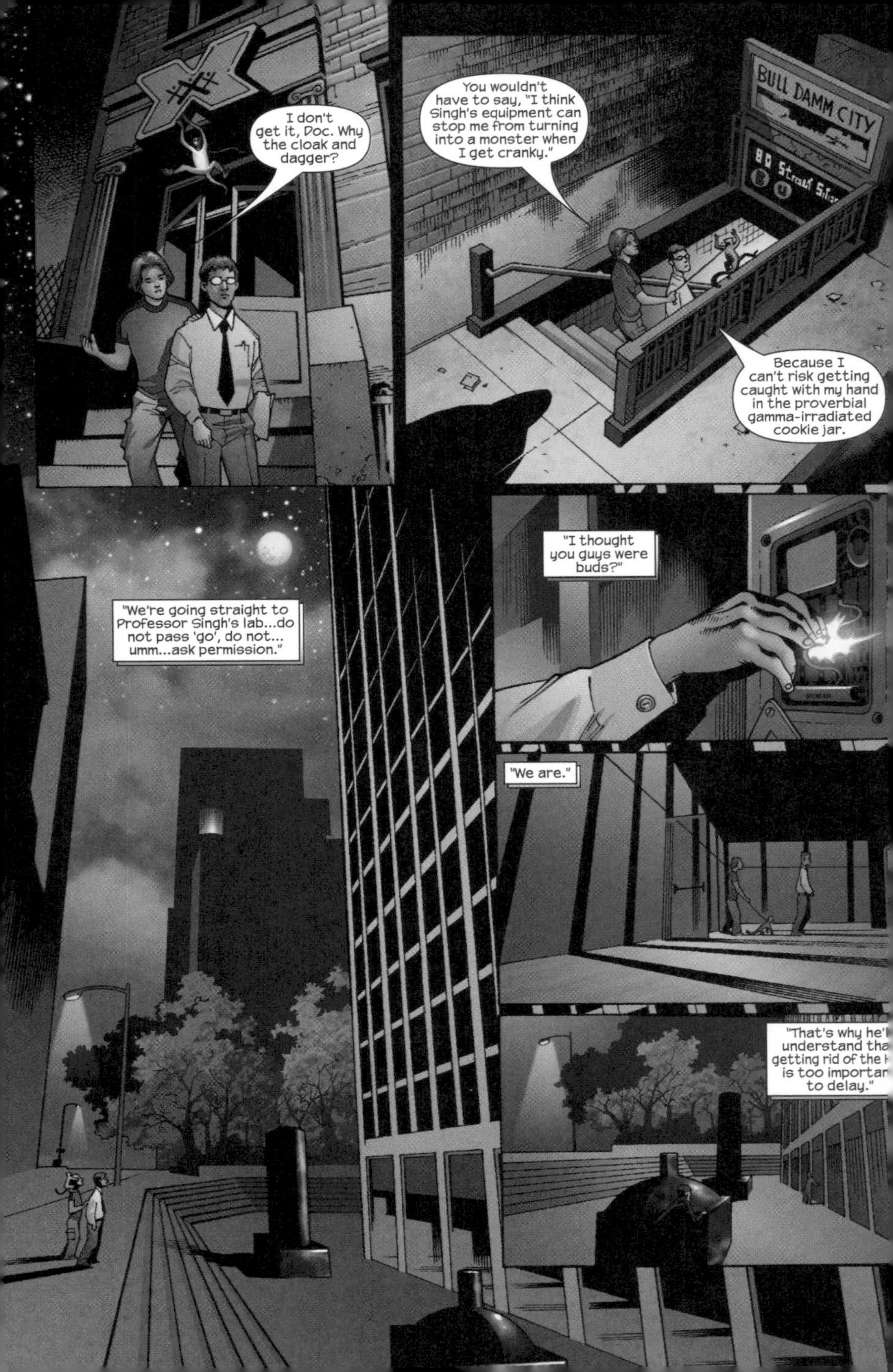
I don't get it, Doc. Why the cloak and dagger?
You wouldn't have to say, "I think Singh's equipment can stop me from turning into a monster when I get cranky."
BULL DAMM CITY
Because I can't risk getting caught with my hand in the proverbial gamma-irradiated cookie jar.
"We're going straight to Professor Singh's lab...do not pass 'go', do not... umm...ask permission."
"I thought you guys were buds?"
"We are."
"That's why he'l understand tha getting rid of the k is too importan to delay."

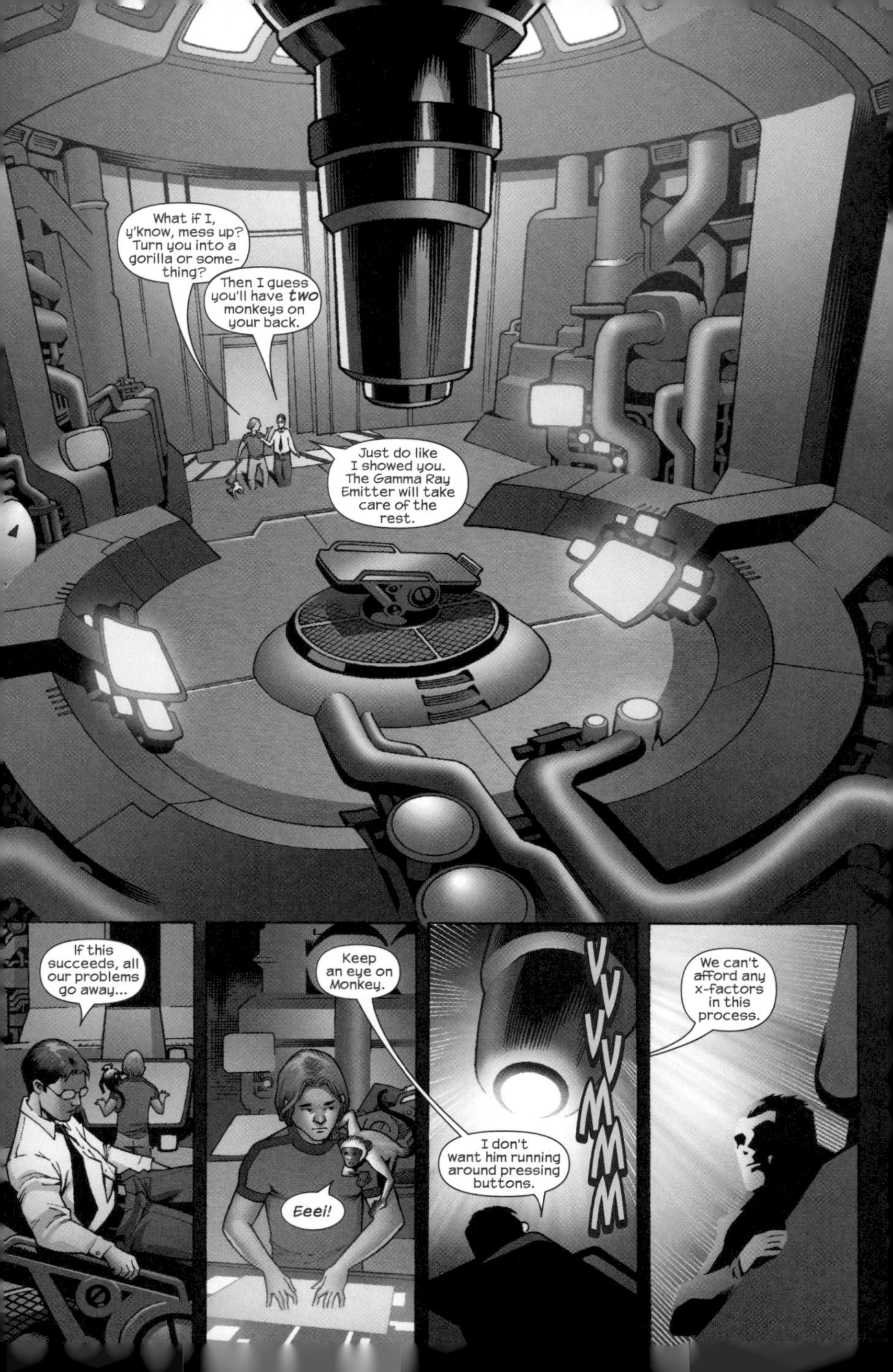
What if I, y'know, mess up? Turn you into a gorilla or something?
Then I guess you'll have *two* monkeys on your back.
Just do like I showed you. The Gamma Ray Emitter will take care of the rest.
If this succeeds, all our problems go away...
Keep an eye on Monkey.
Eeei!
I don't want him running around pressing buttons.
VVVVMMMM
We can't afford any x-factors in this process.

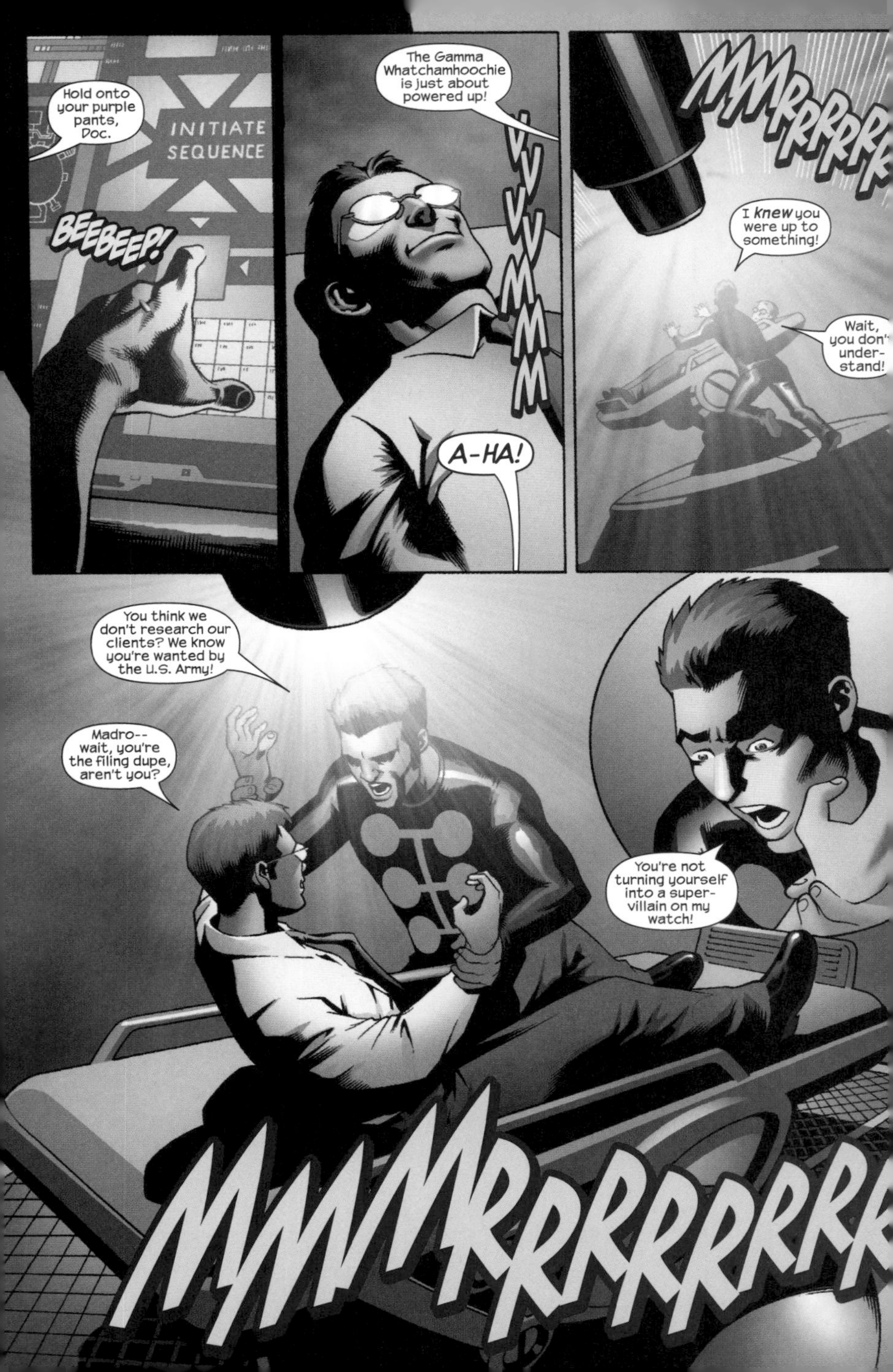
Hold onto your purple pants, Doc.
INITIATE SEQUENCE
BEEBEEP!
The Gamma Whatchamhoochie is just about powered up!
VVVVMMMMM
A-HA!
MMRRRRR
I knew you were up to something!
Wait, you don't under-stand!
You think we don't research our clients? We know you're wanted by the U.S. Army!
Madro-- wait, you're the filing dupe, aren't you?
You're not turning yourself into a super-villain on my watch!
MMMRRRRRRR

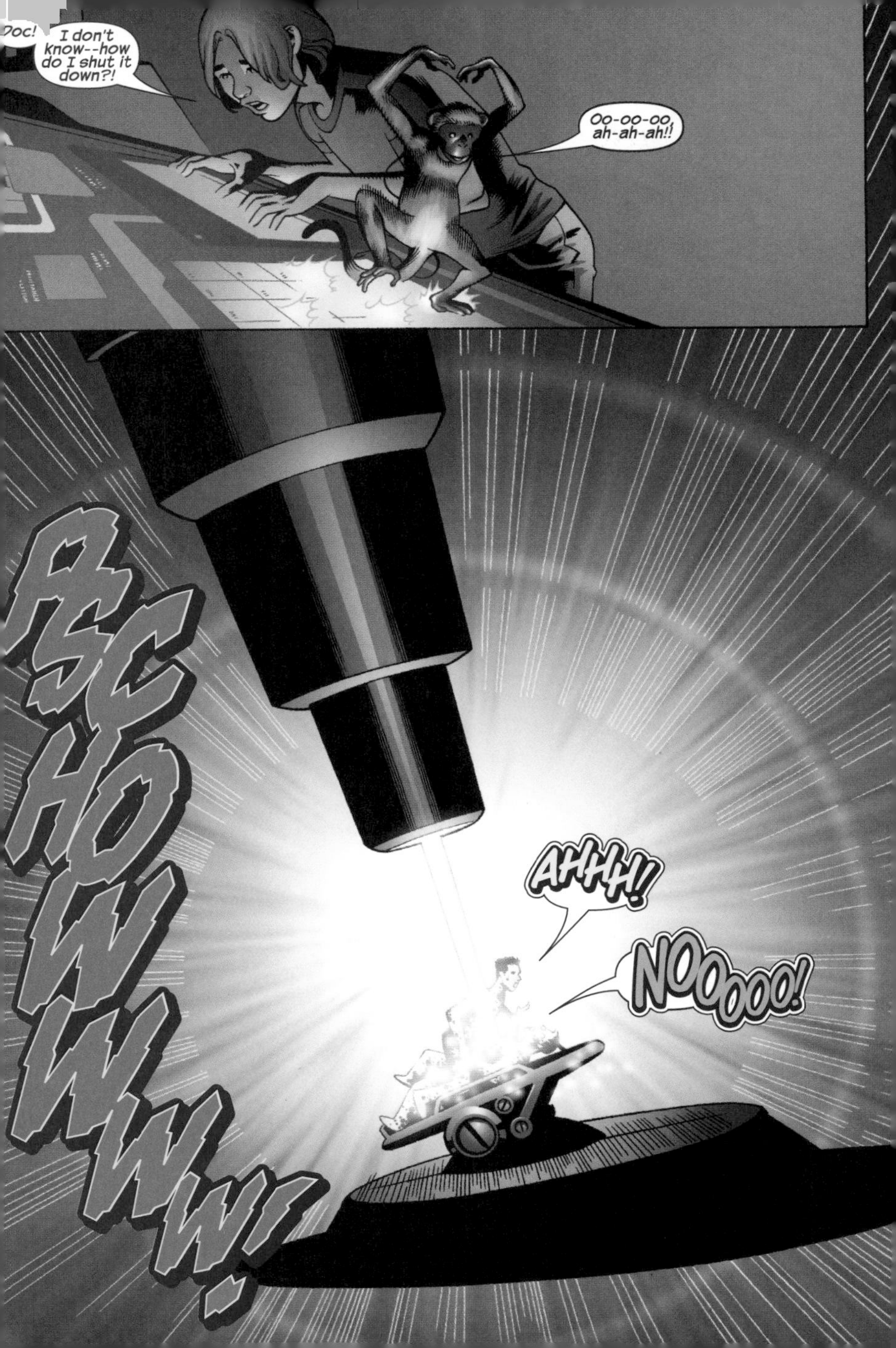
Doc!
I don't know--how do I shut it down?!
Oo-oo-oo, ah-ah-ah!!
ASCHOOWWW!
AHHH!
NOOOOO!

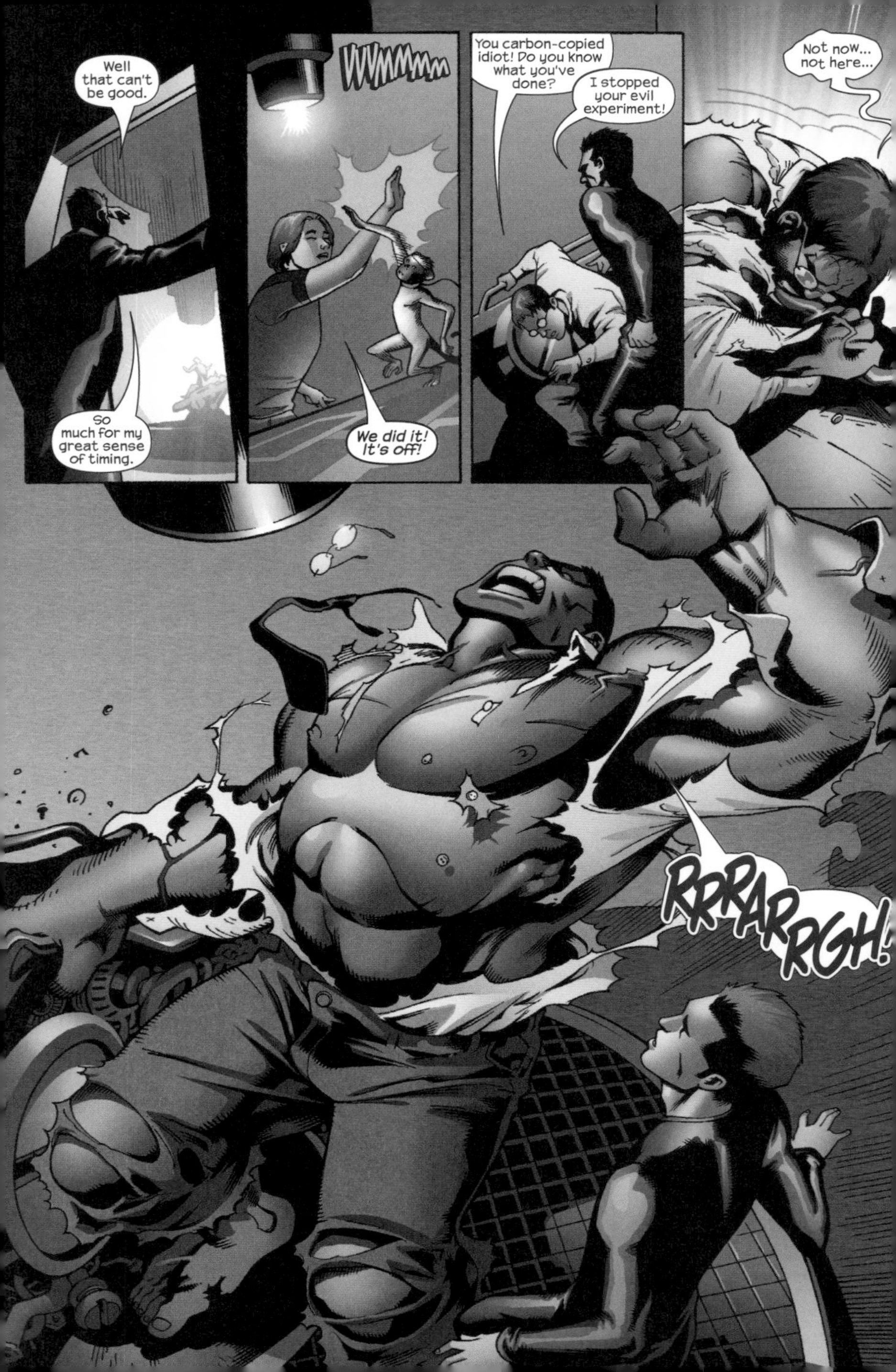

Well that can't be good.
So much for my great sense of timing.
VVVMMMmm
We did it! It's off!
You carbon-copied idiot! Do you know what you've done?
I stopped your evil experiment!
Not now... not here...
RRRARRGH!

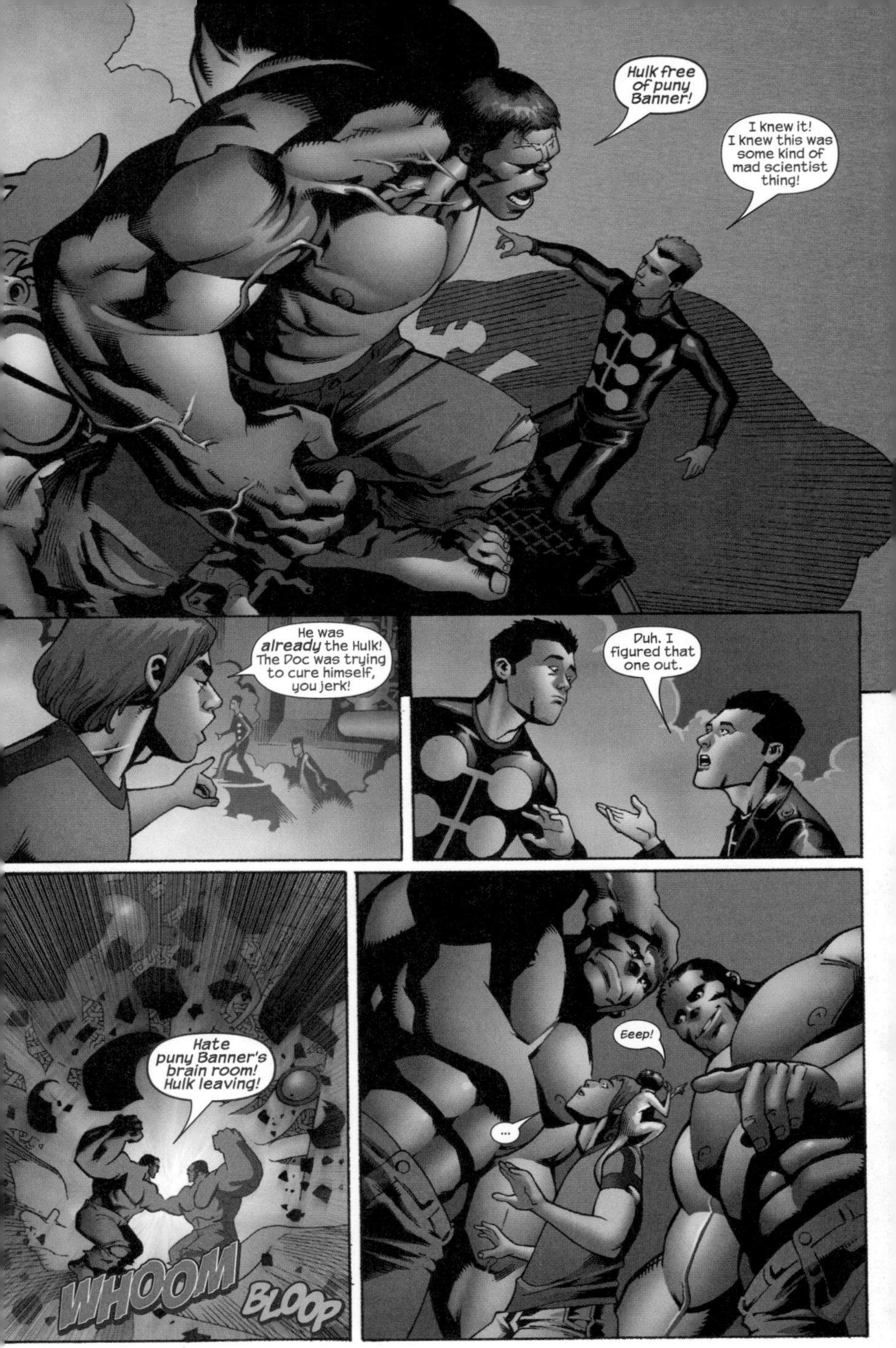
Hulk free of puny Banner!
I knew it! I knew this was some kind of mad scientist thing!
He was *already* the Hulk! The Doc was trying to cure himself, you jerk!
Duh. I figured that one out.
Hate puny Banner's brain room! Hulk leaving!
WHOOM
BLOOP
Eeep!
...

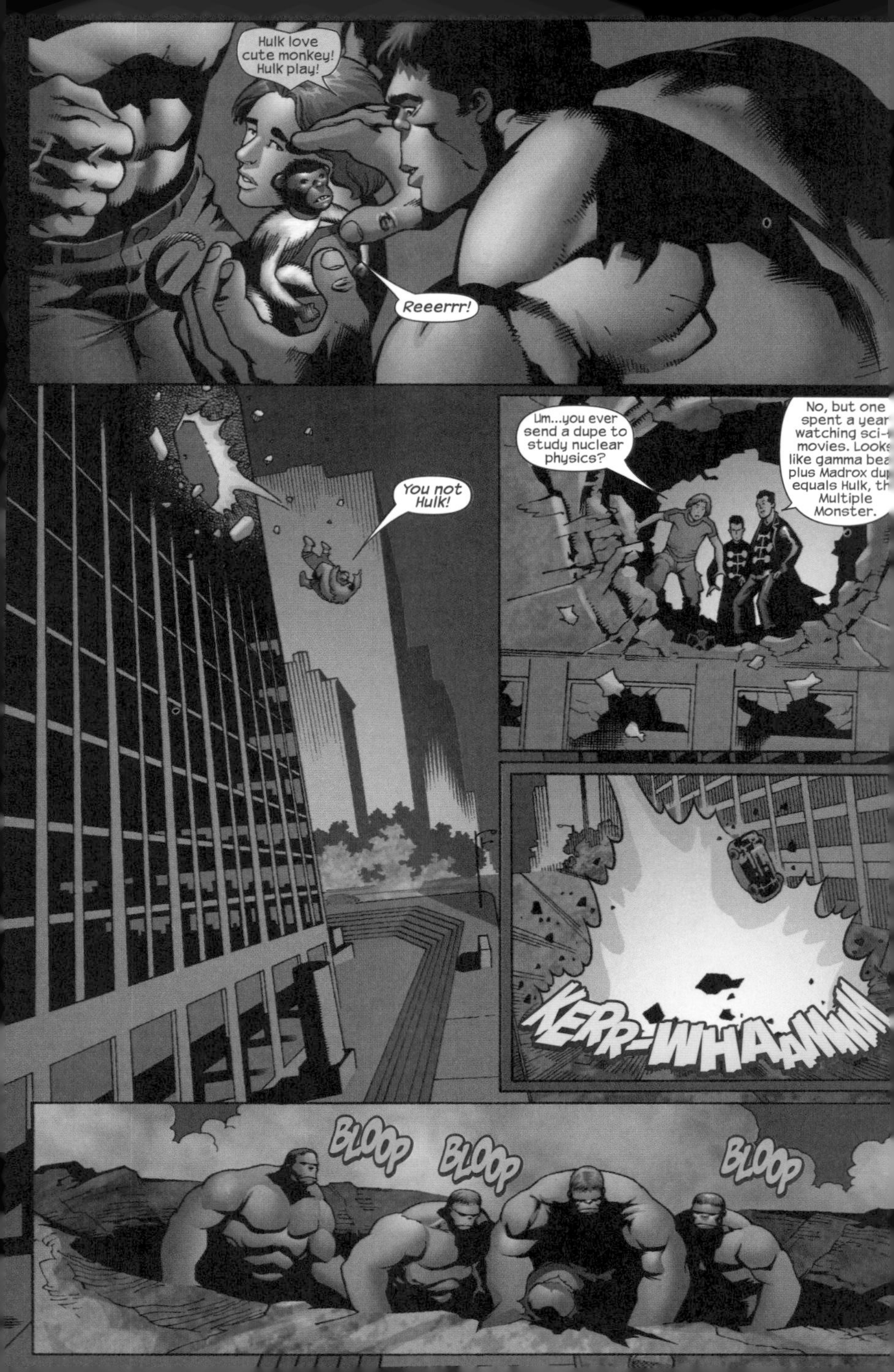

Hulk love cute monkey! Hulk play!
Reeerrr!
You not Hulk!
Um...you ever send a dupe to study nuclear physics?
No, but one spent a year watching sci-
movies. Looks like gamma bea
plus Madrox dup equals Hulk, th
Multiple Monster.
KERR-WHAAMMM
BLOOP
BLOOP
BLOOP

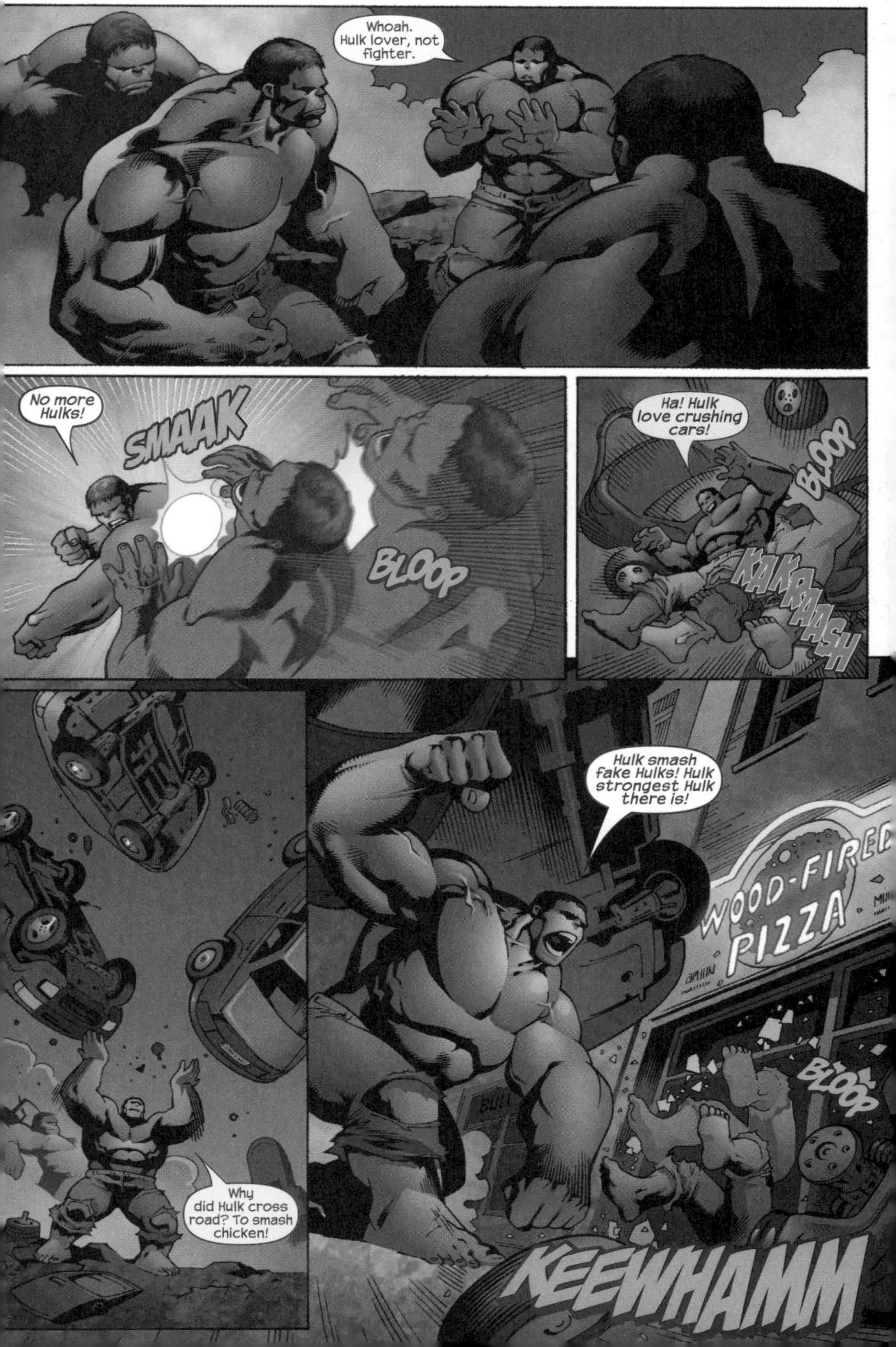
Whoah. Hulk lover, not fighter.
No more Hulks!
SMAAK
BLOOP
Ha! Hulk love crushing cars!
BLOOP
KAKRAASH
Why did Hulk cross road? To smash chicken!
Hulk smash fake Hulks! Hulk strongest Hulk there is!
WOOD-FIRED PIZZA
BLOOP
KEEWHAMM

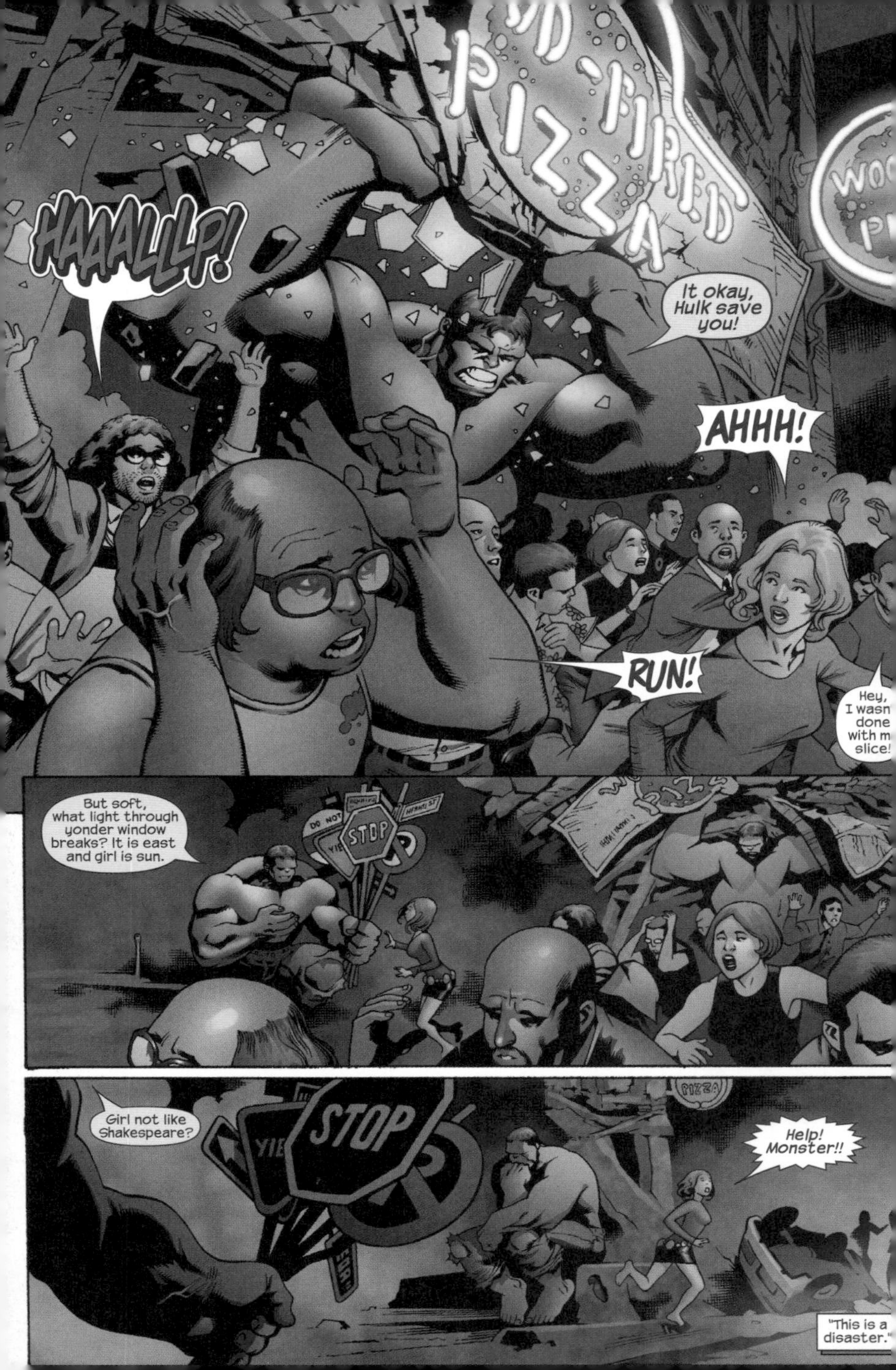
WOOD-FIRED PIZZA
HAAALLLP!
It okay, Hulk save you!
AHHH!
RUN!
Hey, I wasn
done with m
slice!
But soft, what light through yonder window breaks? It is east and girl is sun.
STOP
Girl not like Shakespeare?
STOP
PIZZA
Help! Monster!!
"This is a disaster."

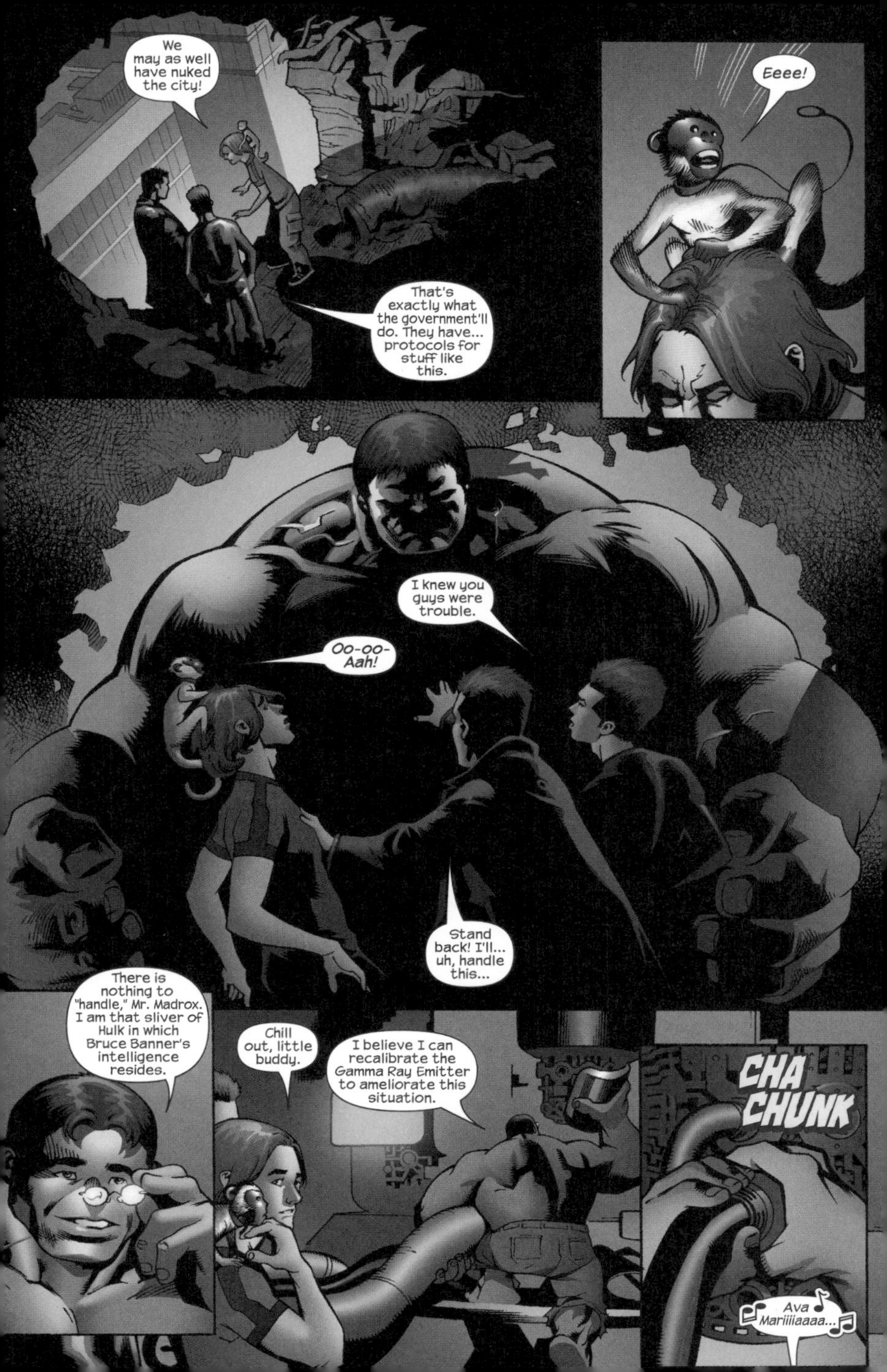
We may as well have nuked the city!
That's exactly what the government'll do. They have... protocols for stuff like this.
Eeee!
I knew you guys were trouble.
Oo-oo-Aah!
Stand back! I'll... uh, handle this...
There is nothing to "handle," Mr. Madrox. I am that sliver of Hulk in which Bruce Banner's intelligence resides.
Chill out, little buddy.
I believe I can recalibrate the Gamma Ray Emitter to ameliorate this situation.
CHA CHUNK
Ava Mariiiaaaa...

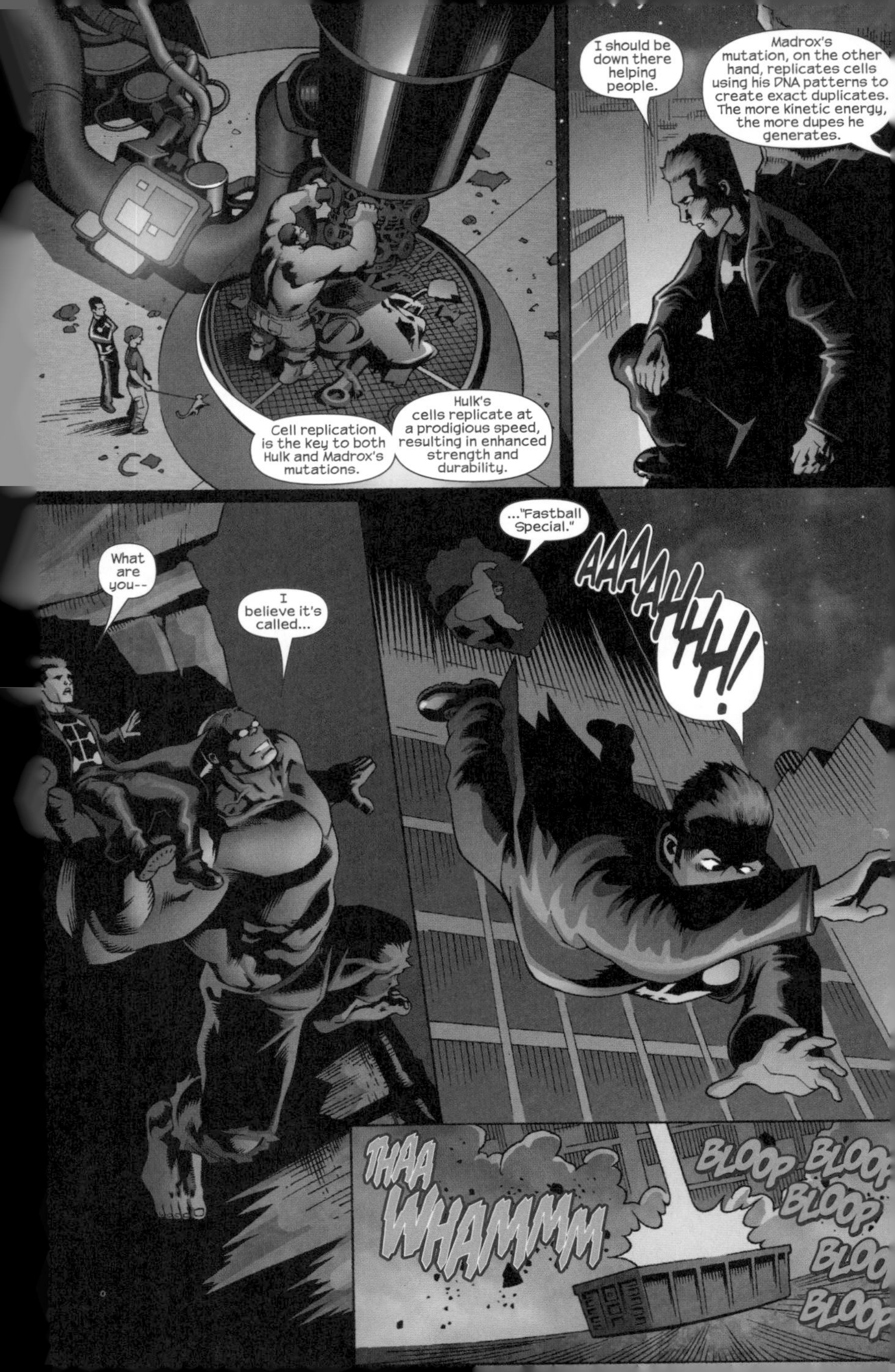
Cell replication is the key to both Hulk and Madrox's mutations.
Hulk's cells replicate at a prodigious speed, resulting in enhanced strength and durability.
I should be down there helping people.
Madrox's mutation, on the other hand, replicates cells using his DNA patterns to create exact duplicates. The more kinetic energy, the more dupes he generates.
What are you--
I believe it's called...
..."Fastball Special."
AAAAHHH!
THAA WHAMMM
BLOOP BLOOP BLOOP BLOOP BLOOP

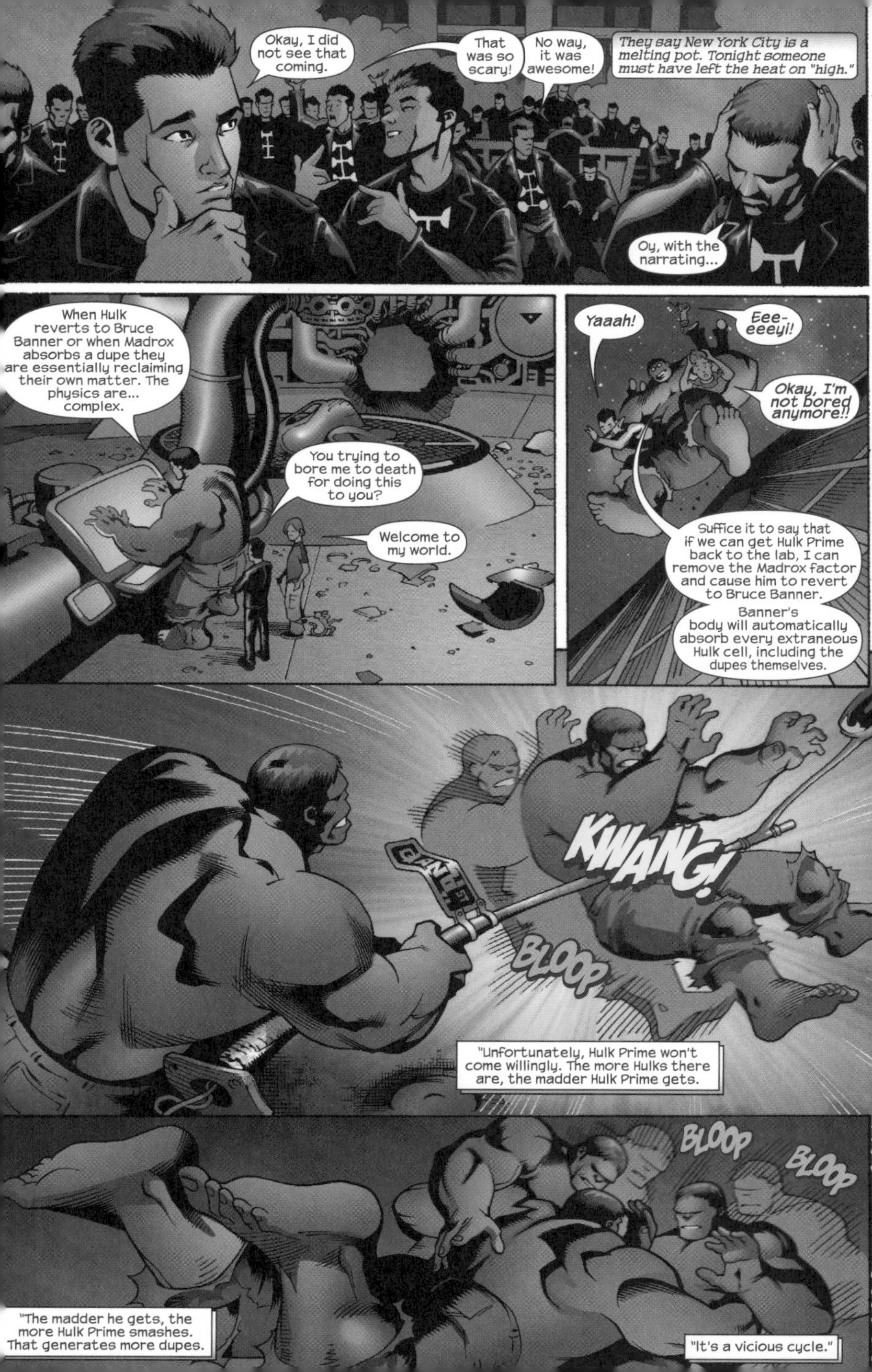
Okay, I did not see that coming.
That was so scary!
No way, it was awesome!
They say New York City is a melting pot. Tonight someone must have left the heat on "high."
Oy, with the narrating...
When Hulk reverts to Bruce Banner or when Madrox absorbs a dupe they are essentially reclaiming their own matter. The physics are... complex.
You trying to bore me to death for doing this to you?
Welcome to my world.
Yaaah!
Eee-eeeyi!
Okay, I'm not bored anymore!!
Suffice it to say that if we can get Hulk Prime back to the lab, I can remove the Madrox factor and cause him to revert to Bruce Banner.
Banner's body will automatically absorb every extraneous Hulk cell, including the dupes themselves.
KWANG!
BLOOP
"Unfortunately, Hulk Prime won't come willingly. The more Hulks there are, the madder Hulk Prime gets.
BLOOP
BLOOP
"The madder he gets, the more Hulk Prime smashes. That generates more dupes.
"It's a vicious cycle."

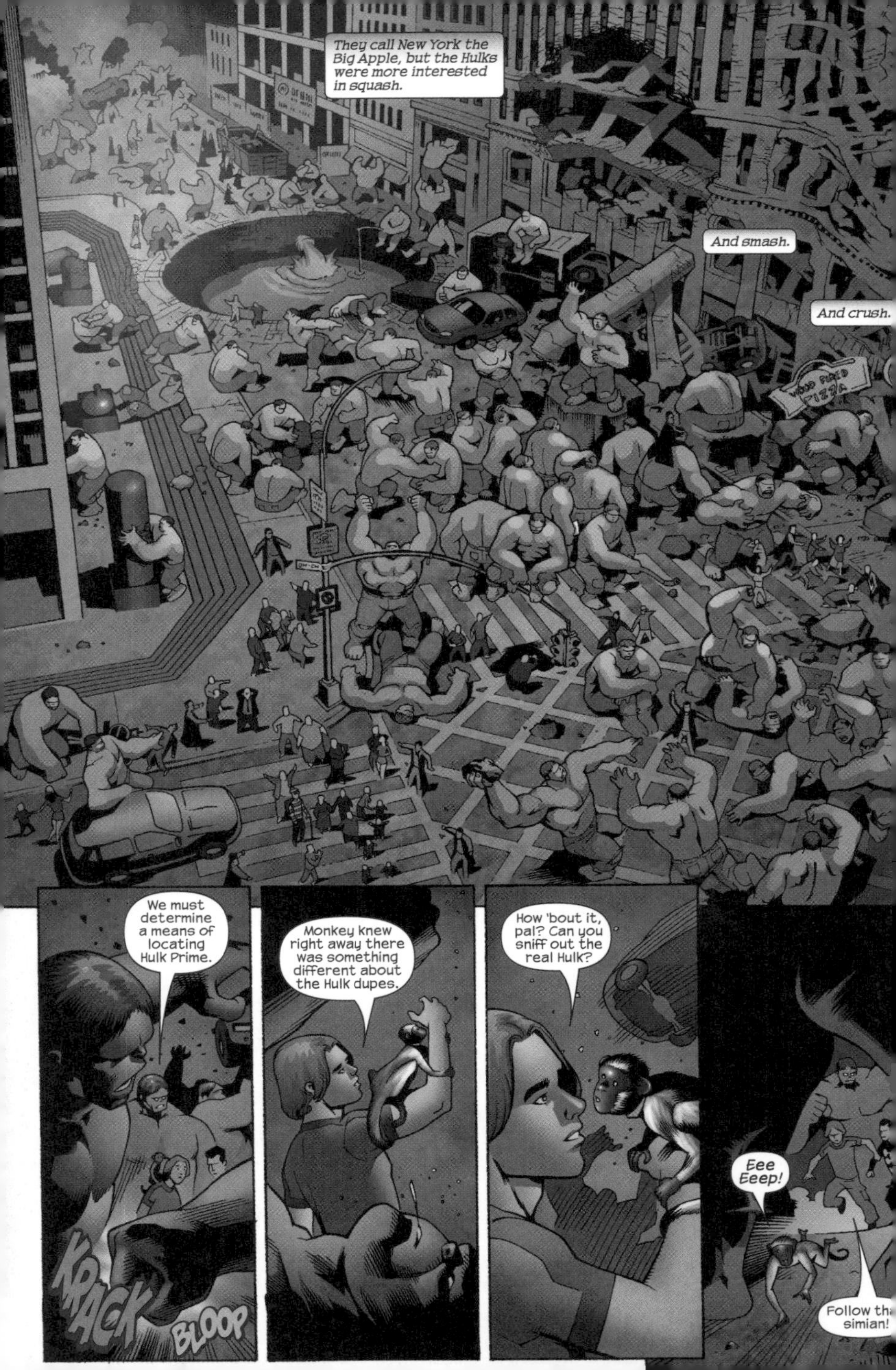

They call New York the Big Apple, but the Hulks were more interested in squash.
And smash.
And crush.
WOOD FIRED PIZZA
We must determine a means of locating Hulk Prime.
KRACK
BLOOP
Monkey knew right away there was something different about the Hulk dupes.
How 'bout it, pal? Can you sniff out the real Hulk?
Eee Eeep!
Follow th
simian!

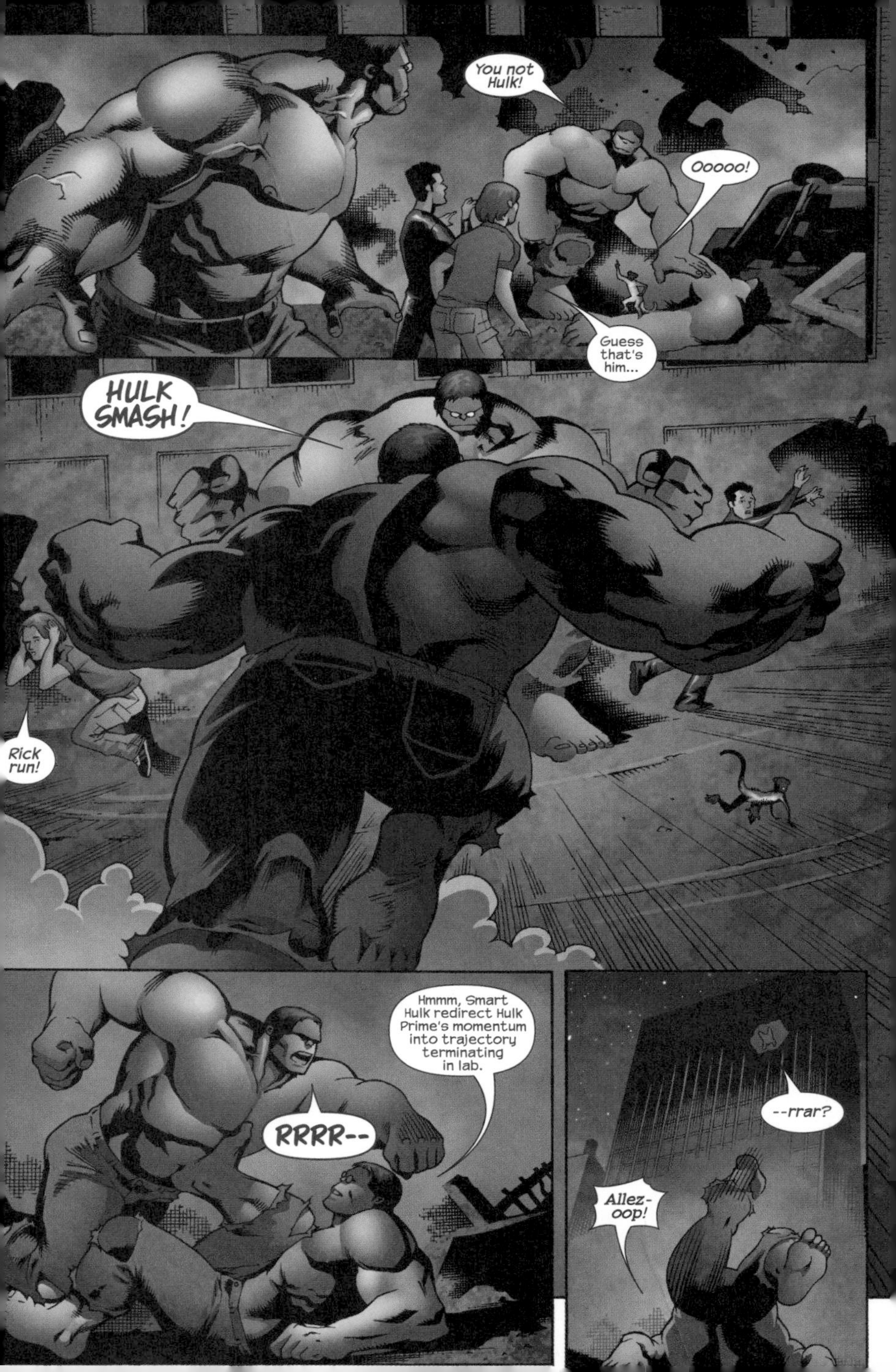
You not Hulk!
Ooooo!
Guess that's him...
HULK SMASH!
Rick run!
Hmmm, Smart Hulk redirect Hulk Prime's momentum into trajectory terminating in lab.
RRRR--
--rrar?
Allez-oop!

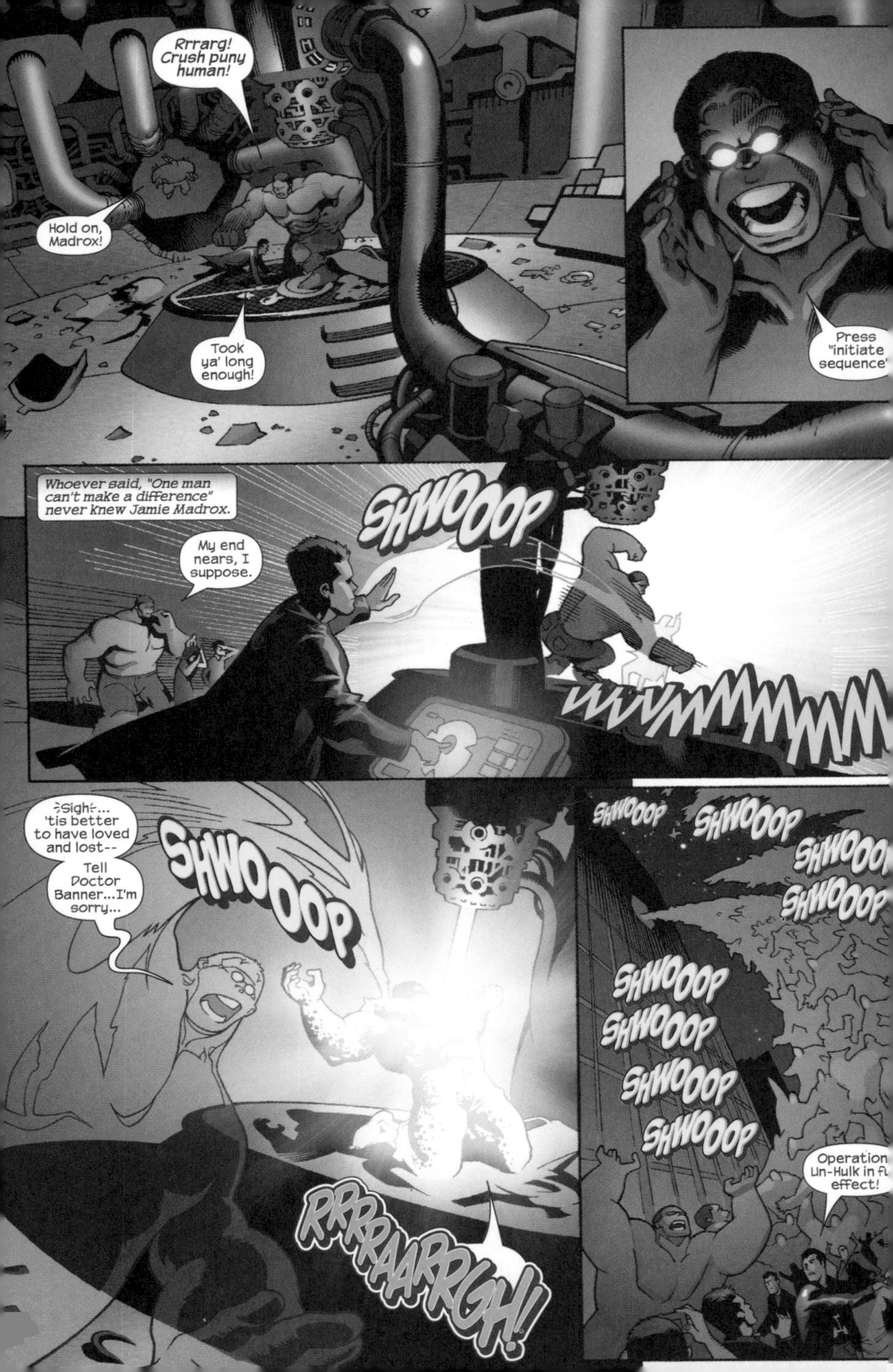
Rrrarg! Crush puny human!
Hold on, Madrox!
Took ya' long enough!
Press "initiate sequence"
Whoever said, "One man can't make a difference" never knew Jamie Madrox.
My end nears, I suppose.
SHWOOOP
WVVMMMMMM
Sigh... 'tis better to have loved and lost--
Tell Doctor Banner...I'm sorry...
SHWOOOP
RRRRAARRGH!
SHWOOOP
SHWOOOP
SHWOOOP
SHWOOOP
SHWOOOP
SHWOOOP
SHWOOOP
SHWOOOP
Operation Un-Hulk in full effect!

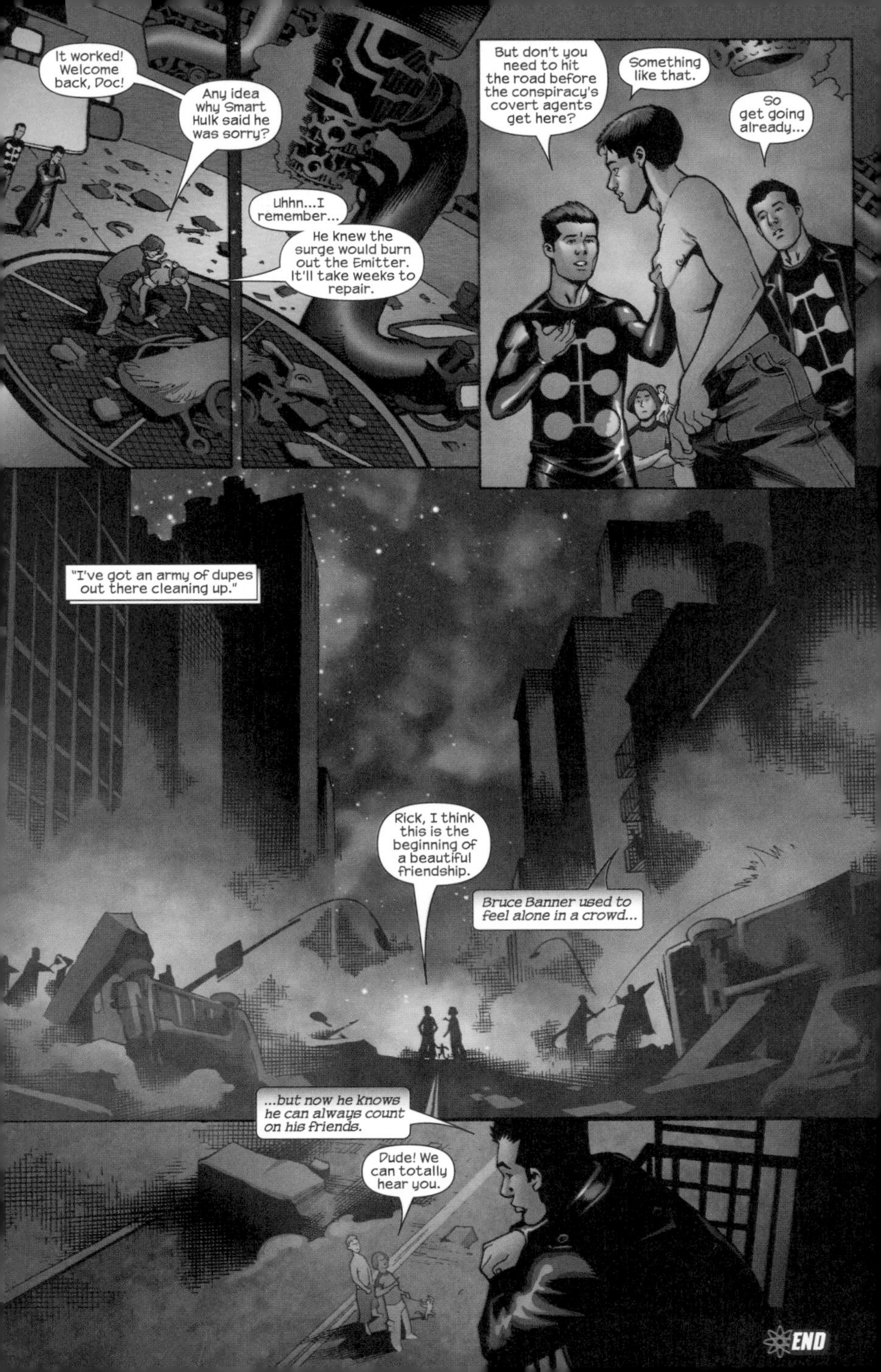

It worked! Welcome back, Doc!
Any idea why Smart Hulk said he was sorry?
Uhhn...I remember...
He knew the surge would burn out the Emitter. It'll take weeks to repair.
But don't you need to hit the road before the conspiracy's covert agents get here?
Something like that.
So get going already...
"I've got an army of dupes out there cleaning up."
Rick, I think this is the beginning of a beautiful friendship.
Bruce Banner used to feel alone in a crowd...
...but now he knows he can always count on his friends.
Dude! We can totally hear you.
END

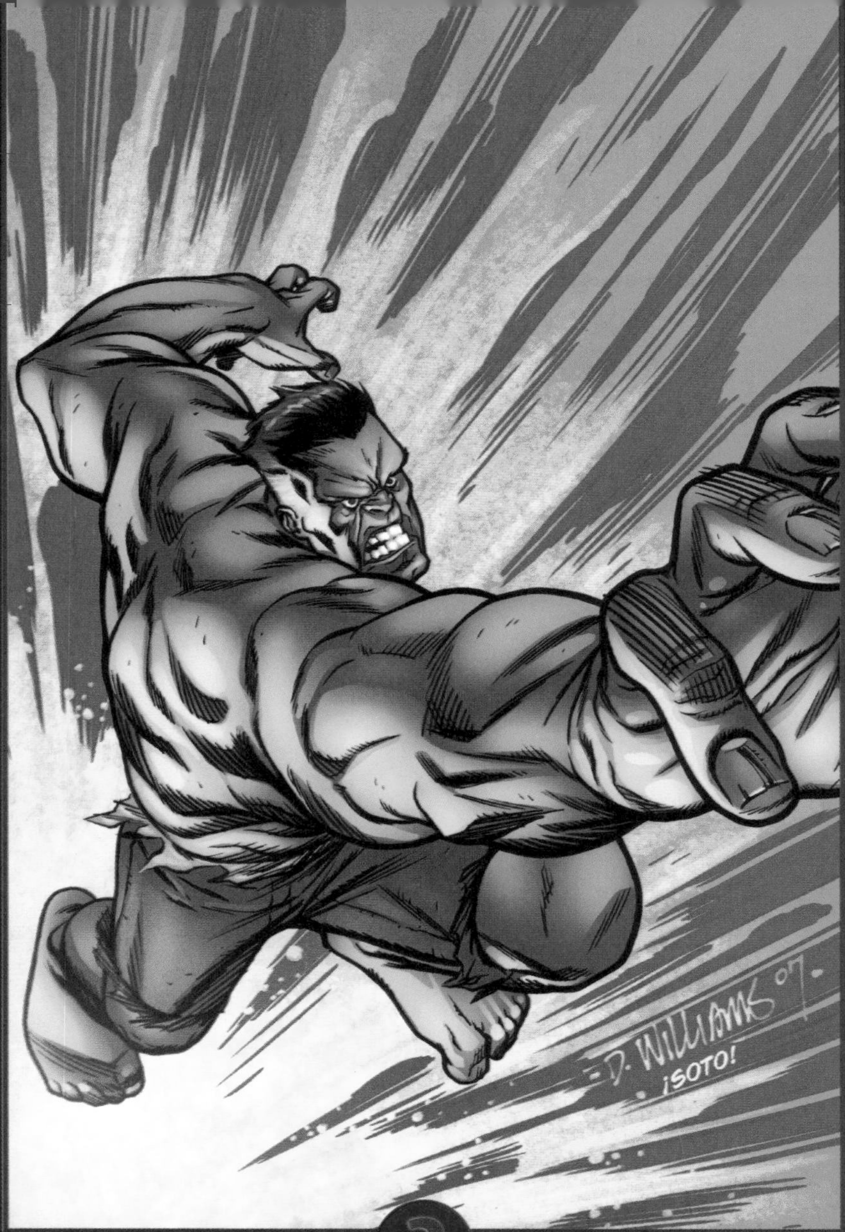
D. WILLIAMS '07
¡SOTO!

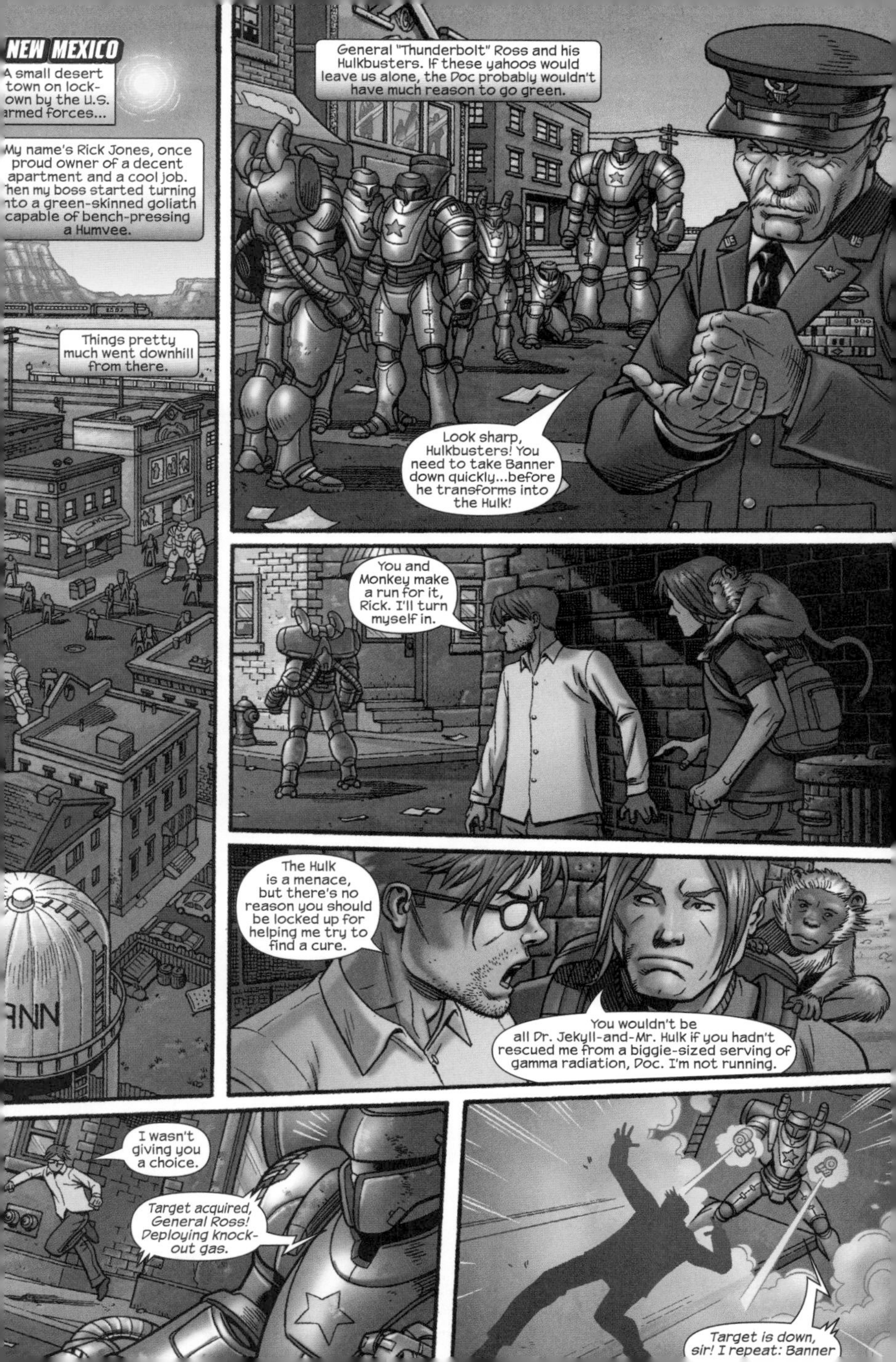
NEW MEXICO
A small desert town on lock-down by the U.S. armed forces...
My name's Rick Jones, once proud owner of a decent apartment and a cool job. Then my boss started turning into a green-skinned goliath capable of bench-pressing a Humvee.
Things pretty much went downhill from there.
General "Thunderbolt" Ross and his Hulkbusters. If these yahoos would leave us alone, the Doc probably wouldn't have much reason to go green.
Look sharp, Hulkbusters! You need to take Banner down quickly...before he transforms into the Hulk!
You and Monkey make a run for it, Rick. I'll turn myself in.
The Hulk is a menace, but there's no reason you should be locked up for helping me try to find a cure.
You wouldn't be all Dr. Jekyll-and-Mr. Hulk if you hadn't rescued me from a biggie-sized serving of gamma radiation, Doc. I'm not running.
I wasn't giving you a choice.
Target acquired, General Ross! Deploying knock-out gas.
Target is down, sir! I repeat: Banner

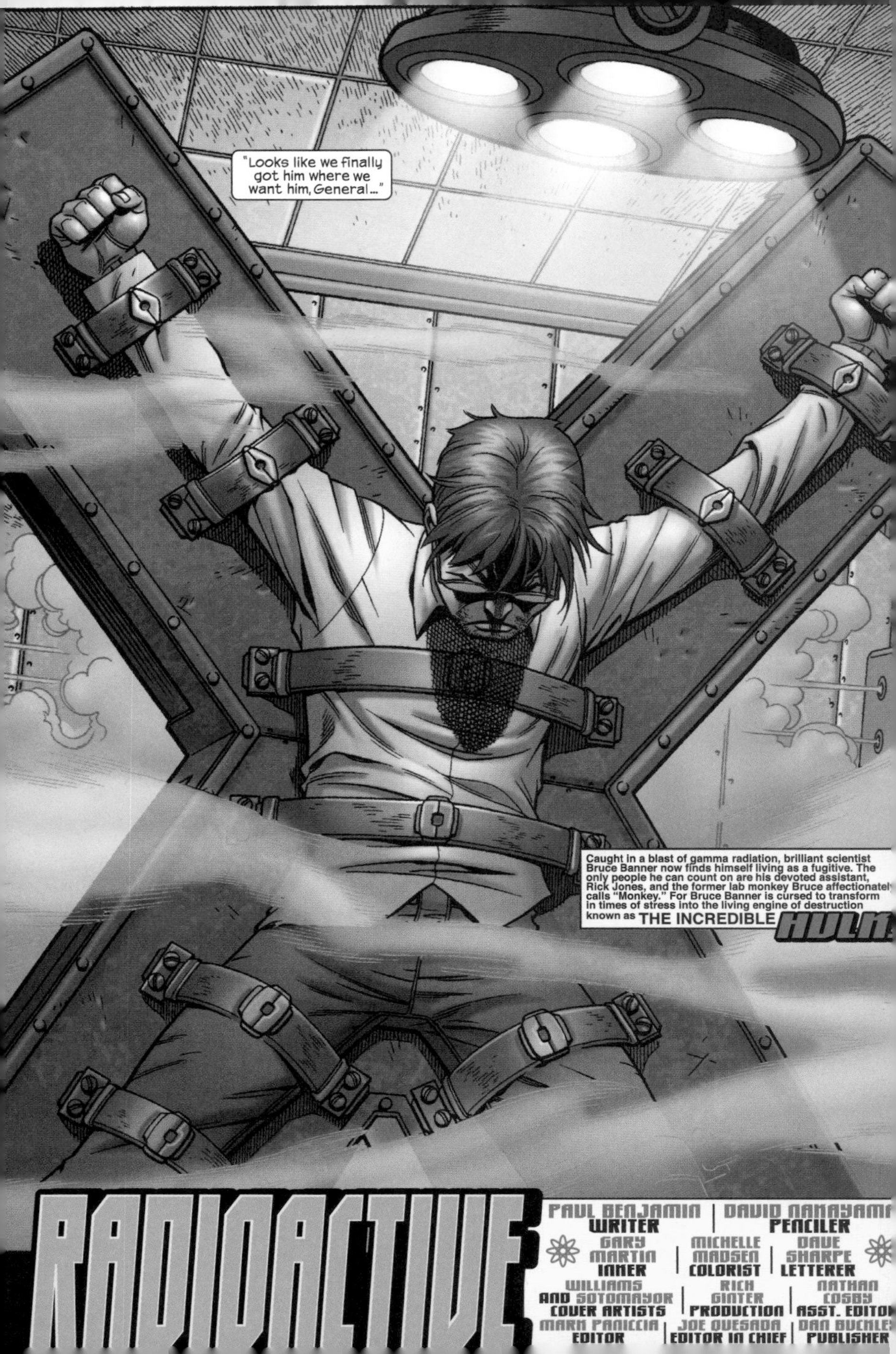
"Looks like we finally got him where we want him, General..."
Caught in a blast of gamma radiation, brilliant scientist Bruce Banner now finds himself living as a fugitive. The only people he can count on are his devoted assistant, Rick Jones, and the former lab monkey Bruce affectionately calls "Monkey." For Bruce Banner is cursed to transform in times of stress into the living engine of destruction known as THE INCREDIBLE HULK!
RADIOACTIVE
PAUL BENJAMIN WRITER
DAVID NAKAYAMA PENCILER
GARY MARTIN INKER
MICHELLE MADSEN COLORIST
DAVE SHARPE LETTERER
WILLIAMS AND SOTOMAYOR COVER ARTISTS
RICH GINTER PRODUCTION
NATHAN COSBY ASST. EDITOR
MARK PANICCIA EDITOR
JOE QUESADA EDITOR IN CHIEF
DAN BUCKLEY PUBLISHER

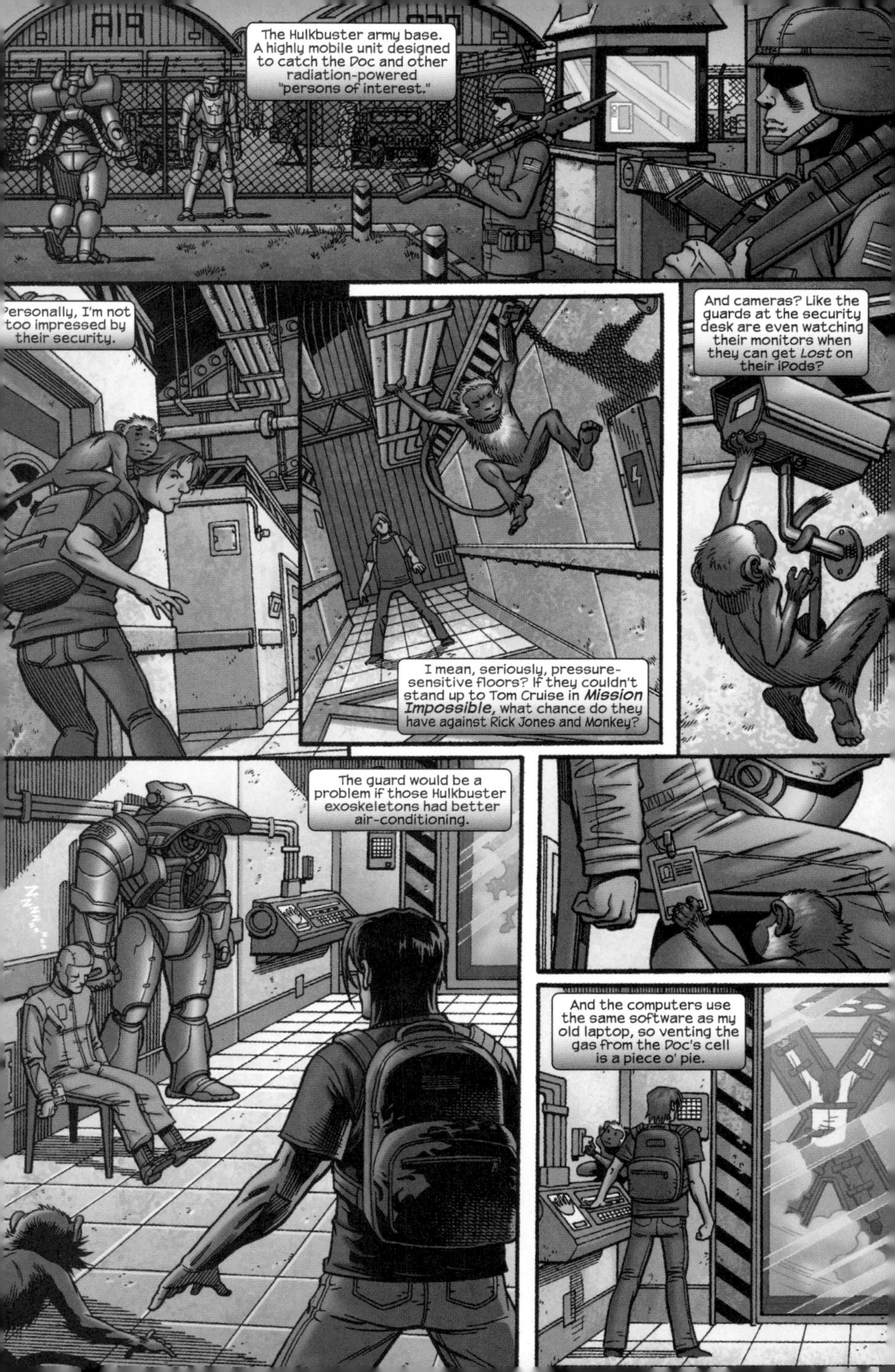

AIR
The Hulkbuster army base. A highly mobile unit designed to catch the Doc and other radiation-powered "persons of interest."
Personally, I'm not too impressed by their security.
I mean, seriously, pressure-sensitive floors? If they couldn't stand up to Tom Cruise in *Mission Impossible,* what chance do they have against Rick Jones and Monkey?
And cameras? Like the guards at the security desk are even watching their monitors when they can get *Lost* on their iPods?
The guard would be a problem if those Hulkbuster exoskeletons had better air-conditioning.
And the computers use the same software as my old laptop, so venting the gas from the Doc's cell is a piece o' pie.

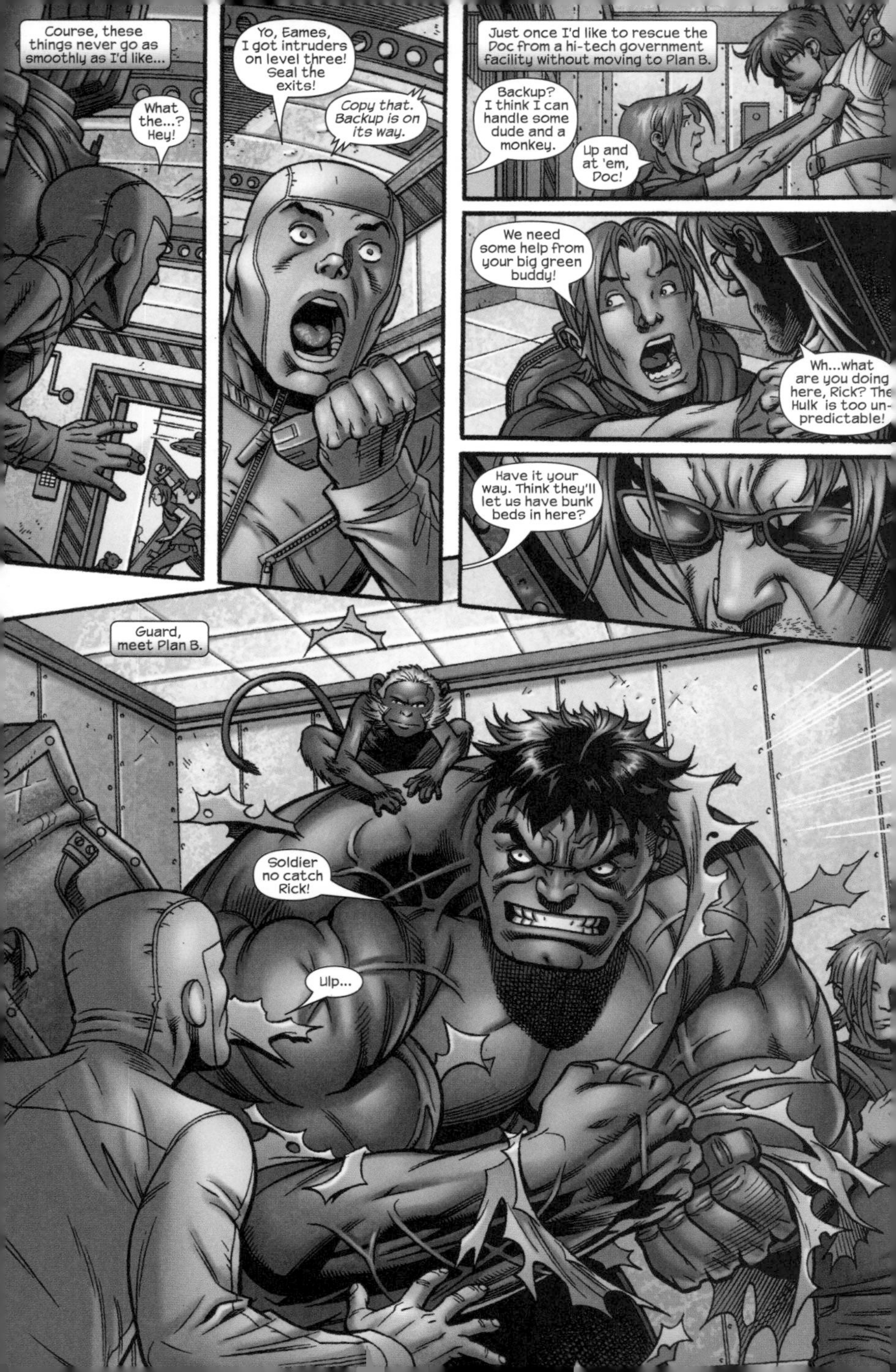
Course, these things never go as smoothly as I'd like...
What the...? Hey!
Yo, Eames, I got intruders on level three! Seal the exits!
Copy that. Backup is on its way.
Just once I'd like to rescue the Doc from a hi-tech government facility without moving to Plan B.
Backup? I think I can handle some dude and a monkey.
Up and at 'em, Doc!
We need some help from your big green buddy!
Wh...what are you doing here, Rick? The Hulk is too un-predictable!
Have it your way. Think they'll let us have bunk beds in here?
Guard, meet Plan B.
Soldier no catch Rick!
Ulp...

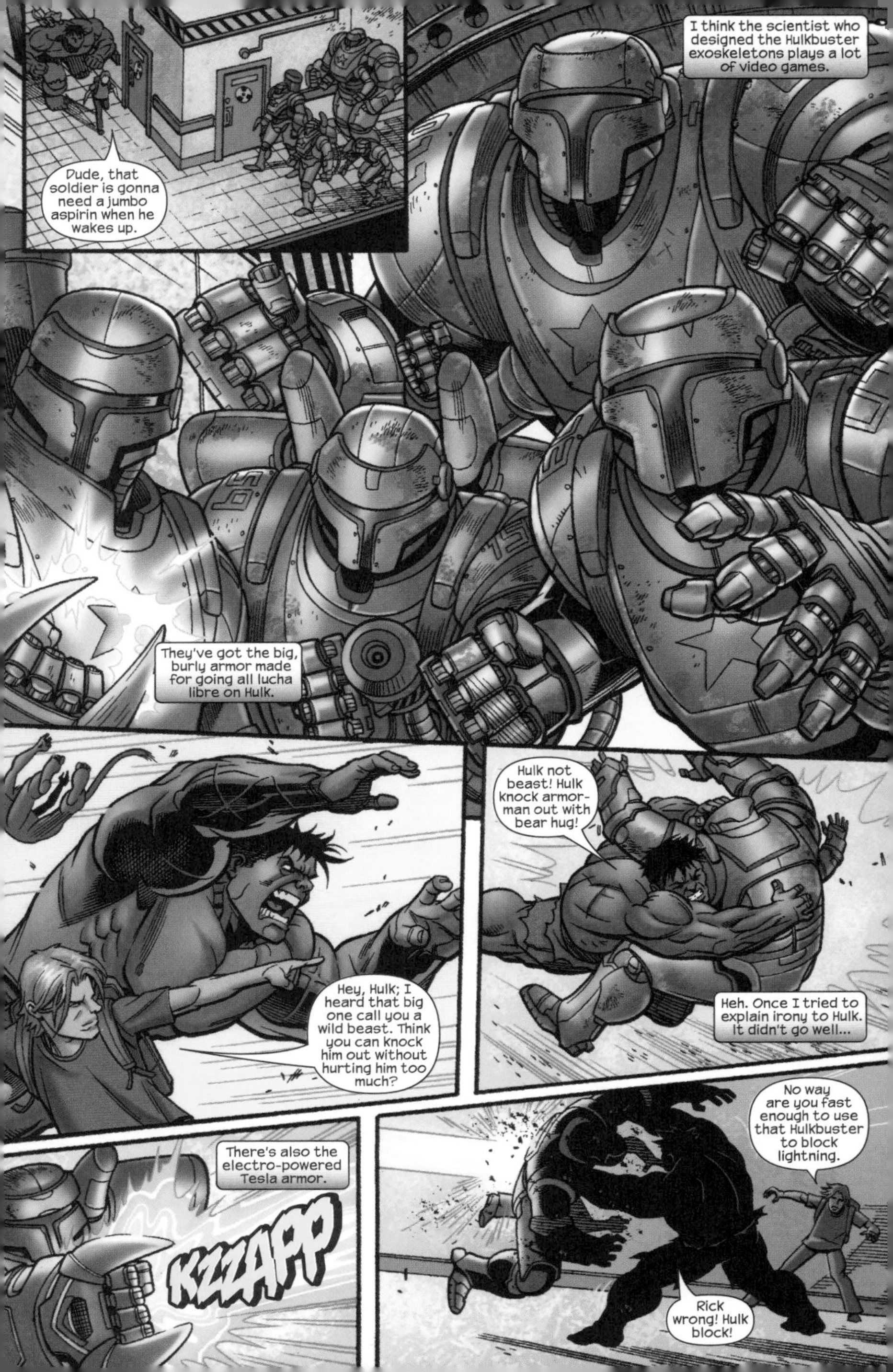
Dude, that soldier is gonna need a jumbo aspirin when he wakes up.
I think the scientist who designed the Hulkbuster exoskeletons plays a lot of video games.
They've got the big, burly armor made for going all lucha libre on Hulk.
Hey, Hulk; I heard that big one call you a wild beast. Think you can knock him out without hurting him too much?
Hulk not beast! Hulk knock armor-man out with bear hug!
Heh. Once I tried to explain irony to Hulk. It didn't go well...
There's also the electro-powered Tesla armor.
KZZAPP
No way are you fast enough to use that Hulkbuster to block lightning.
Rick wrong! Hulk block!

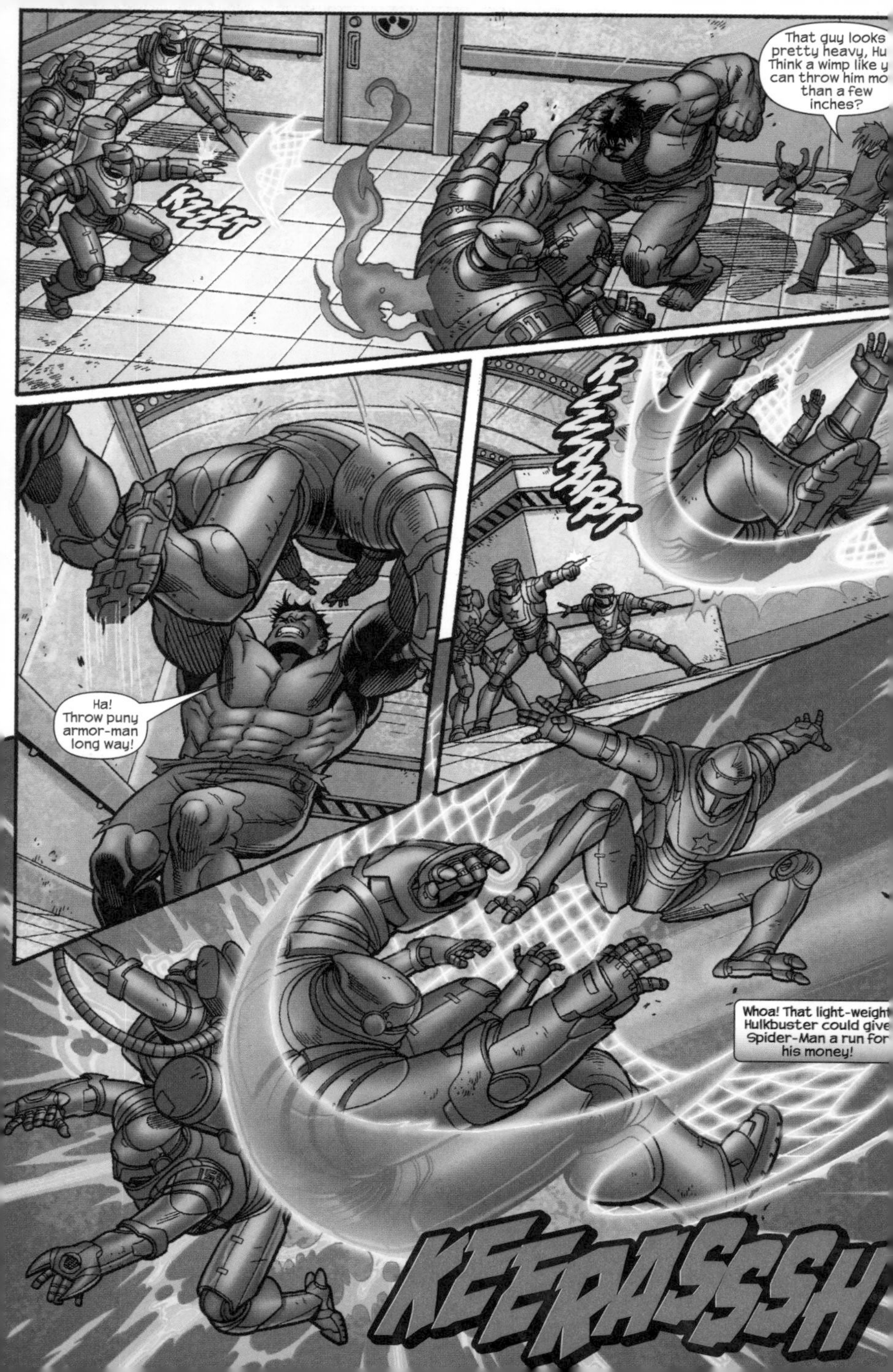

That guy looks pretty heavy, Hu Think a wimp like y can throw him mo than a few inches?
KZZZT
Ha! Throw puny armor-man long way!
KZZZAPPT
Whoa! That light-weight Hulkbuster could give Spider-Man a run for his money!
KEERASSSH

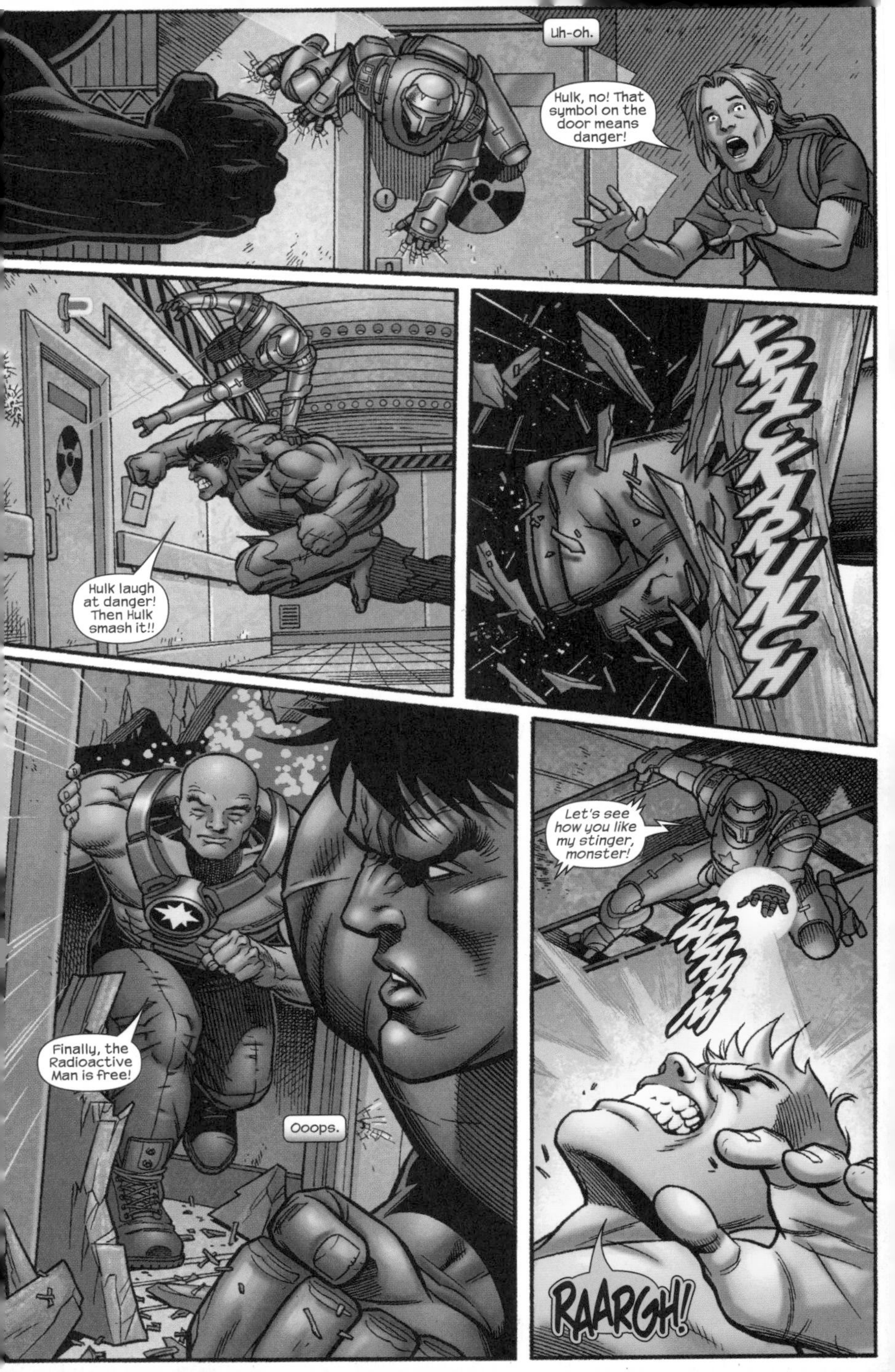

Uh-oh.
Hulk, no! That symbol on the door means danger!
Hulk laugh at danger! Then Hulk smash it!!
KRACKARUNCH
Finally, the Radioactive Man is free!
Ooops.
Let's see how you like my stinger, monster!
RAARGH!

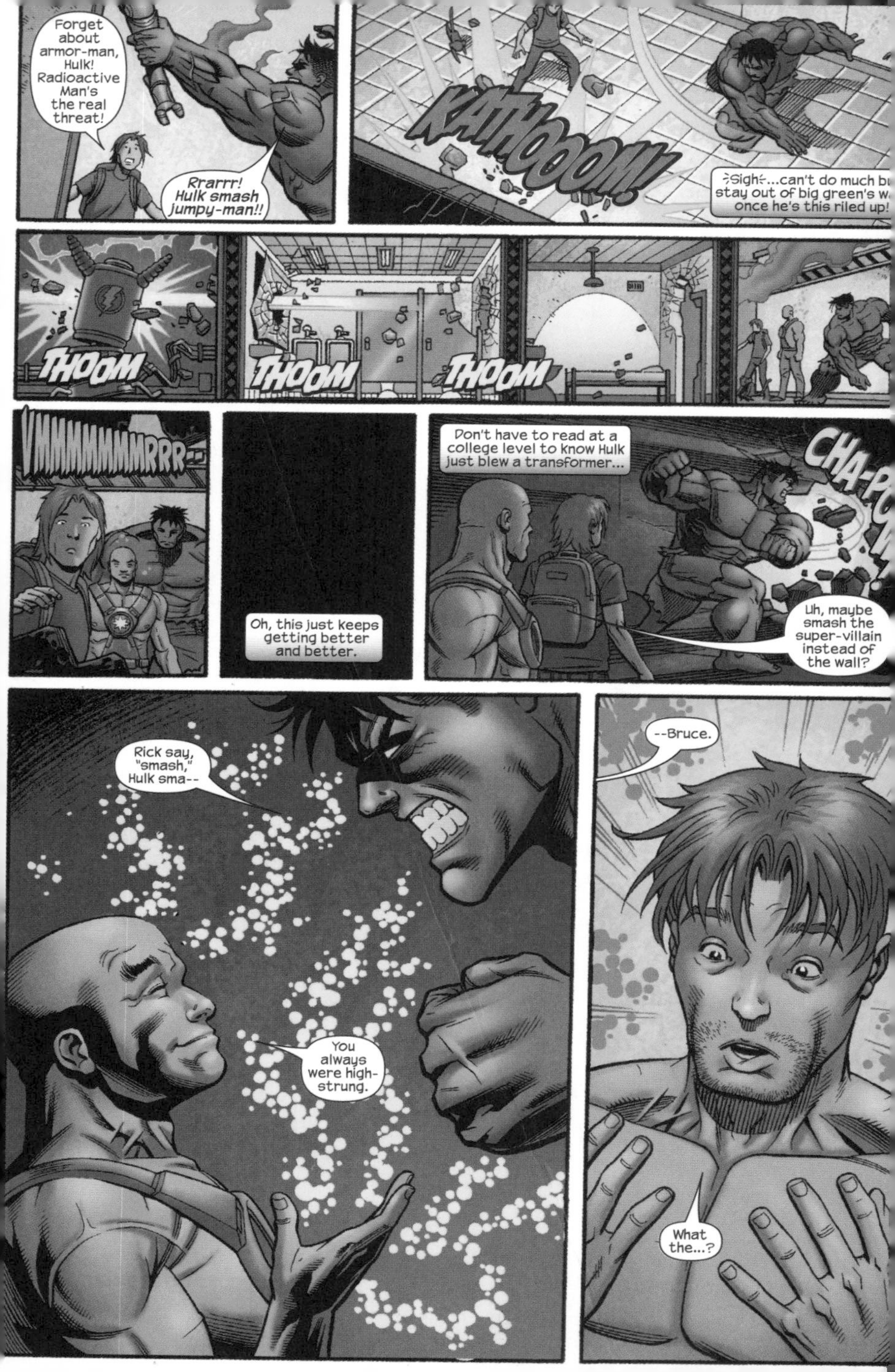
Forget about armor-man, Hulk! Radioactive Man's the real threat!
Rrarrr! Hulk smash jumpy-man!!
KATHOOOOM!!
Sigh...can't do much bu stay out of big green's wa once he's this riled up!
THOOM
THOOM
THOOM
VMMMMMMMRRR
Oh, this just keeps getting better and better.
Don't have to read at a college level to know Hulk just blew a transformer...
CHA-POW
Uh, maybe smash the super-villain instead of the wall?
Rick say, "smash," Hulk sma--
You always were high-strung.
--Bruce.
What the...?

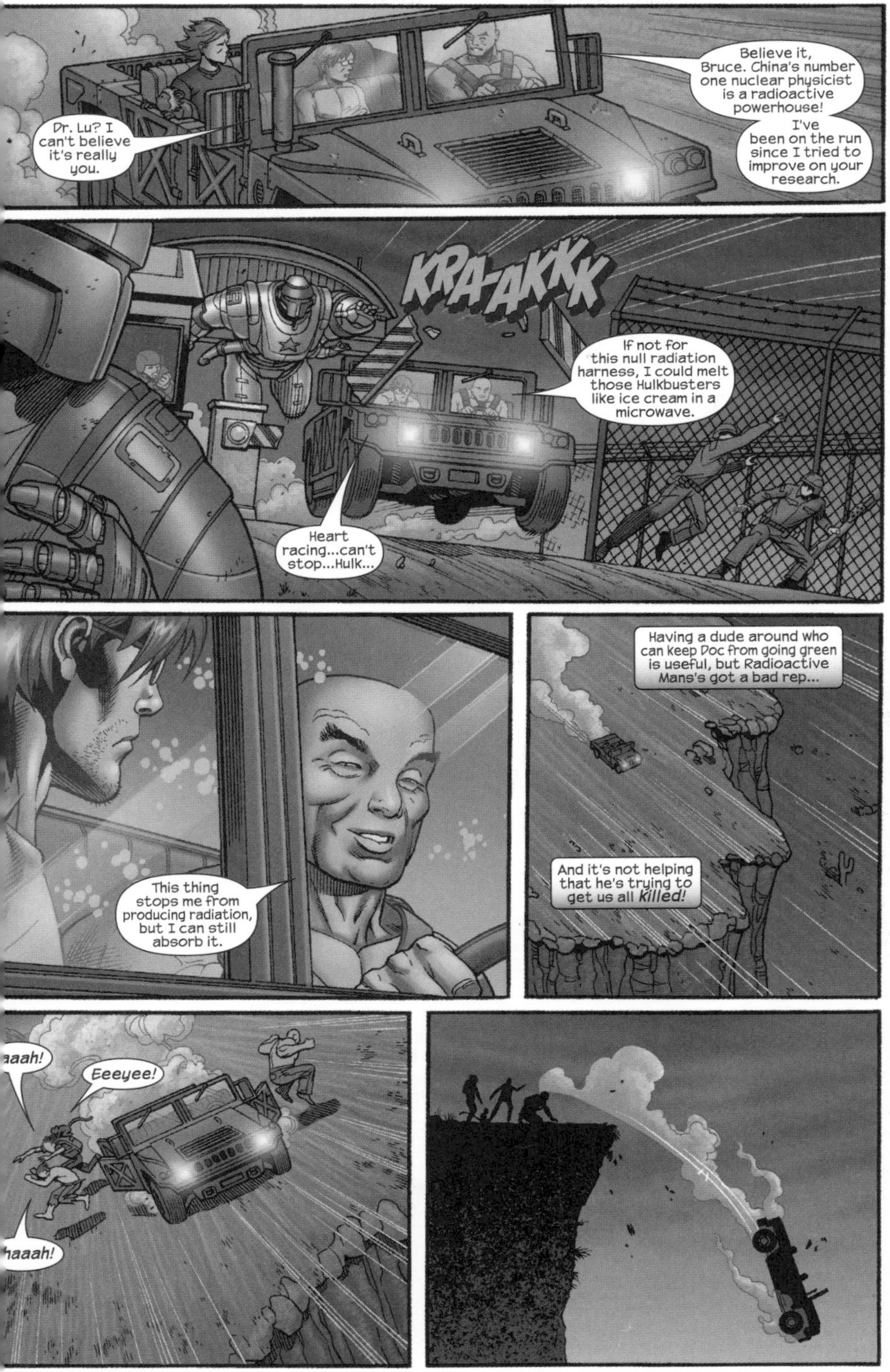
Dr. Lu? I can't believe it's really you.
Believe it, Bruce. China's number one nuclear physicist is a radioactive powerhouse!
I've been on the run since I tried to improve on your research.
KRA-AKKK
If not for this null radiation harness, I could melt those Hulkbusters like ice cream in a microwave.
Heart racing...can't stop...Hulk...
This thing stops me from producing radiation, but I can still absorb it.
Having a dude around who can keep Doc from going green is useful, but Radioactive Mans's got a bad rep...
And it's not helping that he's trying to get us all *killed!*
aaah!
Eeeyee!
haaah!

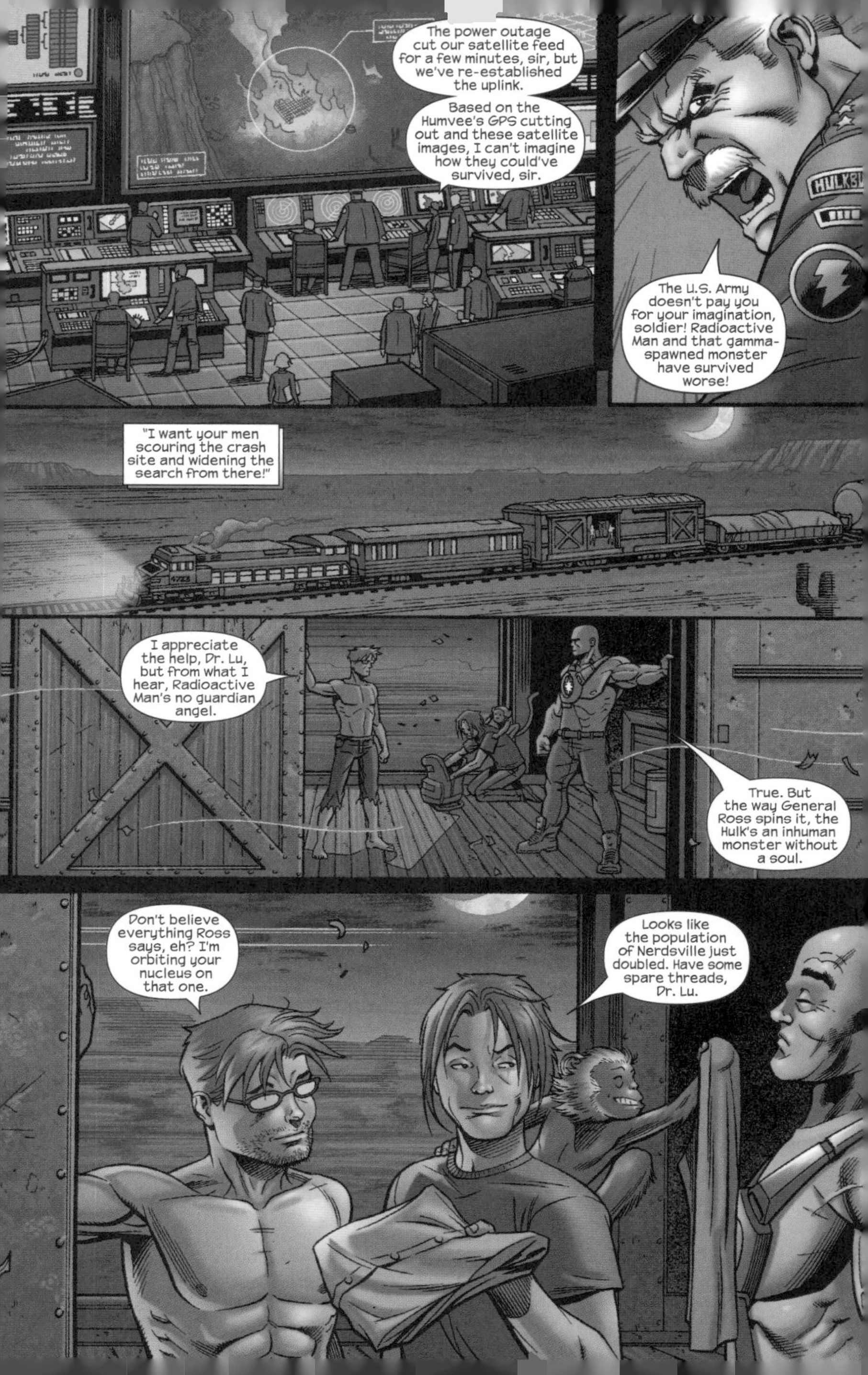
The power outage cut our satellite feed for a few minutes, sir, but we've re-established the uplink.
Based on the Humvee's GPS cutting out and these satellite images, I can't imagine how they could've survived, sir.
The U.S. Army doesn't pay you for your imagination, soldier! Radioactive Man and that gamma-spawned monster have survived worse!
HULKBU
"I want your men scouring the crash site and widening the search from there!"
I appreciate the help, Dr. Lu, but from what I hear, Radioactive Man's no guardian angel.
True. But the way General Ross spins it, the Hulk's an inhuman monster without a soul.
Don't believe everything Ross says, eh? I'm orbiting your nucleus on that one.
Looks like the population of Nerdsville just doubled. Have some spare threads, Dr. Lu.

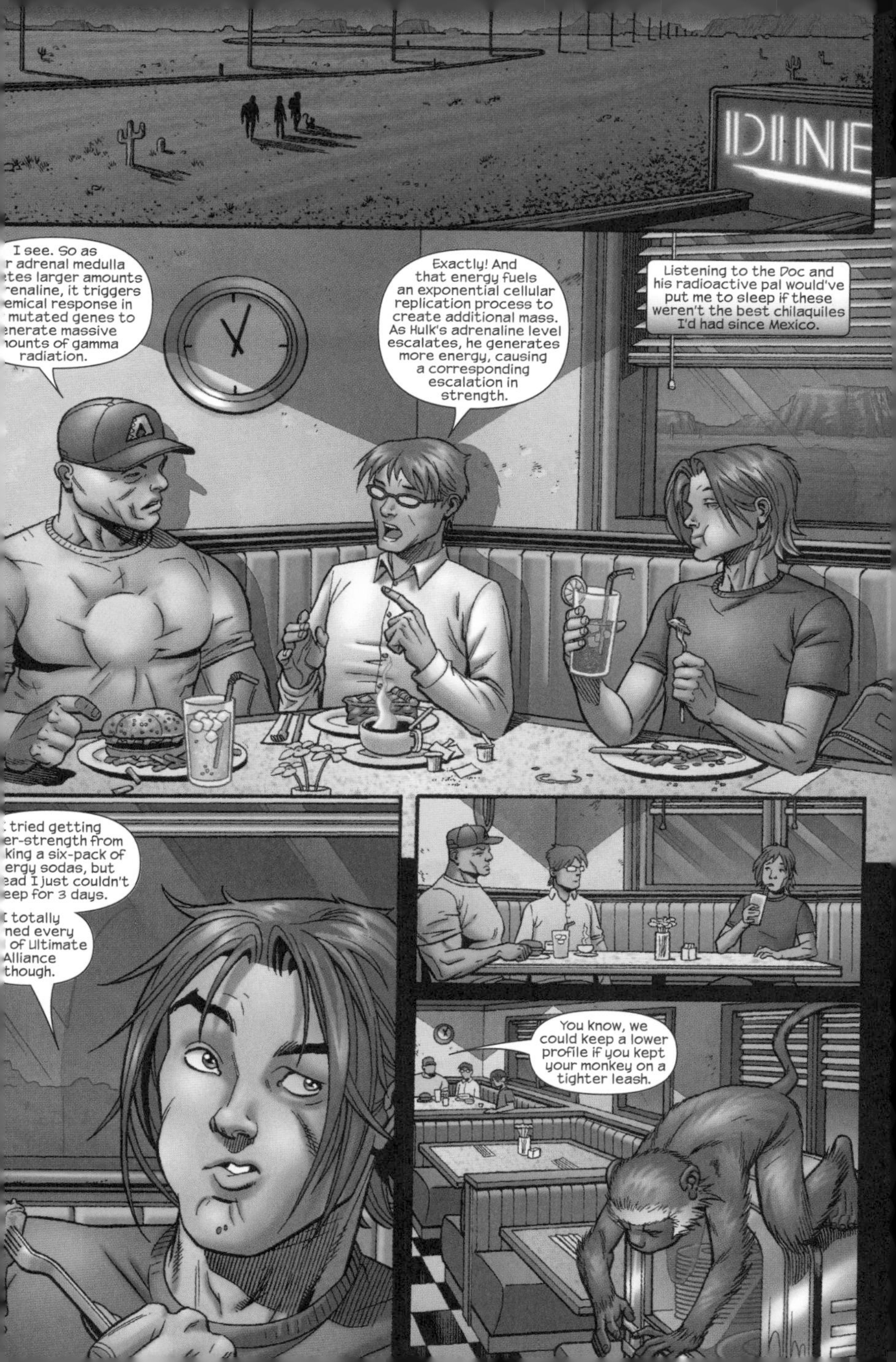
DINE
I see. So as
r adrenal medulla
etes larger amounts
renaline, it triggers
emical response in
mutated genes to
enerate massive
nounts of gamma
radiation.
Exactly! And that energy fuels an exponential cellular replication process to create additional mass. As Hulk's adrenaline level escalates, he generates more energy, causing a corresponding escalation in strength.
Listening to the Doc and his radioactive pal would've put me to sleep if these weren't the best chilaquiles I'd had since Mexico.
tried getting
er-strength from
king a six-pack of
ergy sodas, but
ead I just couldn't
eep for 3 days.
totally
ned every
of Ultimate
Alliance
though.
You know, we could keep a lower profile if you kept your monkey on a tighter leash.

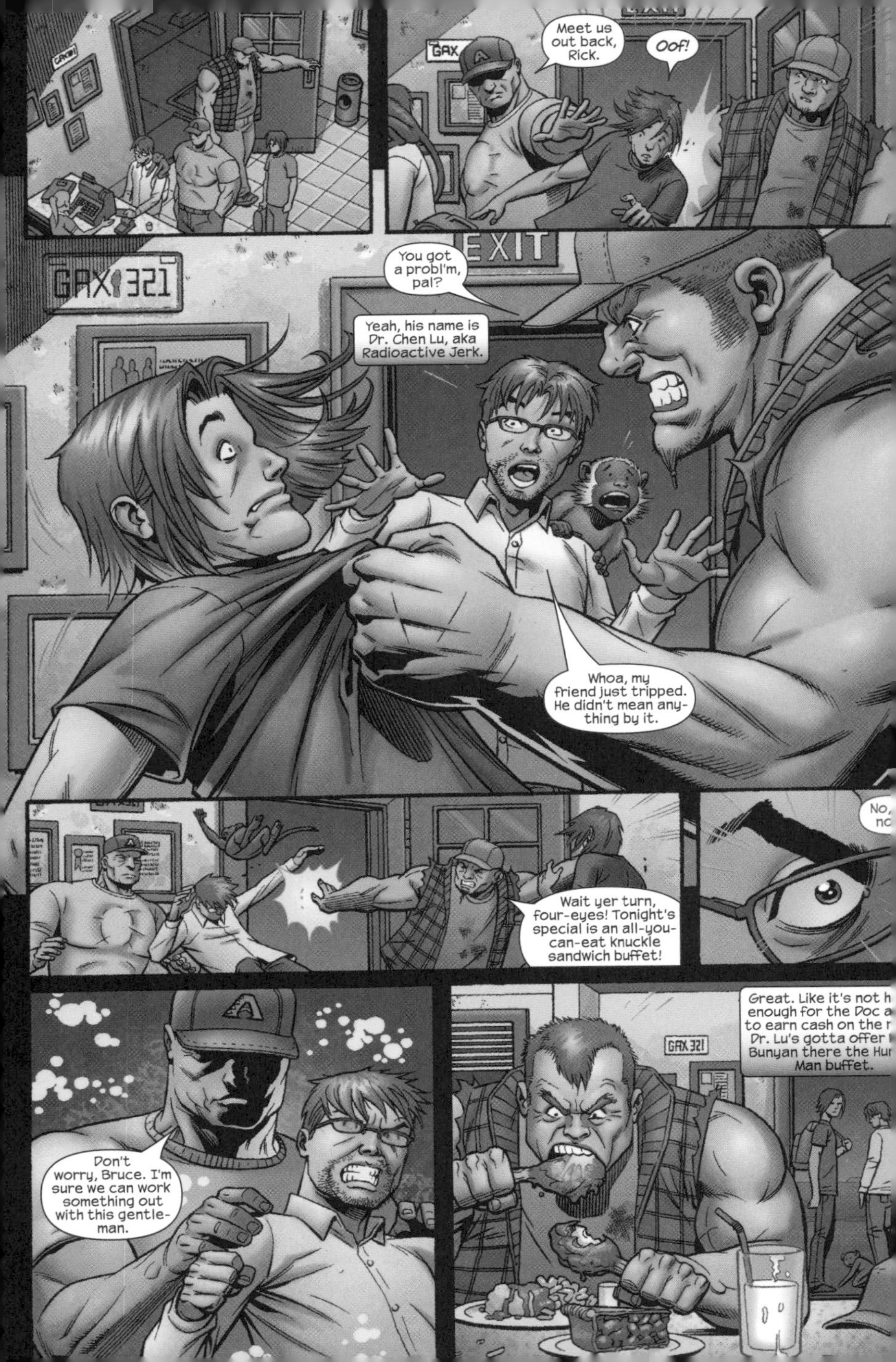
Meet us out back, Rick.
Oof!
EXIT
GAX 321
You got a probl'm, pal?
Yeah, his name is Dr. Chen Lu, aka Radioactive Jerk.
Whoa, my friend just tripped. He didn't mean any-thing by it.
Wait yer turn, four-eyes! Tonight's special is an all-you-can-eat knuckle sandwich buffet!
No,
Don't worry, Bruce. I'm sure we can work something out with this gentle-man.
Great. Like it's not h
enough for the Doc a
to earn cash on the r
Dr. Lu's gotta offer
Bunyan there the Hu
Man buffet.

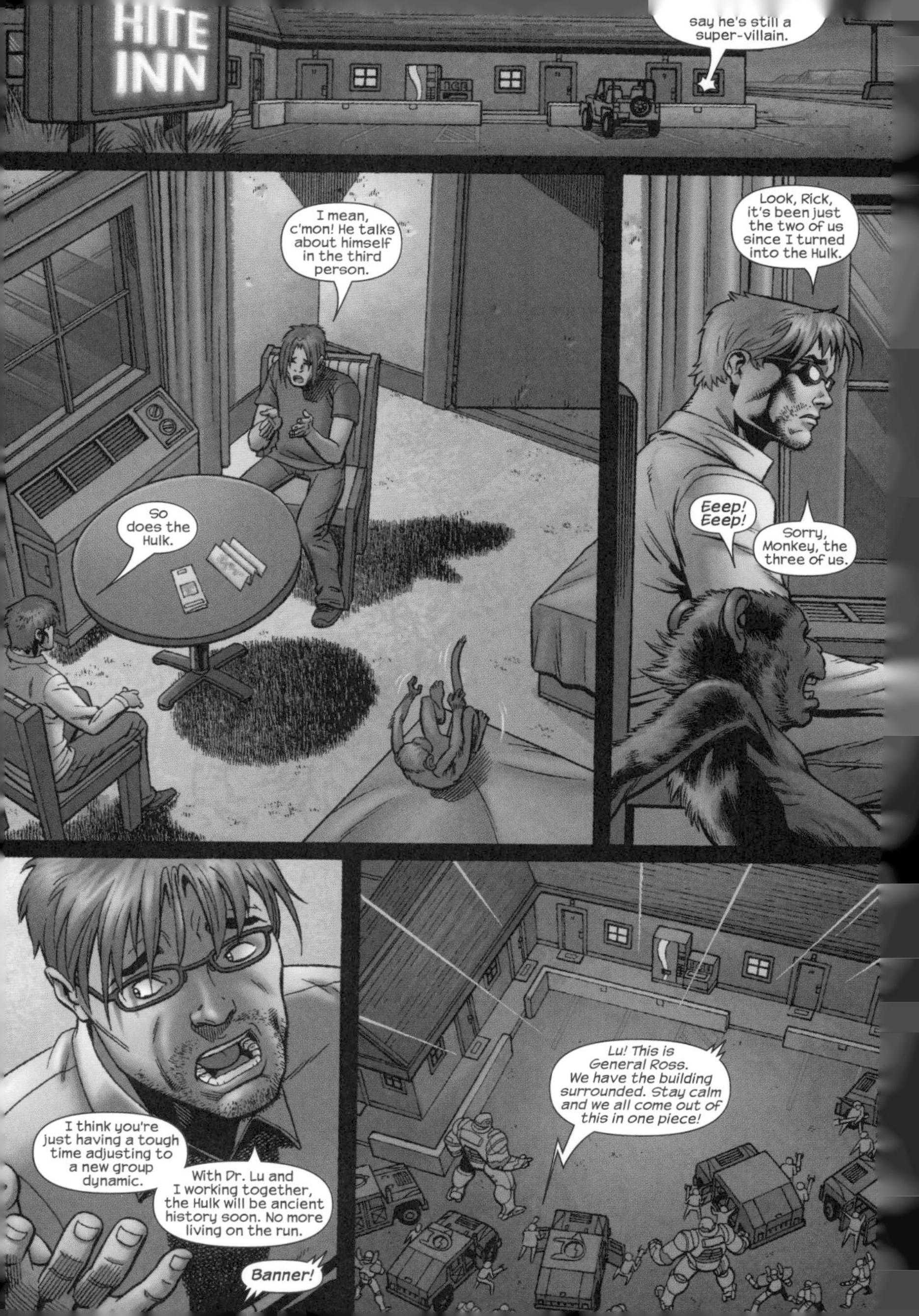
HITE
INN
say he's still a super-villain.
I mean, c'mon! He talks about himself in the third person.
So does the Hulk.
Look, Rick, it's been just the two of us since I turned into the Hulk.
Eeep! Eeep!
Sorry, Monkey, the three of us.
I think you're just having a tough time adjusting to a new group dynamic.
With Dr. Lu and I working together, the Hulk will be ancient history soon. No more living on the run.
Banner!
Lu! This is General Ross. We have the building surrounded. Stay calm and we all come out of this in one piece!

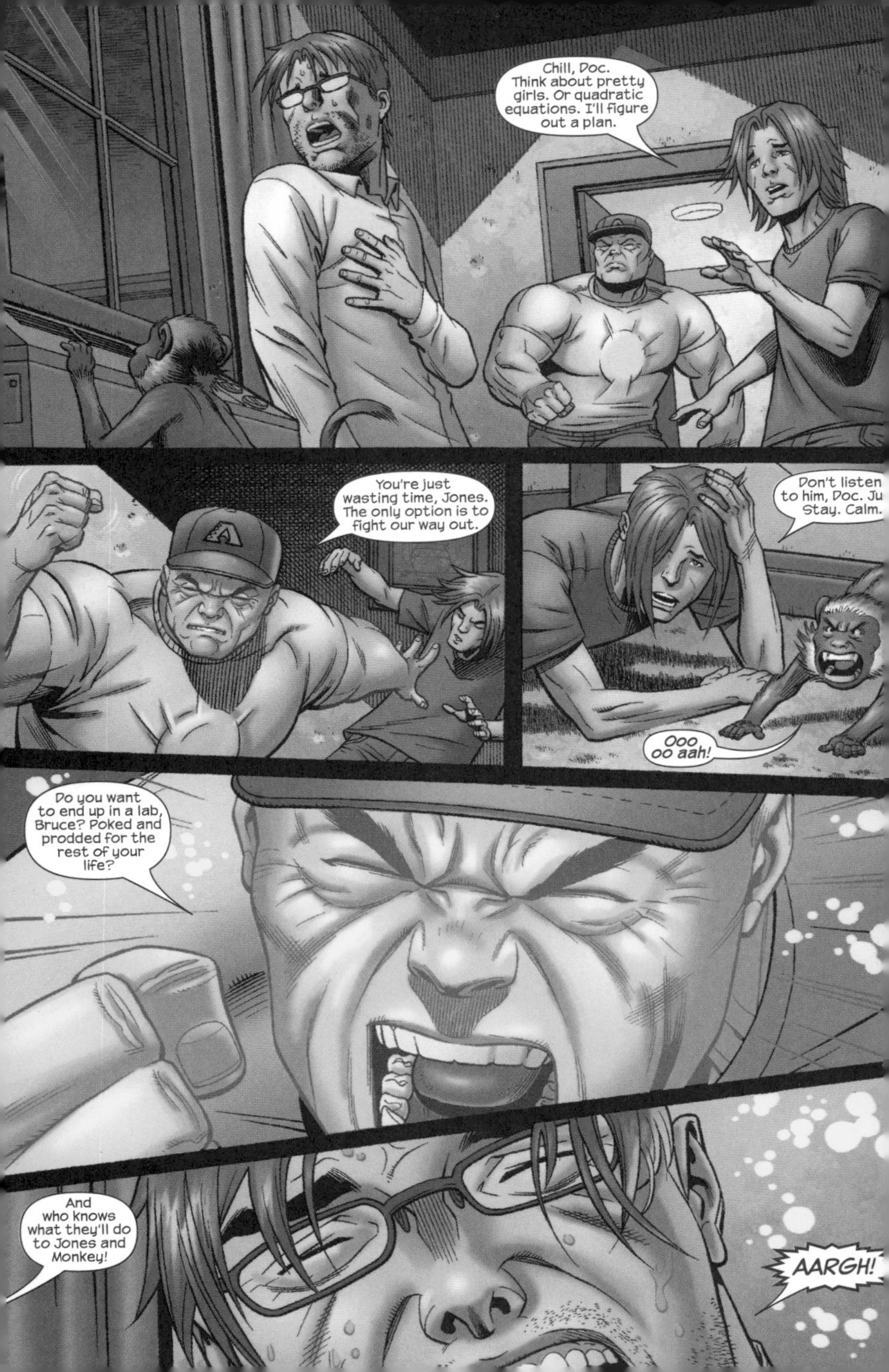
Chill, Doc. Think about pretty girls. Or quadratic equations. I'll figure out a plan.
You're just wasting time, Jones. The only option is to fight our way out.
Don't listen to him, Doc. Ju Stay. Calm.
Ooo oo aah!
Do you want to end up in a lab, Bruce? Poked and prodded for the rest of your life?
And who knows what they'll do to Jones and Monkey!
AARGH!

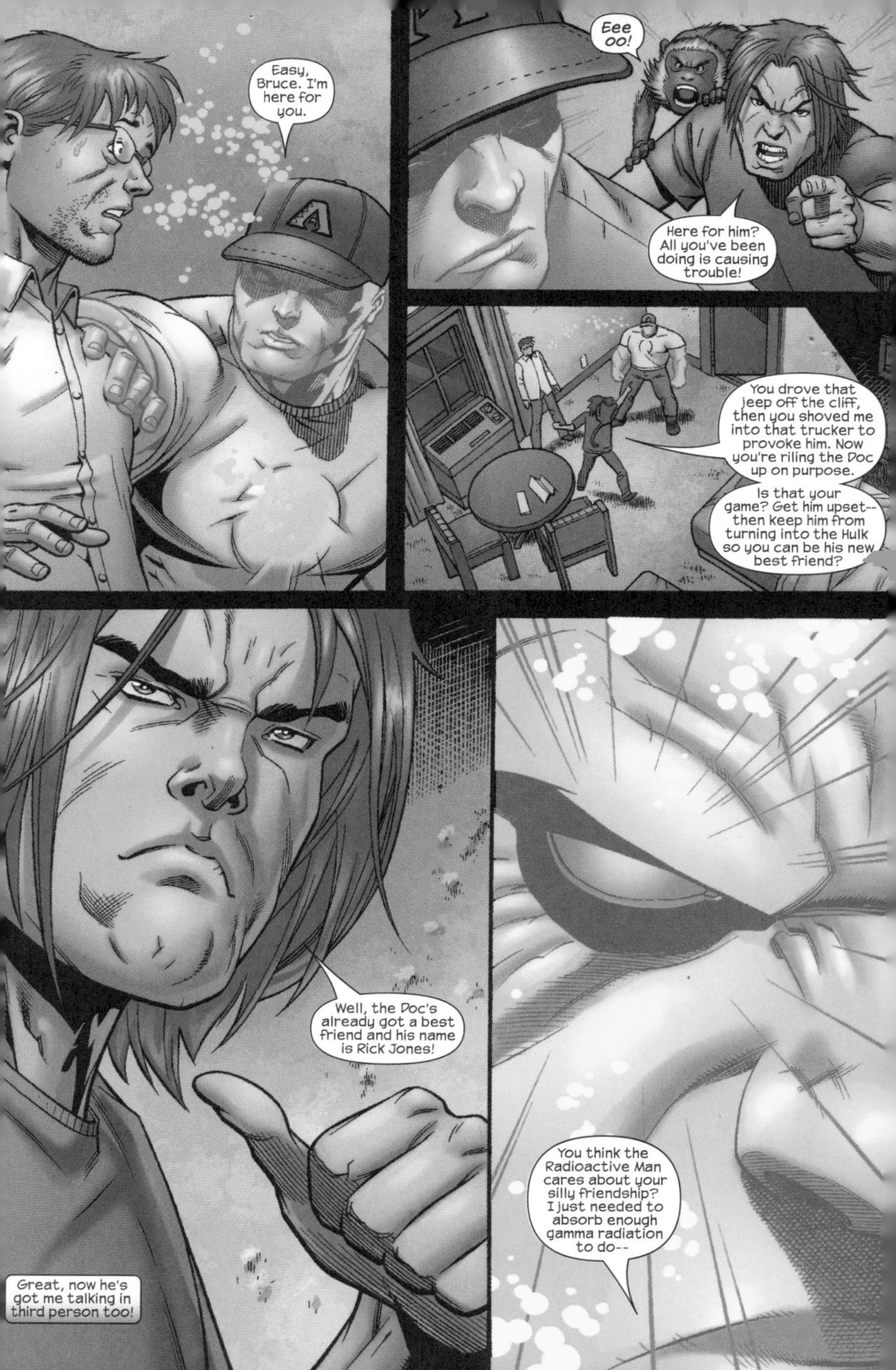
Easy, Bruce. I'm here for you.
Eee oo!
Here for him? All you've been doing is causing trouble!
You drove that jeep off the cliff, then you shoved me into that trucker to provoke him. Now you're riling the Doc up on purpose.
Is that your game? Get him upset--then keep him from turning into the Hulk so you can be his new best friend?
Well, the Doc's already got a best friend and his name is Rick Jones!
Great, now he's got me talking in third person too!
You think the Radioactive Man cares about your silly friendship? I just needed to absorb enough gamma radiation to do--

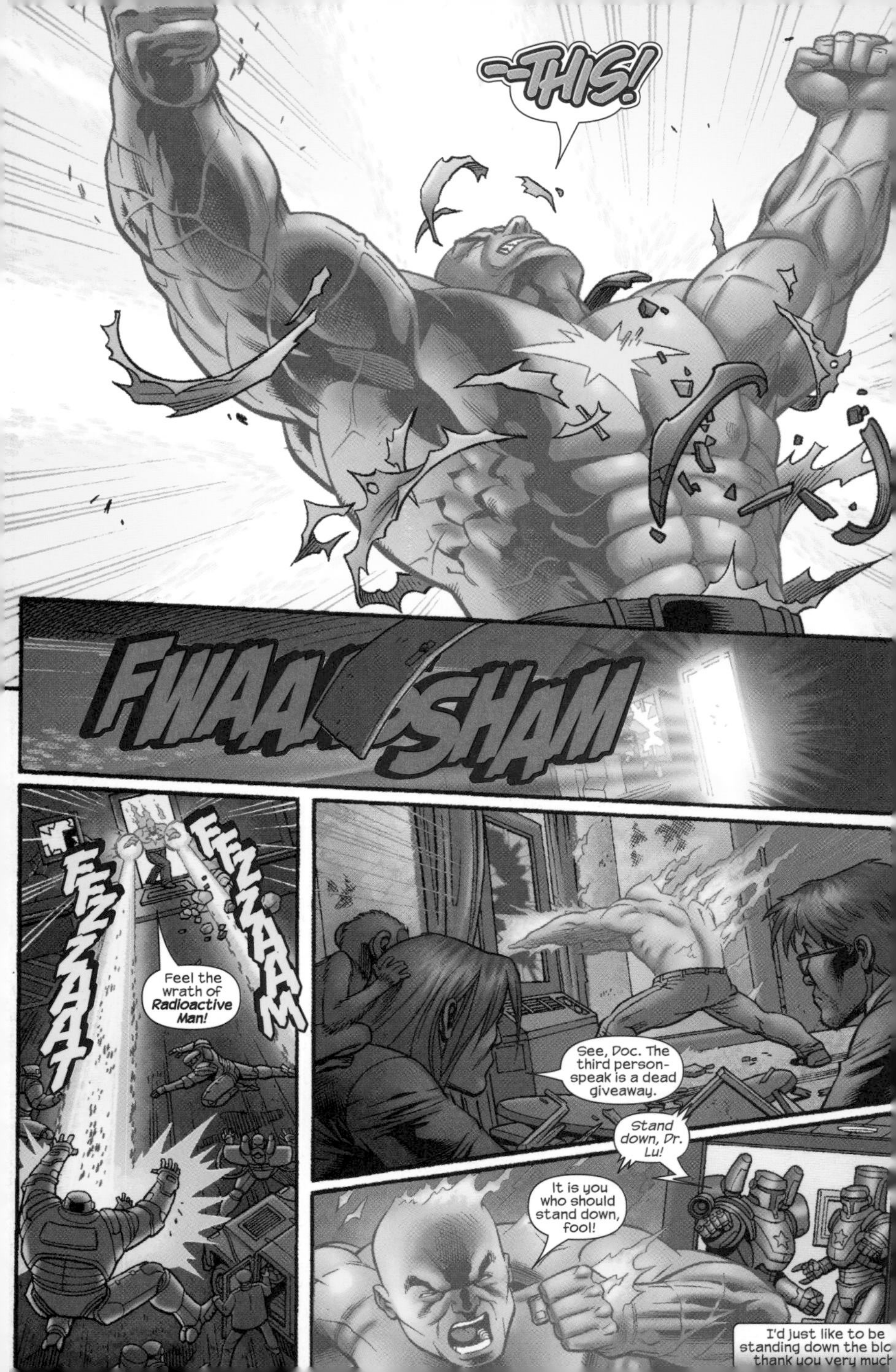
--THIS!
FWAAM SHAM
FFZZAAT
FFZZAAM
Feel the wrath of *Radioactive Man!*
See, Doc. The third person-speak is a dead giveaway.
Stand down, Dr. Lu!
It is you who should stand down, fool!
I'd just like to be standing down the blo thank you very much

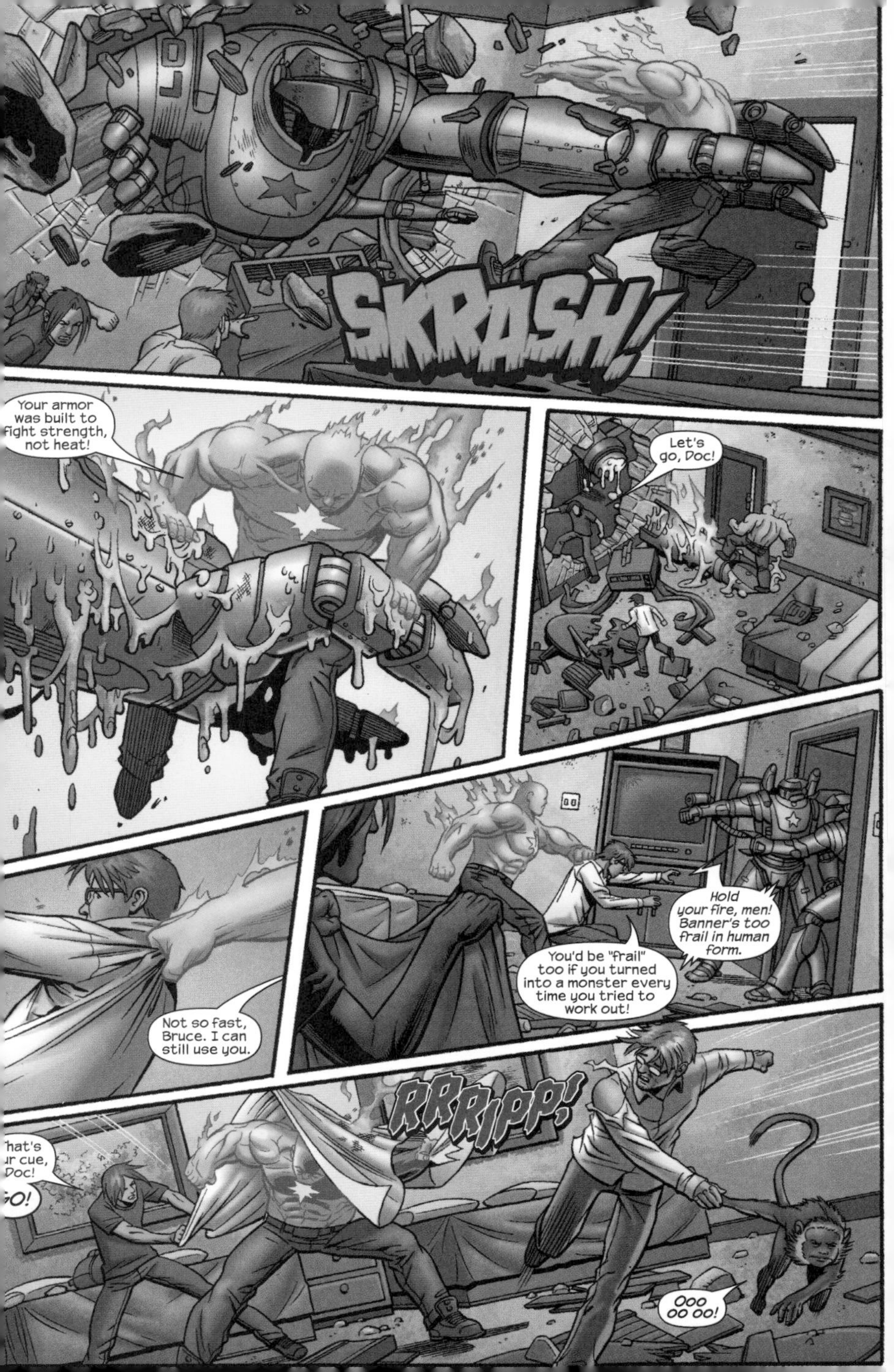
SKRASH!
Your armor was built to fight strength, not heat!
Let's go, Doc!
Not so fast, Bruce. I can still use you.
Hold your fire, men! Banner's too frail in human form.
You'd be "frail" too if you turned into a monster every time you tried to work out!
RRRIPP!
hat's ur cue, Doc!
GO!
OOO OO OO!

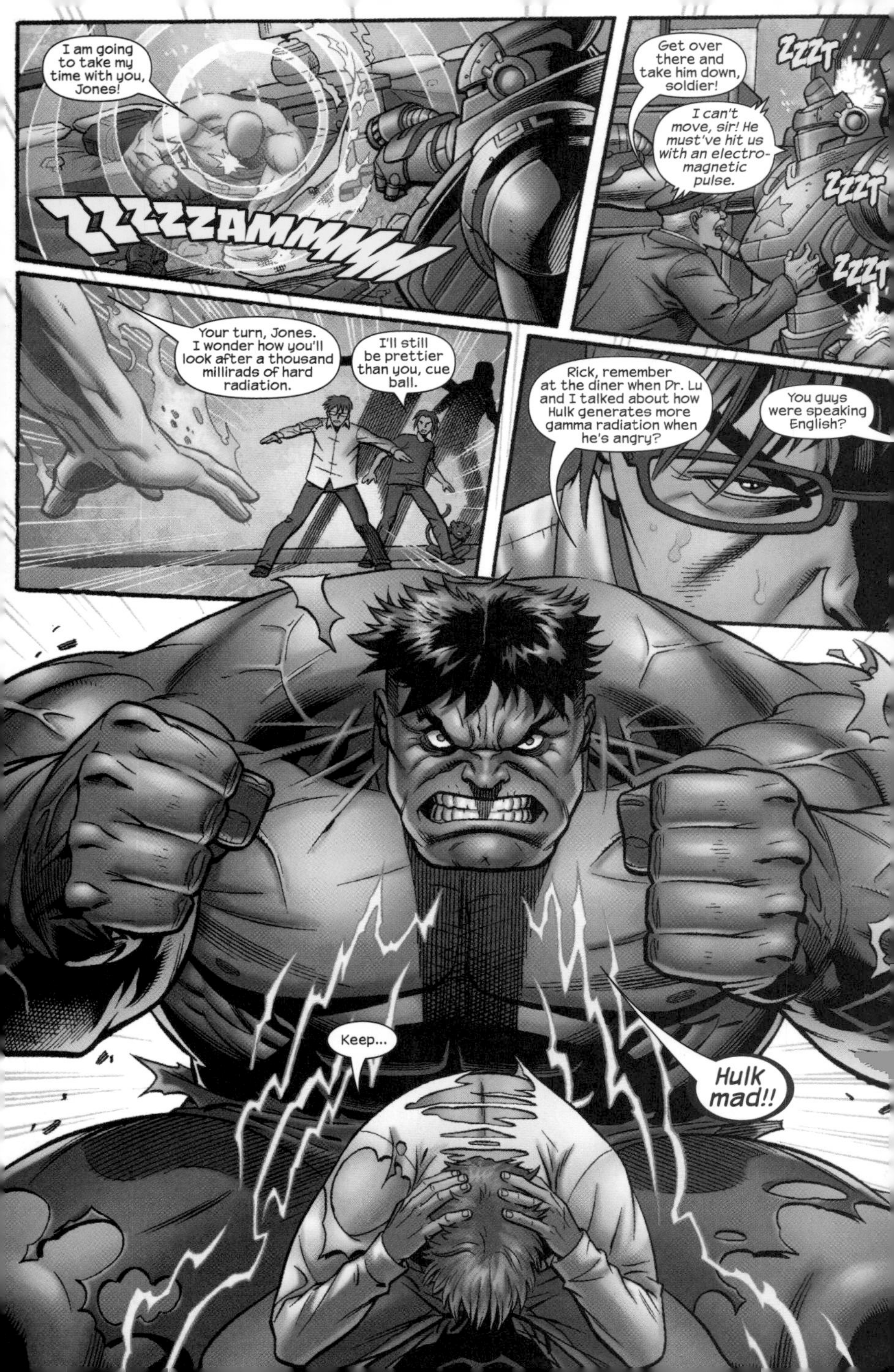
I am going to take my time with you, Jones!
ZZZZZAMMMMM
Get over there and take him down, soldier!
I can't move, sir! He must've hit us with an electro-magnetic pulse.
ZZZT
ZZZT
ZZZT
Your turn, Jones. I wonder how you'll look after a thousand millirads of hard radiation.
I'll still be prettier than you, cue ball.
Rick, remember at the diner when Dr. Lu and I talked about how Hulk generates more gamma radiation when he's angry?
You guys were speaking English?
Keep...
Hulk mad!!

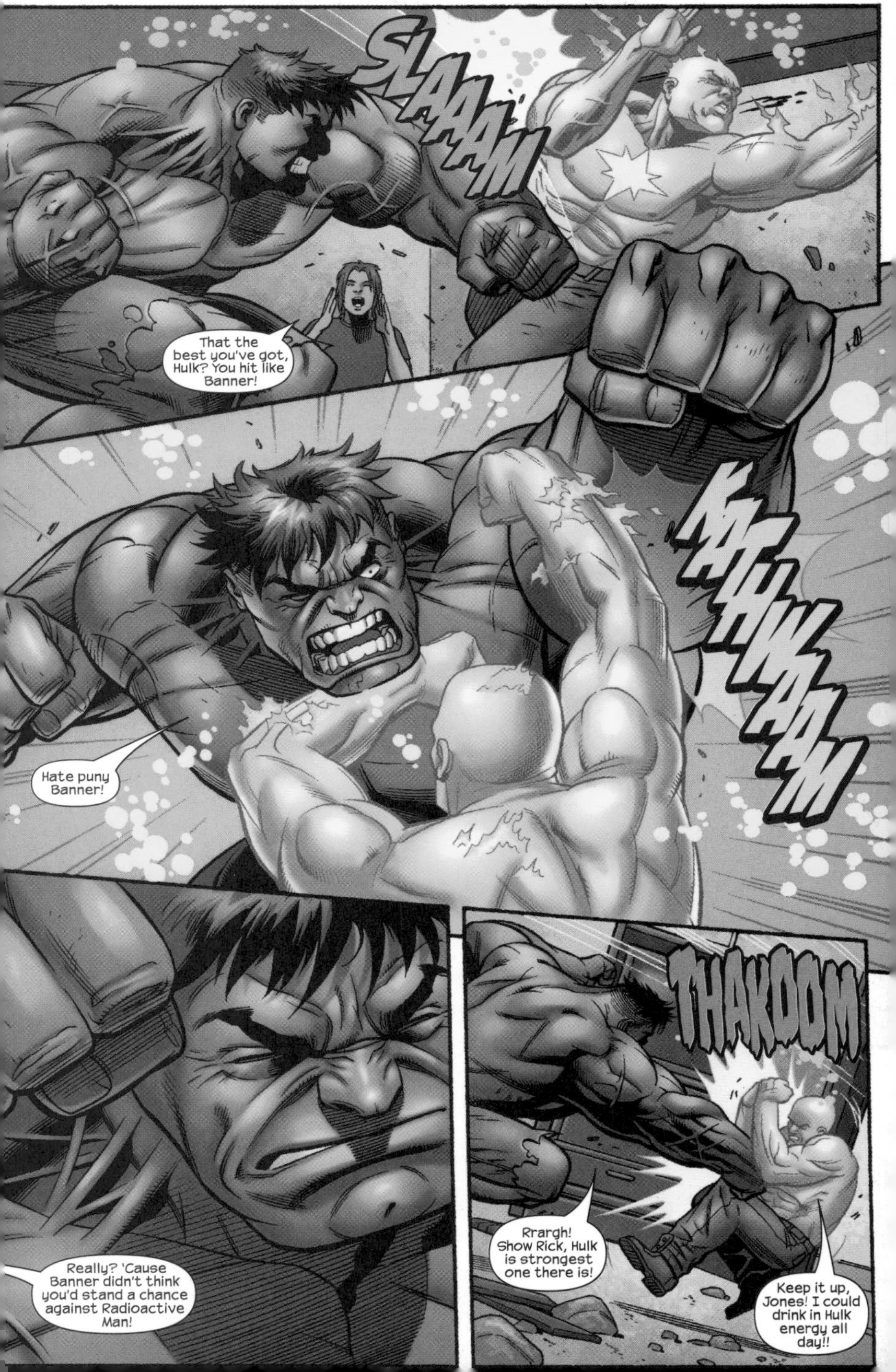
SLAAAAM
That the best you've got, Hulk? You hit like Banner!
KATHWAAAM
Hate puny Banner!
Really? 'Cause Banner didn't think you'd stand a chance against Radioactive Man!
THAKOOM
Rrargh! Show Rick, Hulk is strongest one there is!
Keep it up, Jones! I could drink in Hulk energy all day!!

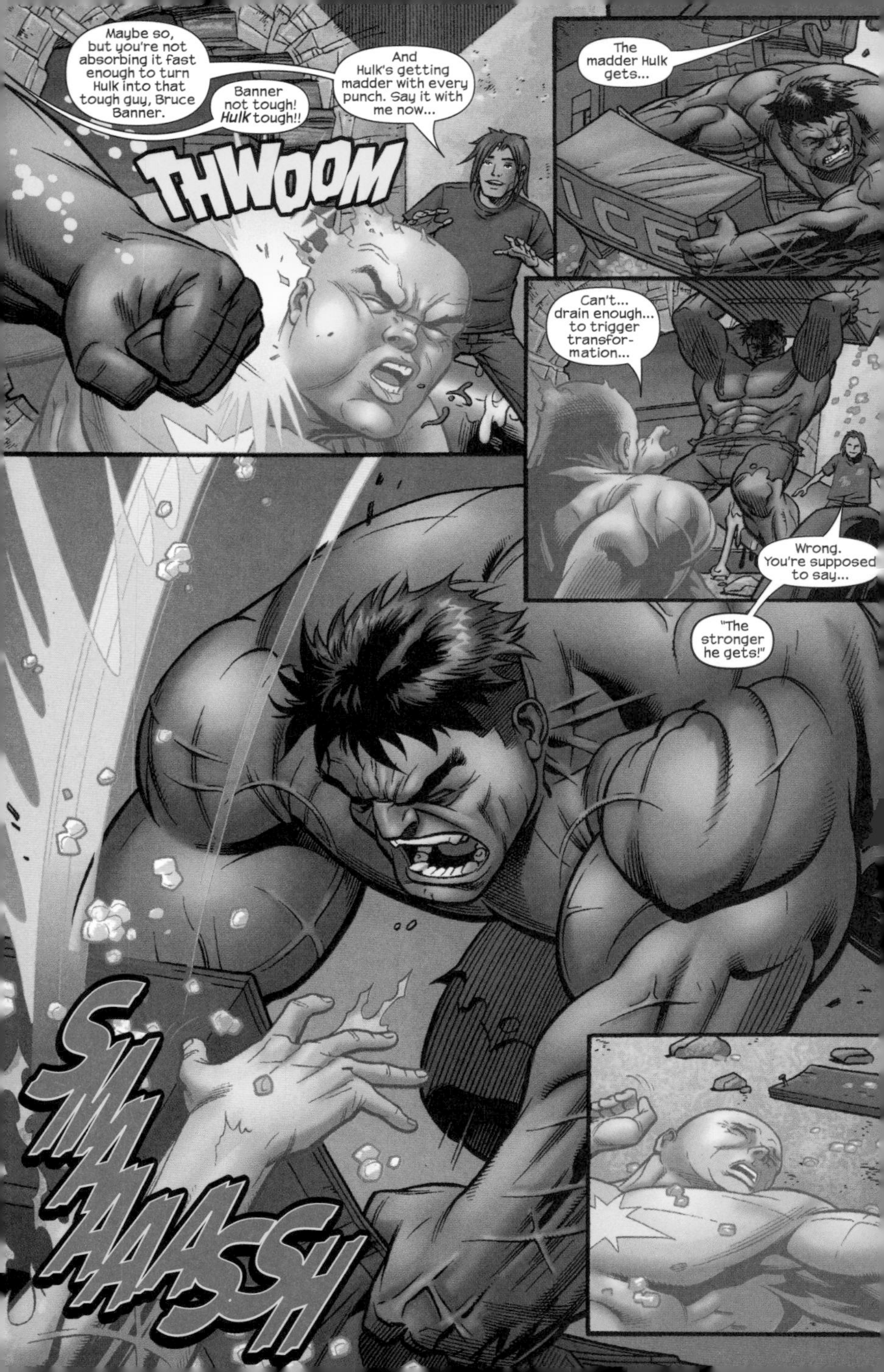

Maybe so, but you're not absorbing it fast enough to turn Hulk into that tough guy, Bruce Banner.
Banner not tough! Hulk tough!!
And Hulk's getting madder with every punch. Say it with me now...
THWOOM
The madder Hulk gets...
Can't... drain enough... to trigger transfor- mation...
Wrong. You're supposed to say...
"The stronger he gets!"
SMAASH

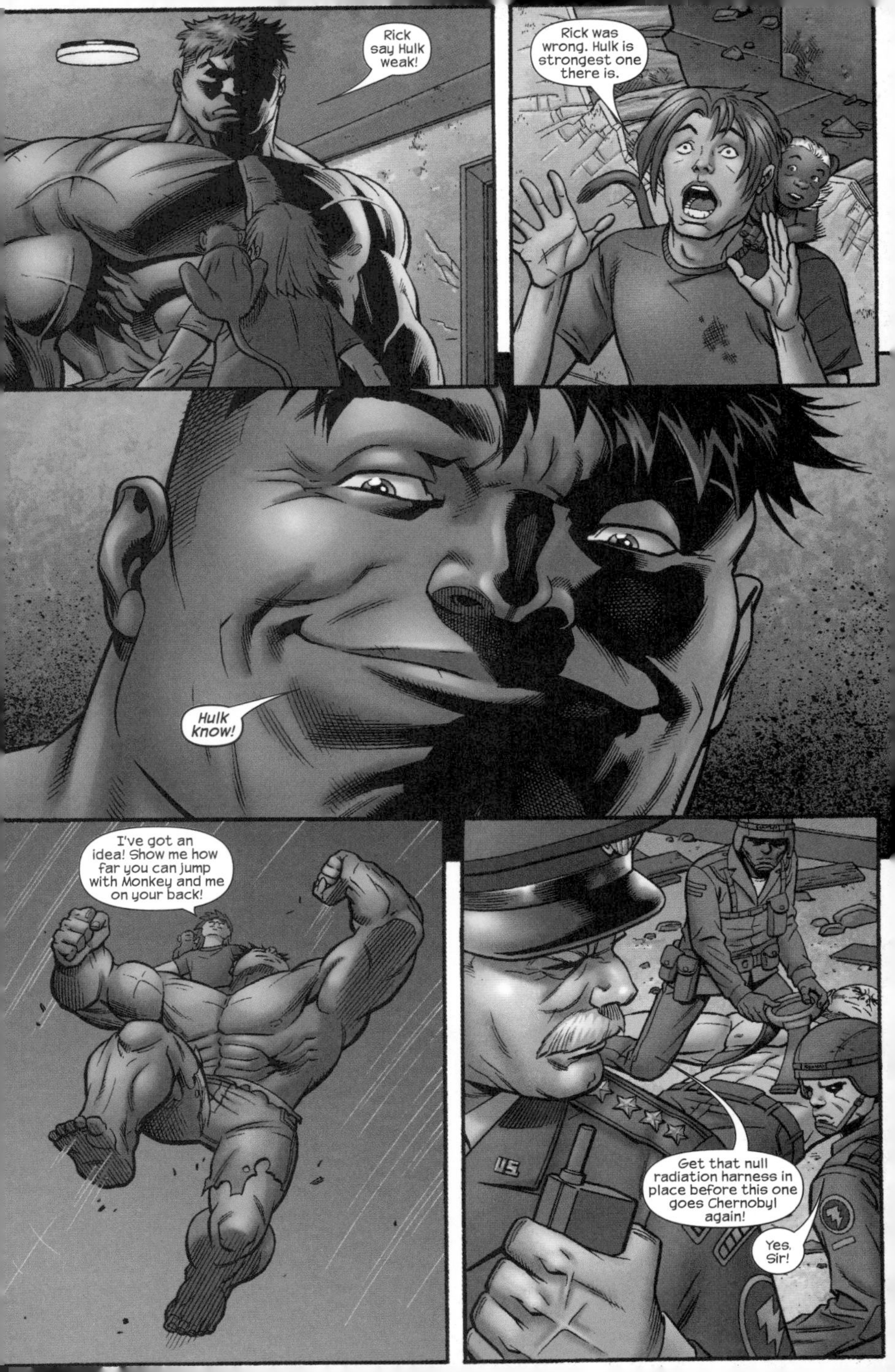
Rick say Hulk weak!
Rick was wrong. Hulk is strongest one there is.
Hulk know!
I've got an idea! Show me how far you can jump with Monkey and me on your back!
Get that null radiation harness in place before this one goes Chernobyl again!
Yes, Sir!

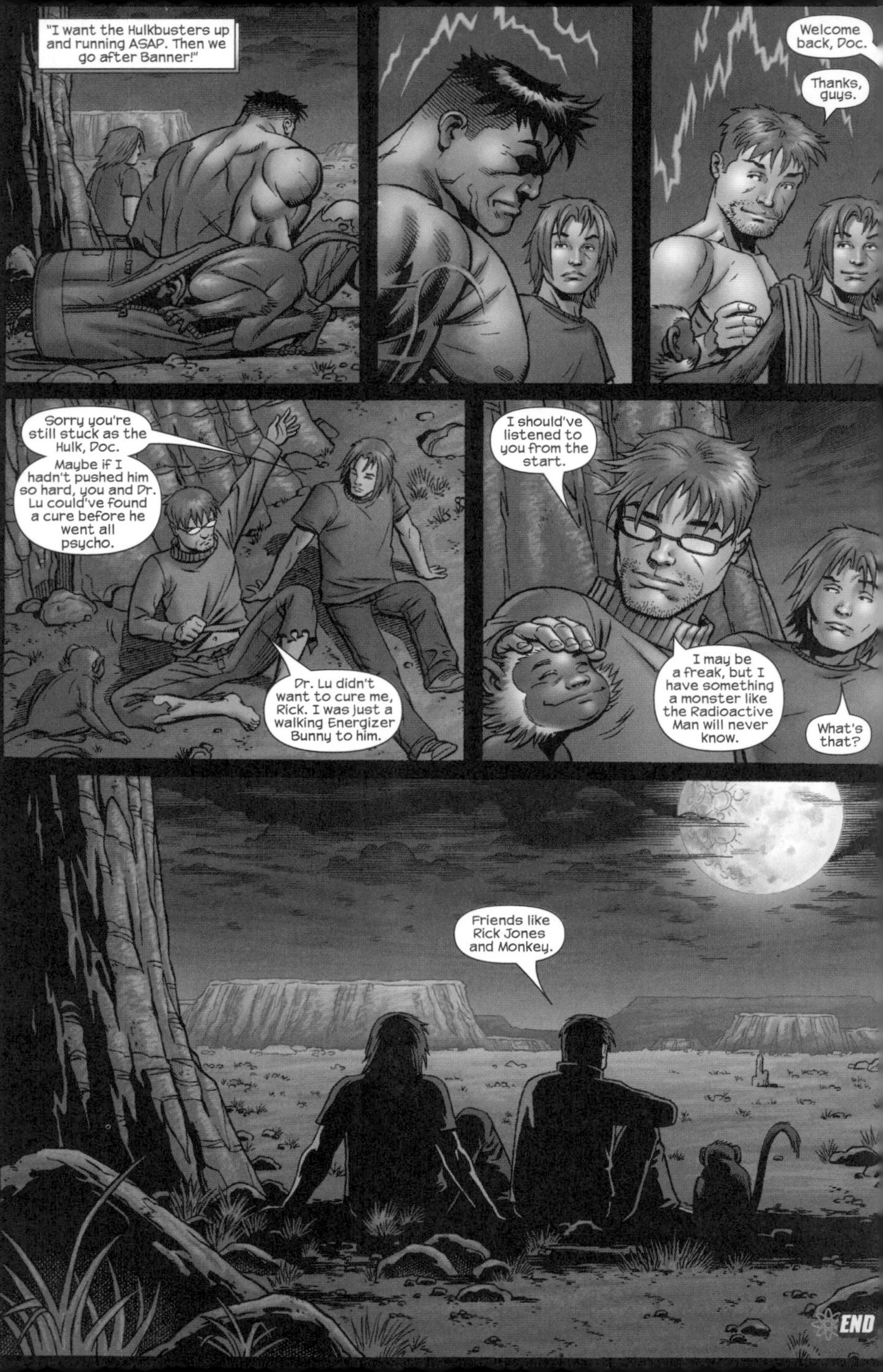
"I want the Hulkbusters up and running ASAP. Then we go after Banner!"
Welcome back, Doc.
Thanks, guys.
Sorry you're still stuck as the Hulk, Doc.
Maybe if I hadn't pushed him so hard, you and Dr. Lu could've found a cure before he went all psycho.
Dr. Lu didn't want to cure me, Rick. I was just a walking Energizer Bunny to him.
I should've listened to you from the start.
I may be a freak, but I have something a monster like the Radioactive Man will never know.
What's that?
Friends like Rick Jones and Monkey.
END

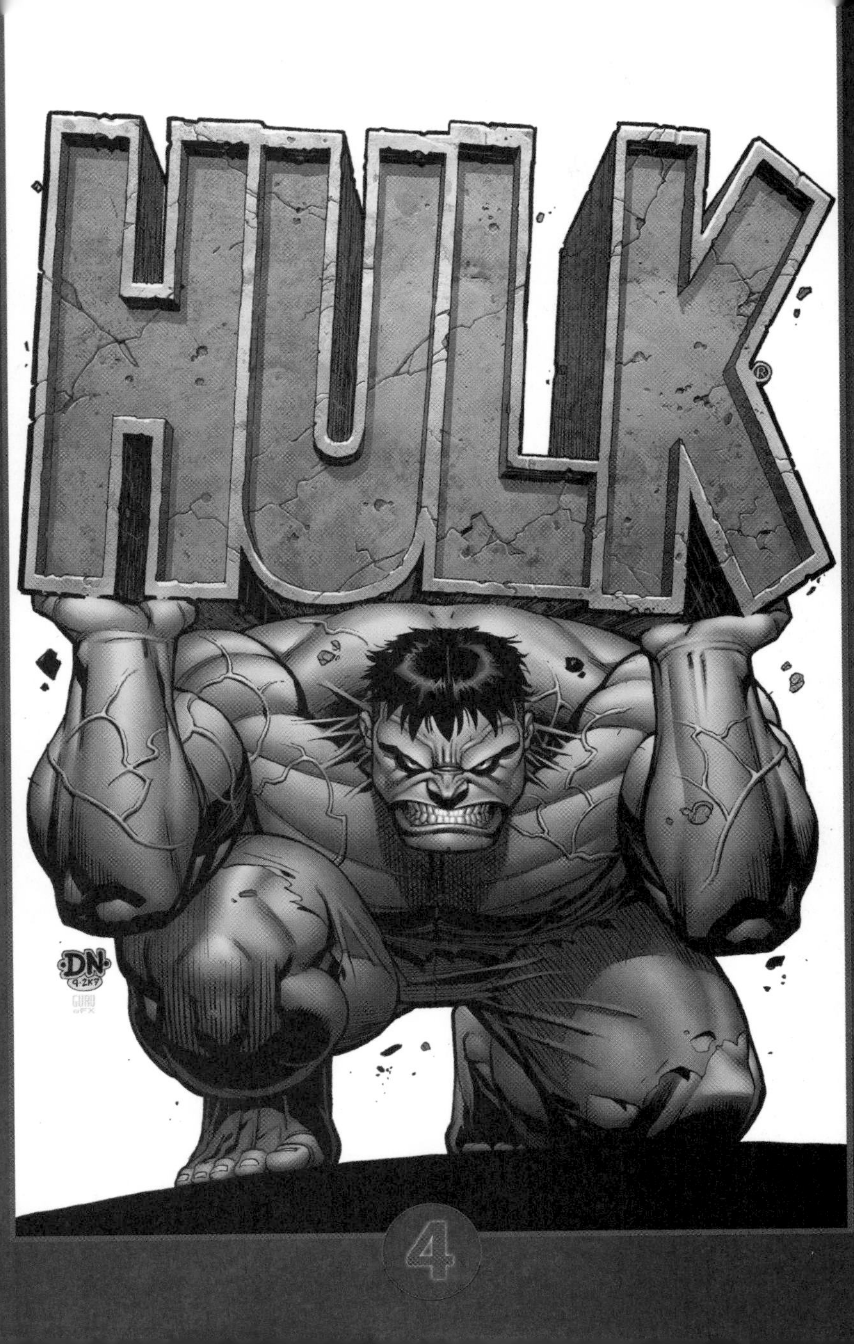
HULK
4

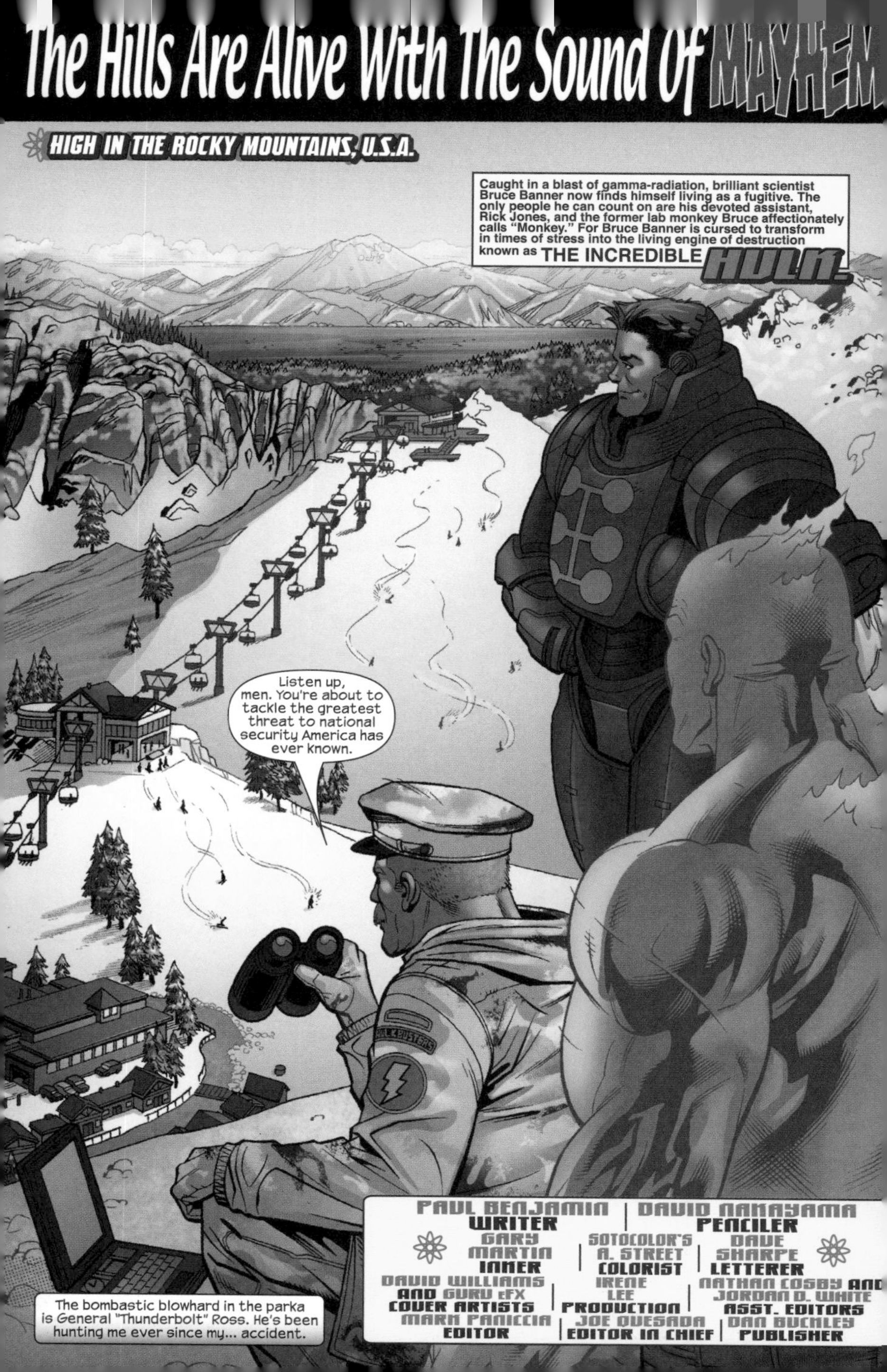
The Hills Are Alive With The Sound Of MAYHEM
HIGH IN THE ROCKY MOUNTAINS, U.S.A.
Caught in a blast of gamma-radiation, brilliant scientist Bruce Banner now finds himself living as a fugitive. The only people he can count on are his devoted assistant, Rick Jones, and the former lab monkey Bruce affectionately calls "Monkey." For Bruce Banner is cursed to transform in times of stress into the living engine of destruction known as THE INCREDIBLE HULK.
Listen up, men. You're about to tackle the greatest threat to national security America has ever known.
The bombastic blowhard in the parka is General "Thunderbolt" Ross. He's been hunting me ever since my... accident.
PAUL BENJAMIN WRITER
DAVID NAKAYAMA PENCILER
GARY MARTIN INKER
SOTOCOLOR'S A. STREET COLORIST
DAVE SHARPE LETTERER
DAVID WILLIAMS AND GURU eFX COVER ARTISTS
IRENE LEE PRODUCTION
NATHAN COSBY AND JORDAN D. WHITE ASST. EDITORS
MARK PANICCIA EDITOR
JOE QUESADA EDITOR IN CHIEF
DAN BUCKLEY PUBLISHER

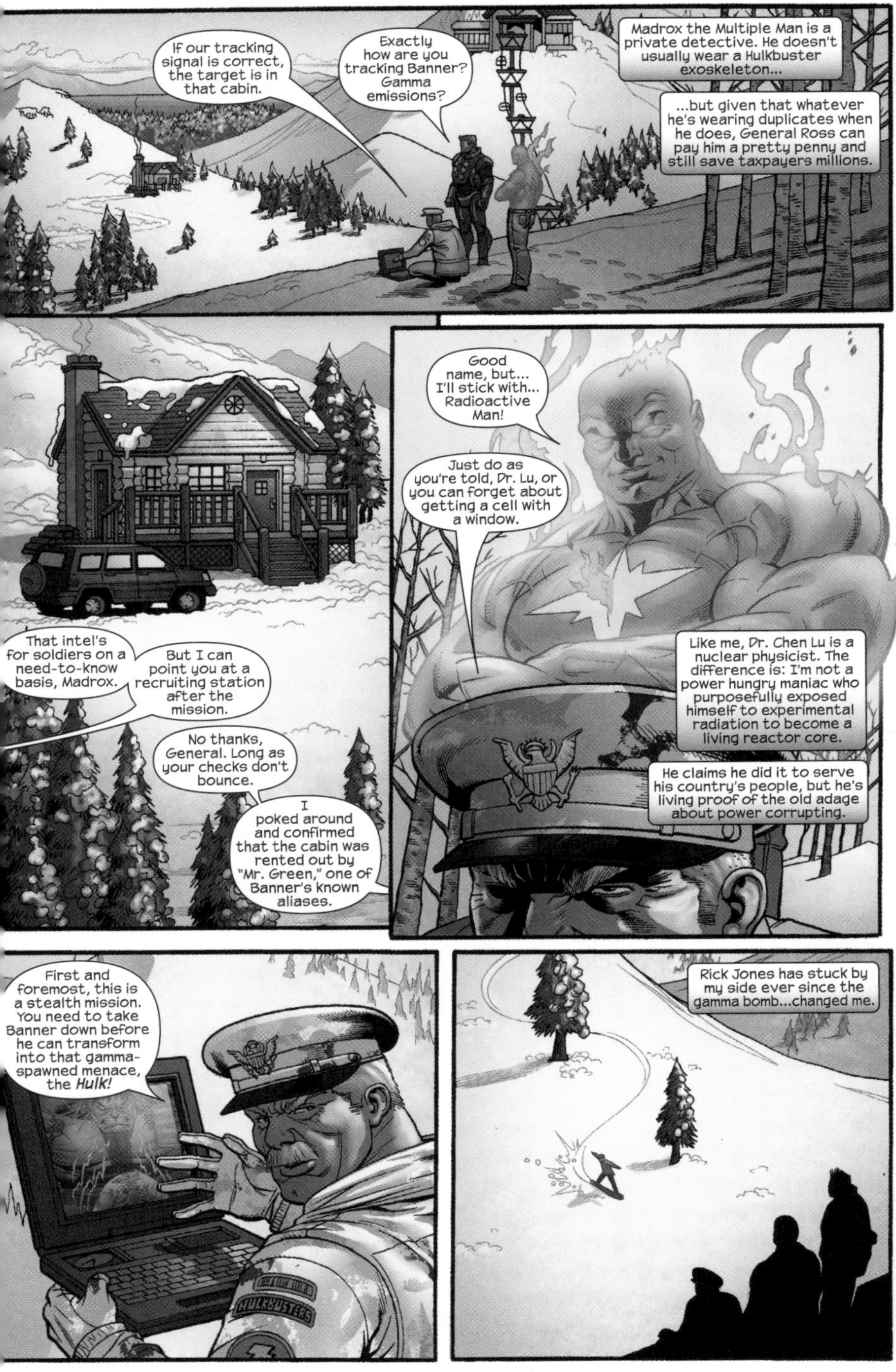
If our tracking signal is correct, the target is in that cabin.
Exactly how are you tracking Banner? Gamma emissions?
Madrox the Multiple Man is a private detective. He doesn't usually wear a Hulkbuster exoskeleton...
...but given that whatever he's wearing duplicates when he does, General Ross can pay him a pretty penny and still save taxpayers millions.
That intel's for soldiers on a need-to-know basis, Madrox.
But I can point you at a recruiting station after the mission.
No thanks, General. Long as your checks don't bounce.
I poked around and confirmed that the cabin was rented out by "Mr. Green," one of Banner's known aliases.
Good name, but... I'll stick with... Radioactive Man!
Just do as you're told, Dr. Lu, or you can forget about getting a cell with a window.
Like me, Dr. Chen Lu is a nuclear physicist. The difference is: I'm not a power hungry maniac who purposefully exposed himself to experimental radiation to become a living reactor core.
He claims he did it to serve his country's people, but he's living proof of the old adage about power corrupting.
First and foremost, this is a stealth mission. You need to take Banner down before he can transform into that gamma-spawned menace, the *Hulk!*
HULKBUSTERS
Rick Jones has stuck by my side ever since the gamma bomb...changed me.

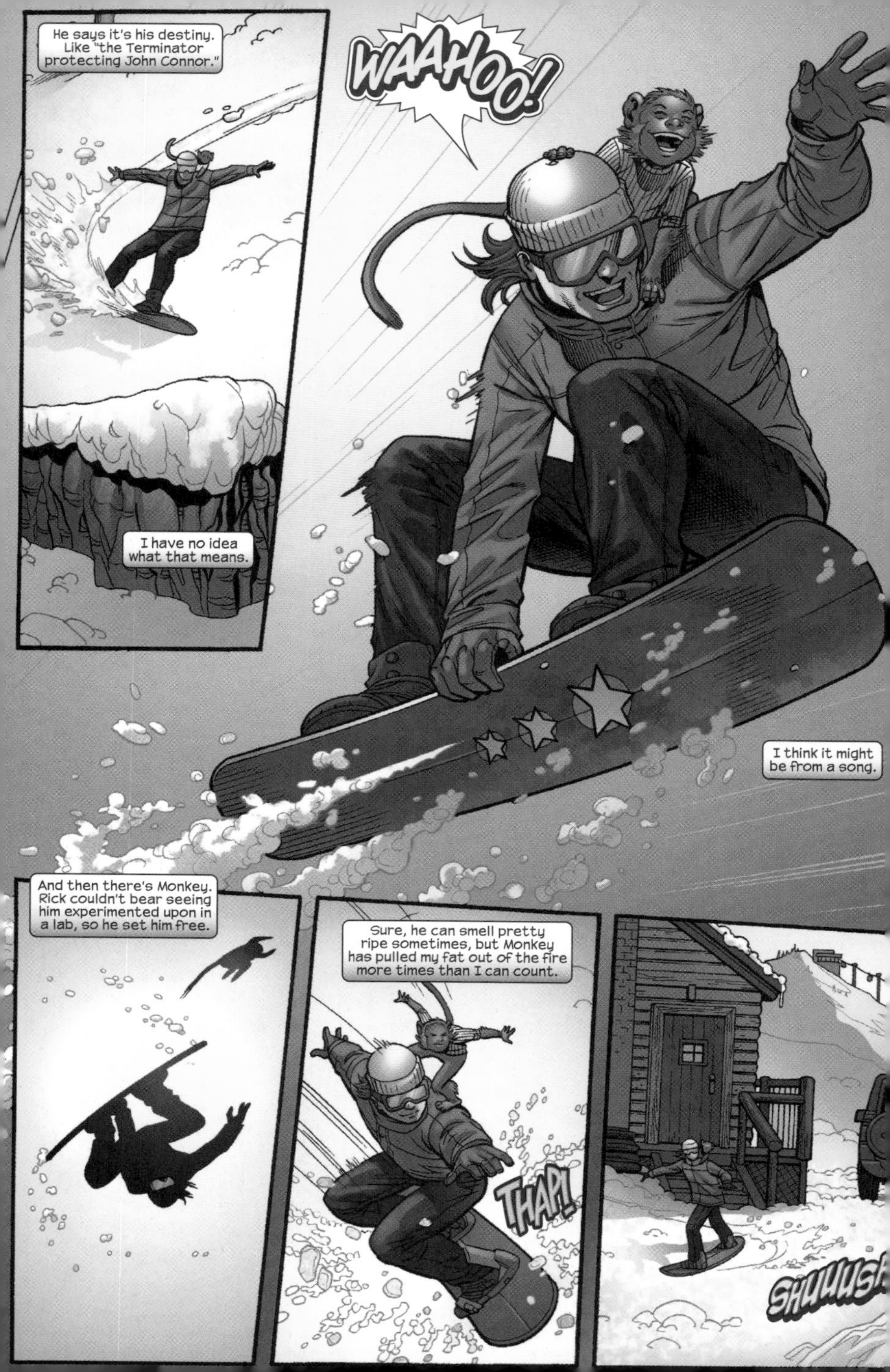
He says it's his destiny. Like "the Terminator protecting John Connor."
WAAHOO!
I have no idea what that means.
I think it might be from a song.
And then there's Monkey. Rick couldn't bear seeing him experimented upon in a lab, so he set him free.
Sure, he can smell pretty ripe sometimes, but Monkey has pulled my fat out of the fire more times than I can count.
THAP!
SHUUUSH

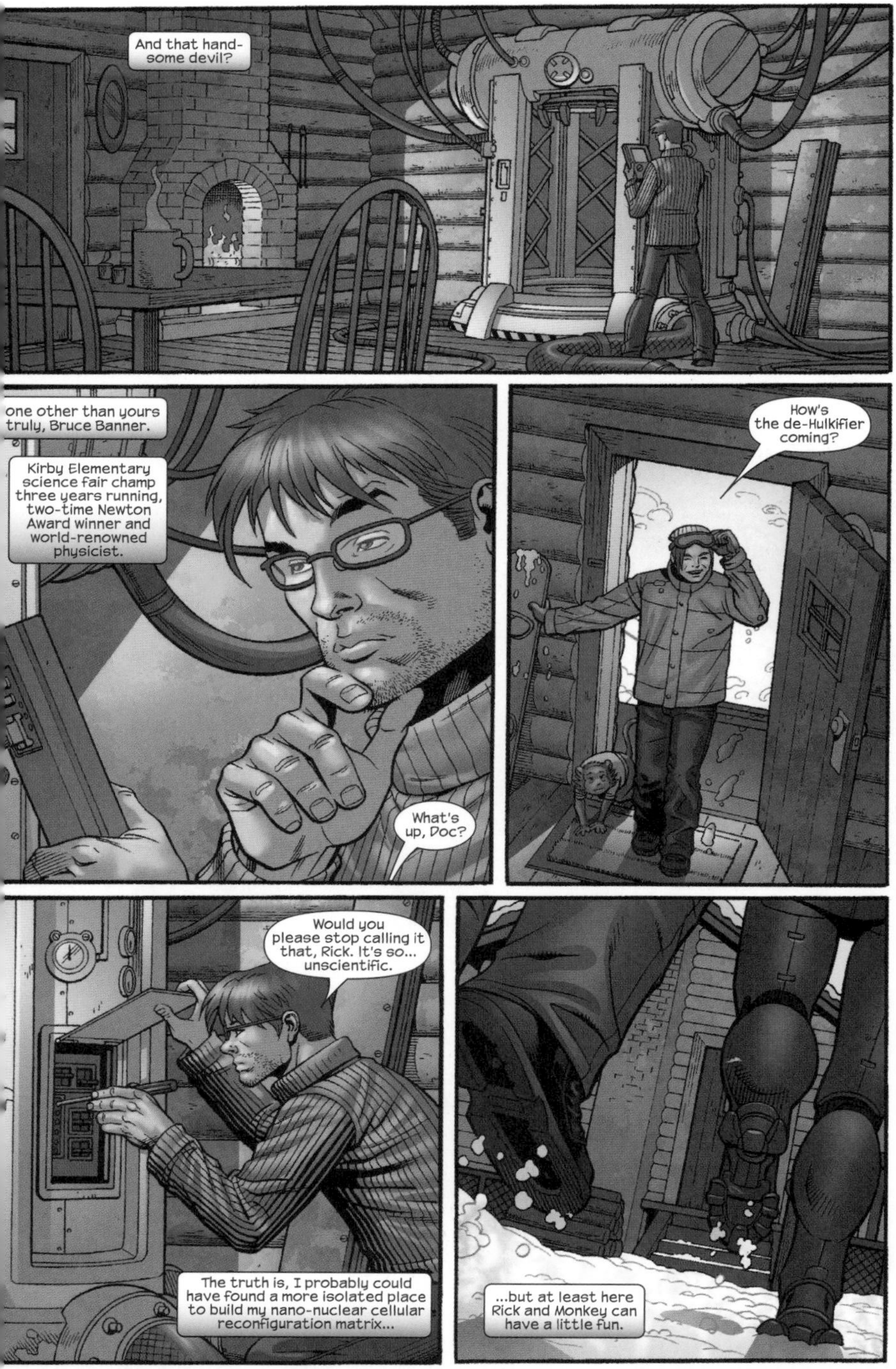

And that hand-some devil?
one other than yours truly, Bruce Banner.
Kirby Elementary science fair champ three years running, two-time Newton Award winner and world-renowned physicist.
What's up, Doc?
How's the de-Hulkifier coming?
Would you please stop calling it that, Rick. It's so... unscientific.
The truth is, I probably could have found a more isolated place to build my nano-nuclear cellular reconfiguration matrix...
...but at least here Rick and Monkey can have a little fun.

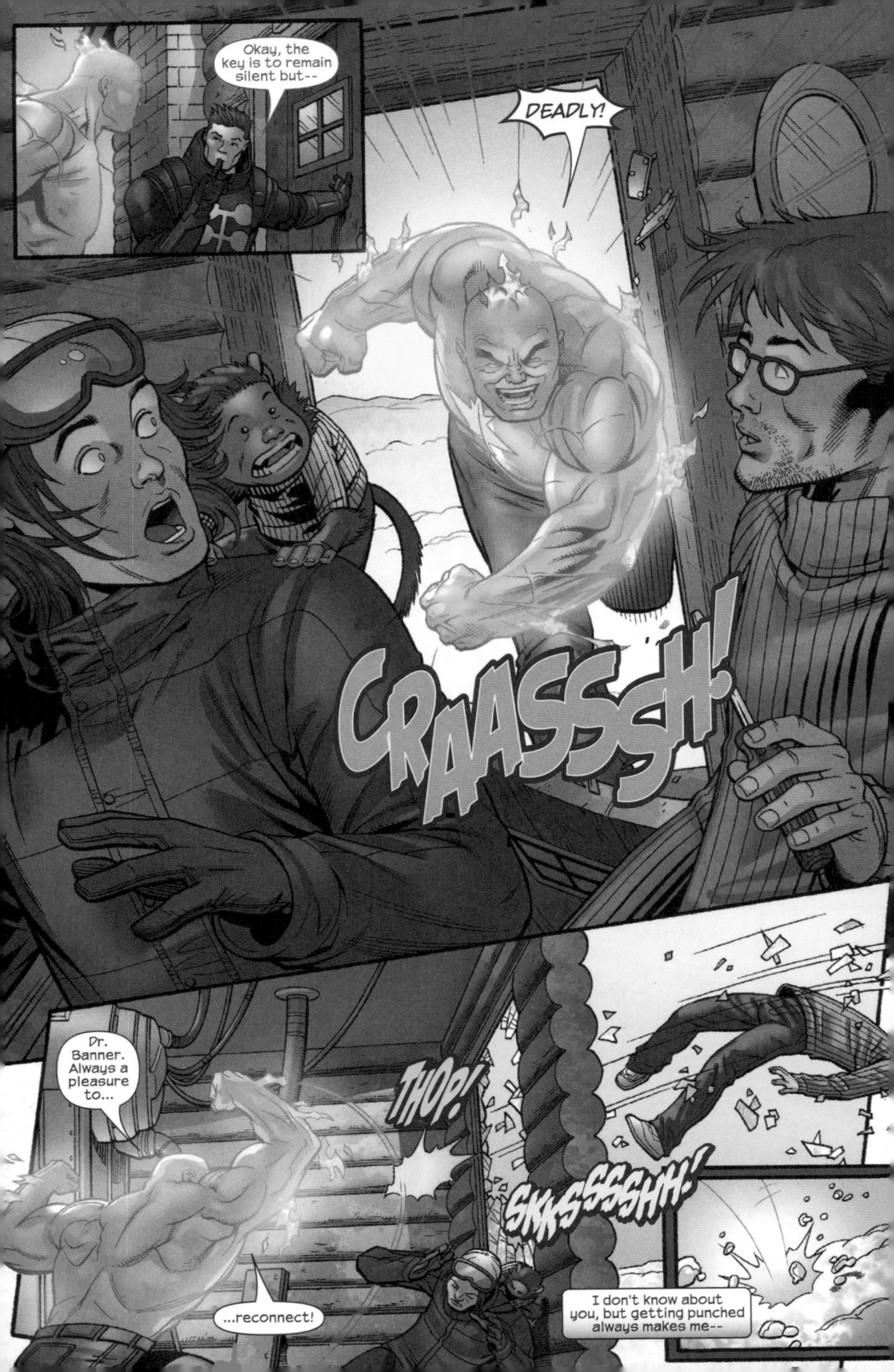
Okay, the key is to remain silent but--
DEADLY!
CRAASSSH!
Dr. Banner. Always a pleasure to...
THOP!
...reconnect!
SKKSSSSHH!
I don't know about you, but getting punched always makes me--

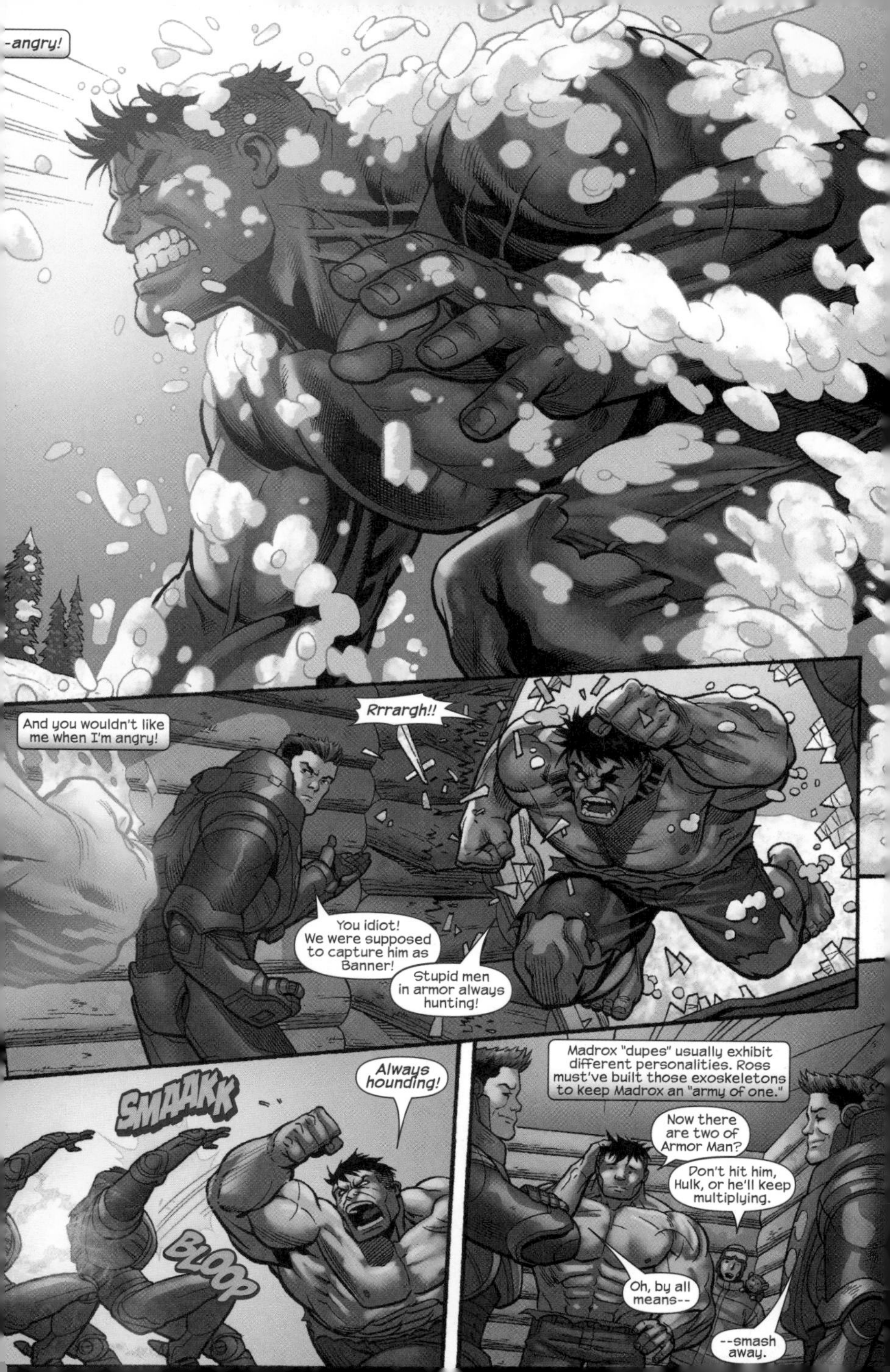
-angry!
And you wouldn't like me when I'm angry!
Rrrargh!!
You idiot! We were supposed to capture him as Banner!
Stupid men in armor always hunting!
Always hounding!
SMAAKK
BLOOP
Madrox "dupes" usually exhibit different personalities. Ross must've built those exoskeletons to keep Madrox an "army of one."
Now there are two of Armor Man?
Don't hit him, Hulk, or he'll keep multiplying.
Oh, by all means--
--smash away.

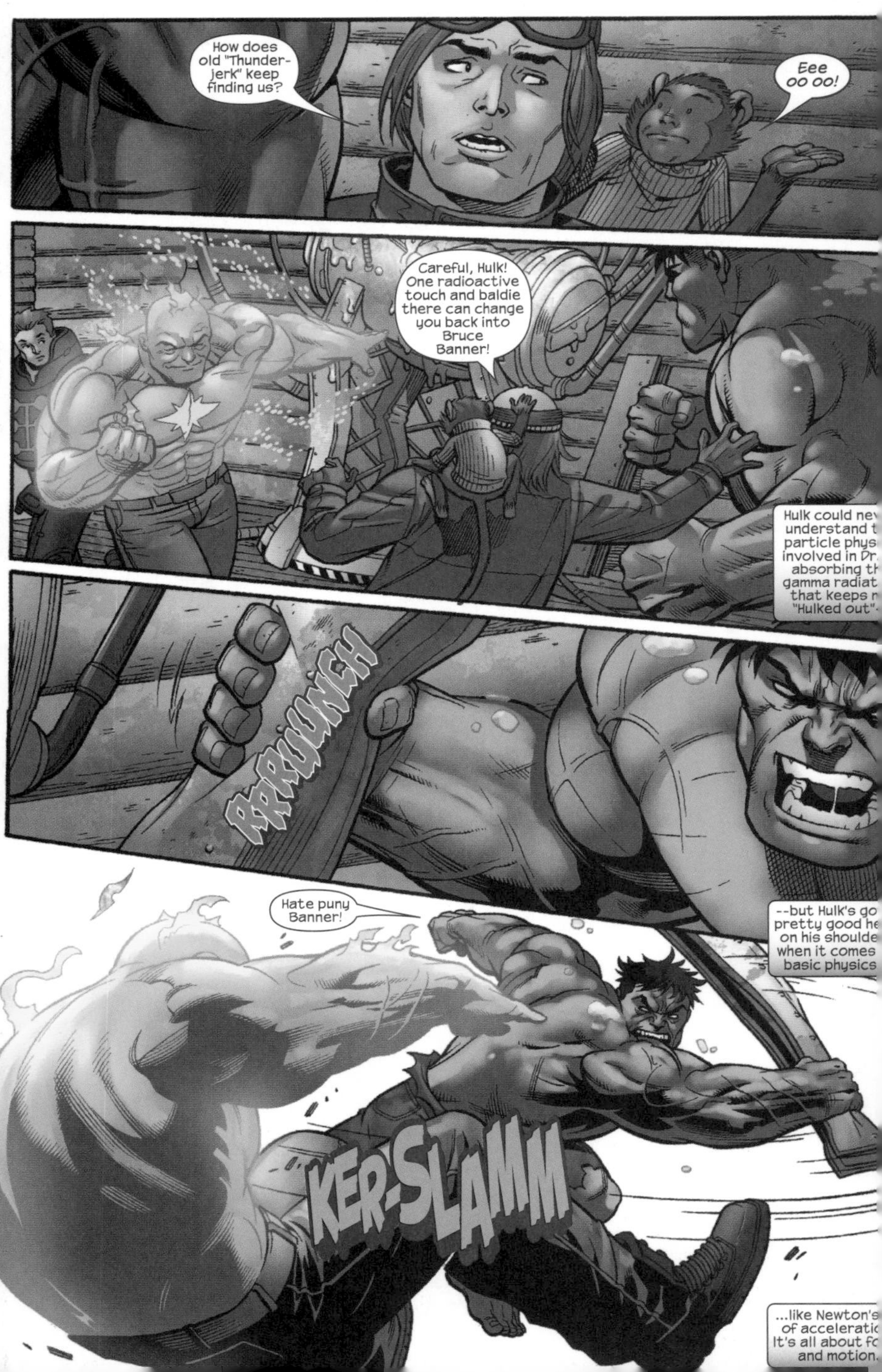
How does old "Thunder-jerk" keep finding us?
Eee oo oo!
Careful, Hulk! One radioactive touch and baldie there can change you back into Bruce Banner!
Hulk could nev understand t particle phys involved in Dr. absorbing th gamma radiat that keeps m "Hulked out"-
RRRUUNCH
Hate puny Banner!
--but Hulk's go pretty good he on his shoulde when it comes basic physics
KER-SLAMM
...like Newton's of acceleratic It's all about fo and motion.

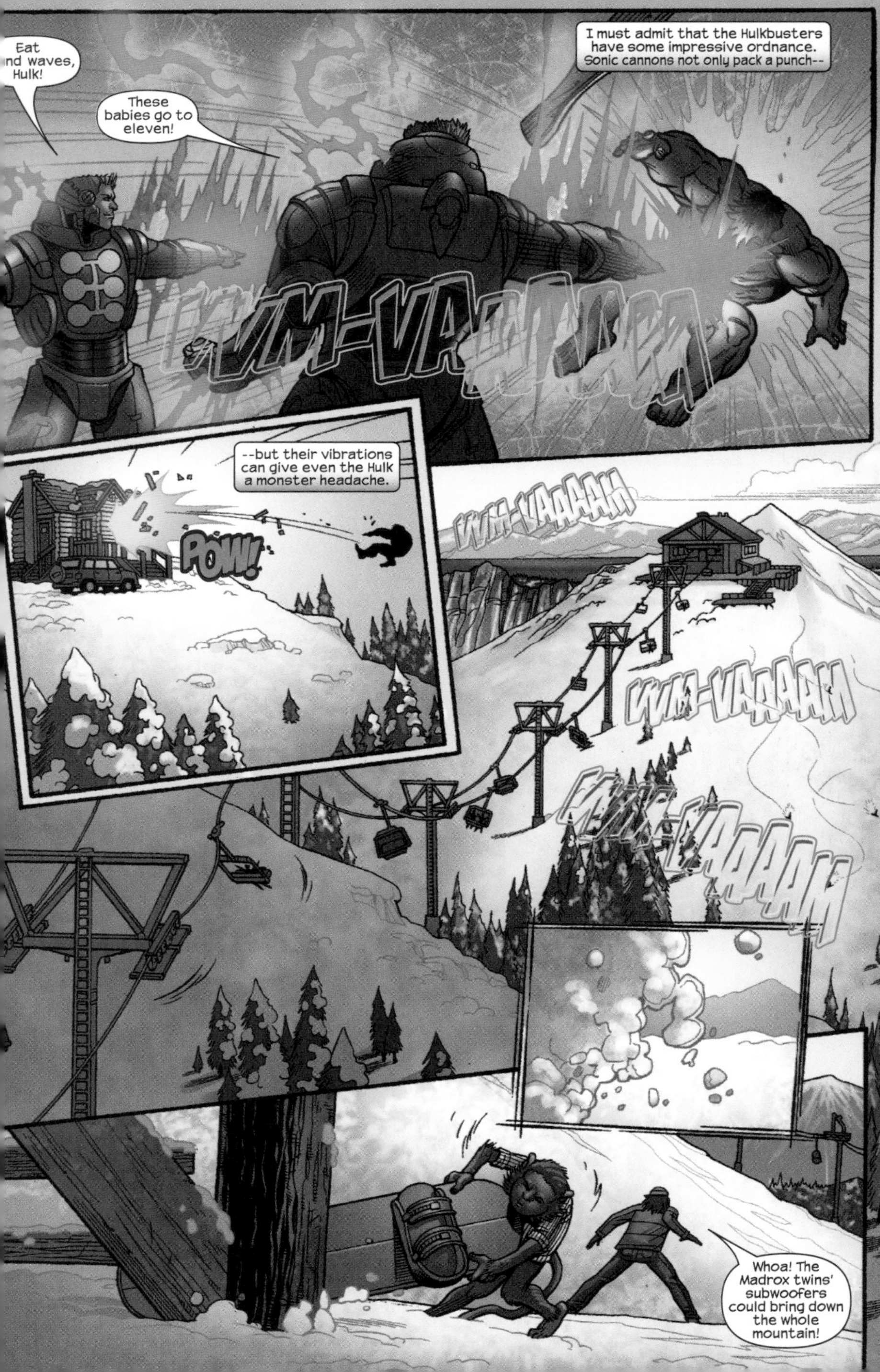
I must admit that the Hulkbusters have some impressive ordnance. Sonic cannons not only pack a punch--
Eat
nd waves,
Hulk!
These babies go to eleven!
--but their vibrations can give even the Hulk a monster headache.
POW!
VVM-VAAAAM
VVM-VAAAAM
Whoa! The Madrox twins' subwoofers could bring down the whole mountain!

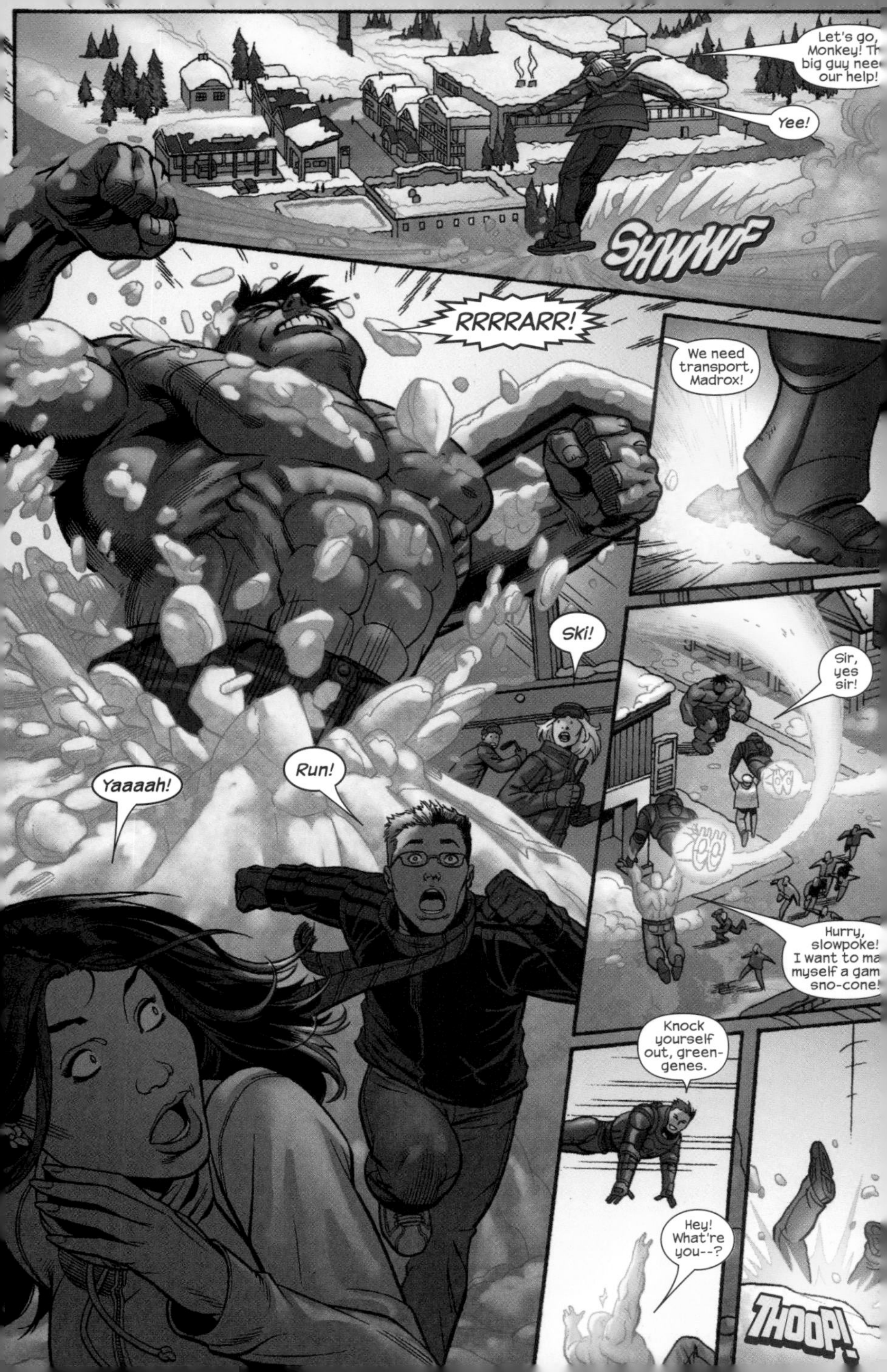

Let's go, Monkey! Th big guy nee our help!
Yee!
SHWWF
RRRRARR!
We need transport, Madrox!
Ski!
Sir, yes sir!
Yaaaah!
Run!
Hurry, slowpoke! I want to ma myself a gam sno-cone!
Knock yourself out, green-genes.
Hey! What're you--?
THOOP!

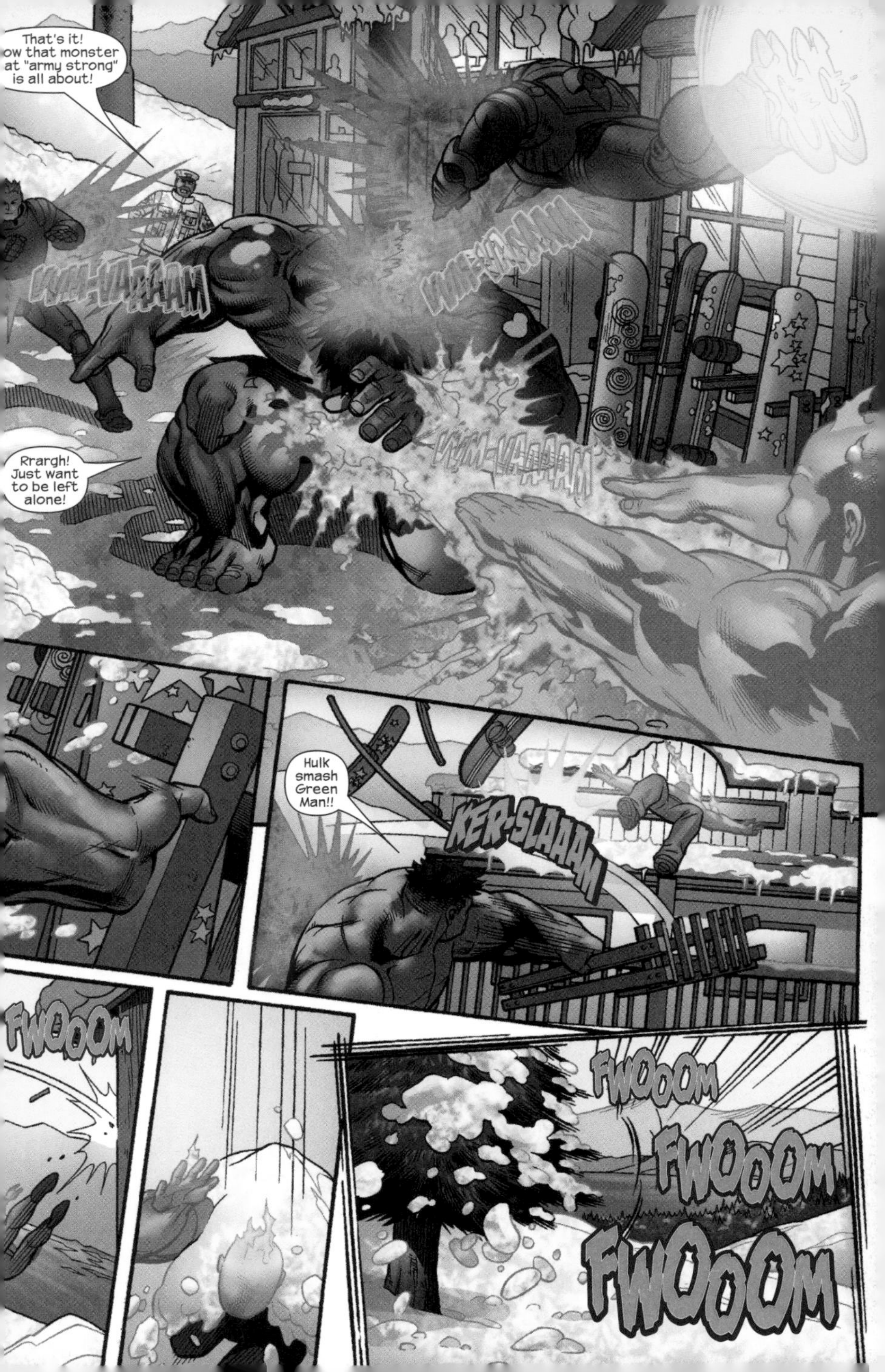
That's it!
ow that monster
at "army strong"
is all about!
Rrargh!
Just want
to be left
alone!
Hulk
smash
Green
Man!!
KER-SLAAAM
FWOOOM
FWOOOM
FWOOOM
FWOOOM

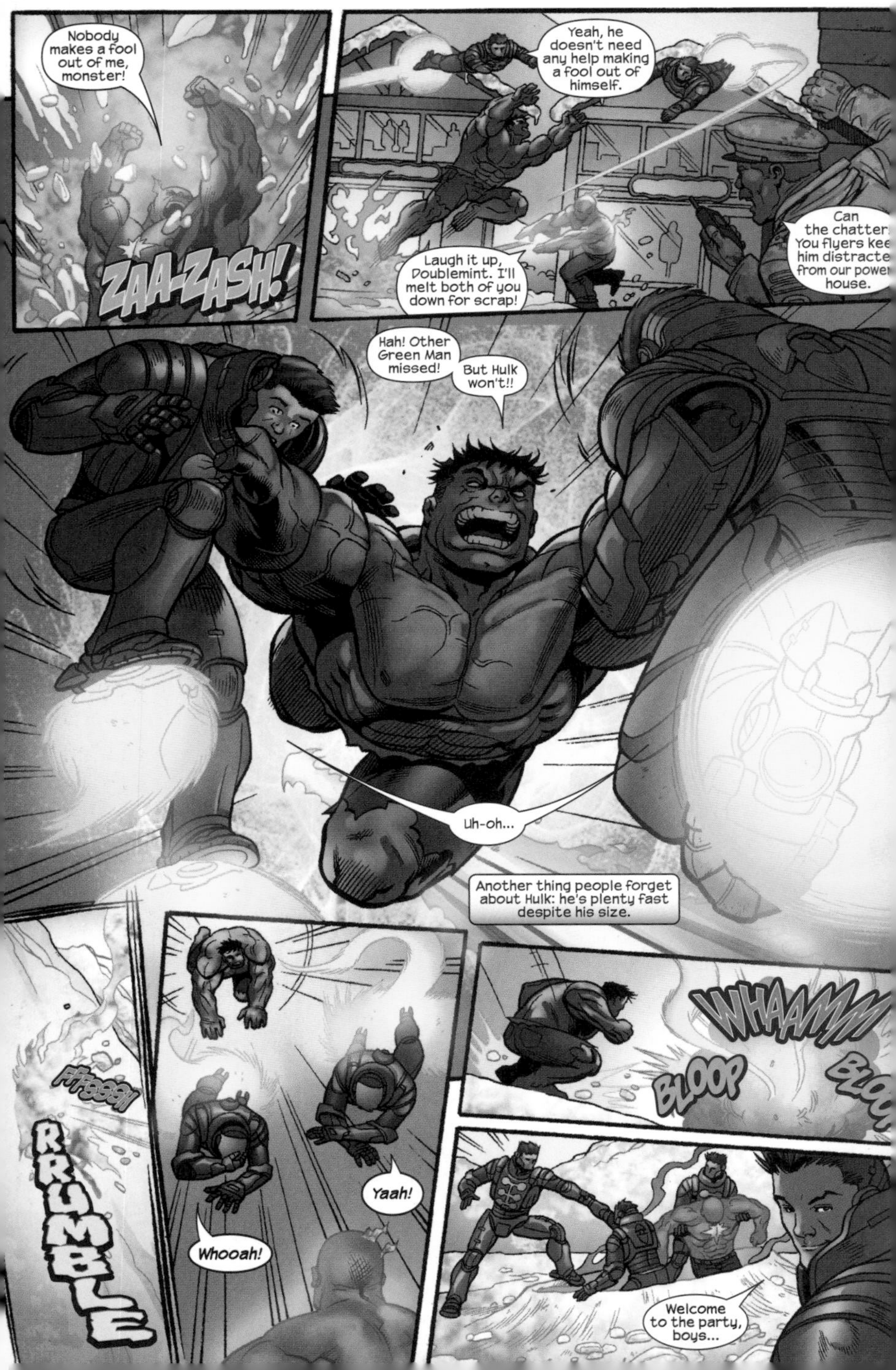
Nobody makes a fool out of me, monster!
ZAA-ZASH!
Yeah, he doesn't need any help making a fool out of himself.
Laugh it up, Doublemint. I'll melt both of you down for scrap!
Can the chatter! You flyers kee him distracte from our powe house.
Hah! Other Green Man missed!
But Hulk won't!!
Uh-oh...
Another thing people forget about Hulk: he's plenty fast despite his size.
FFSSSH
RRUMBLE
Yaah!
Whooah!
WHAAMM
BLOOP
BLOO
Welcome to the party, boys...

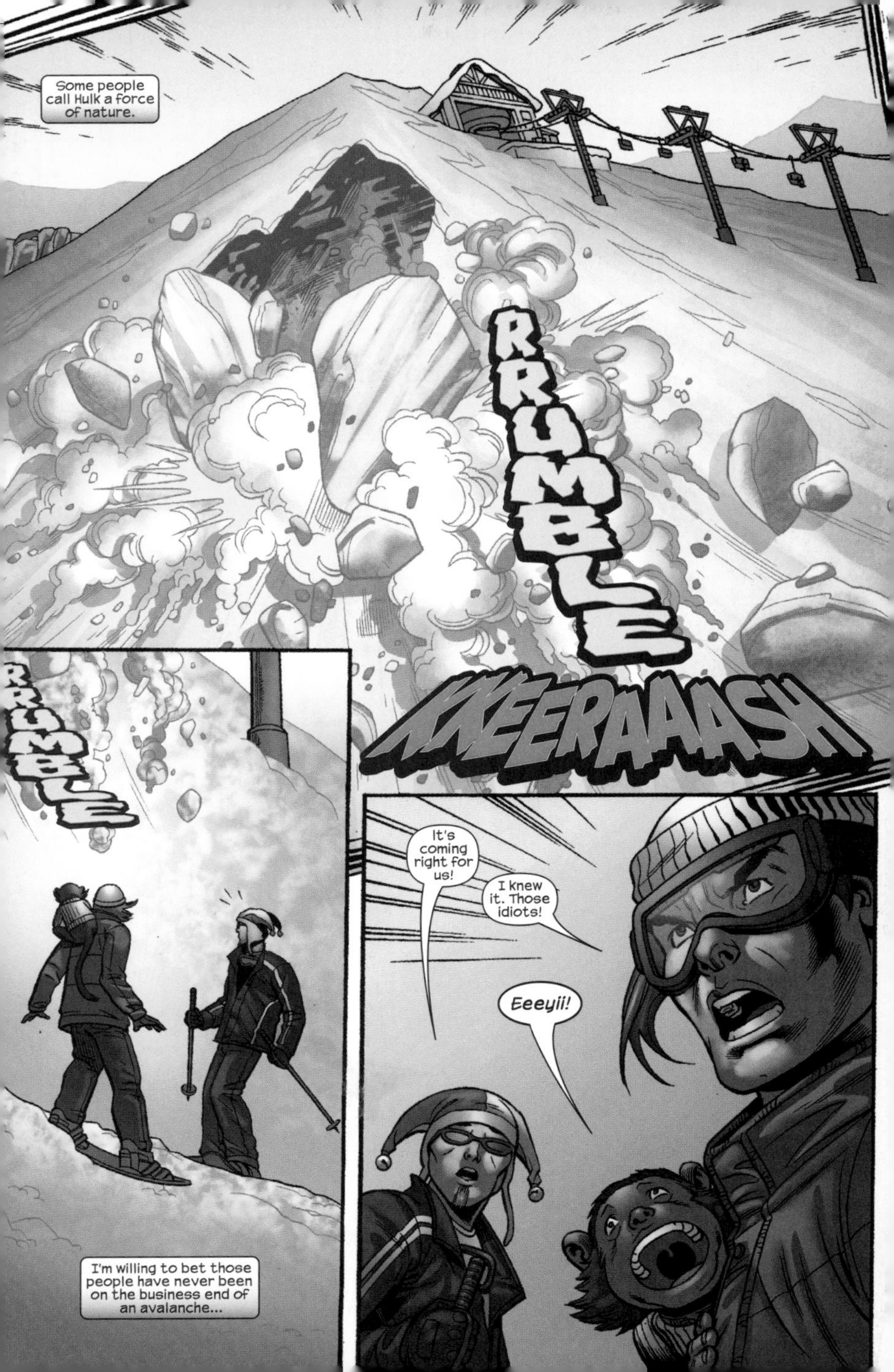
Some people call Hulk a force of nature.
RRUMBLE
KKEERAAASH
RRUMBLE
I'm willing to bet those people have never been on the business end of an avalanche...
It's coming right for us!
I knew it. Those idiots!
Eeeyii!

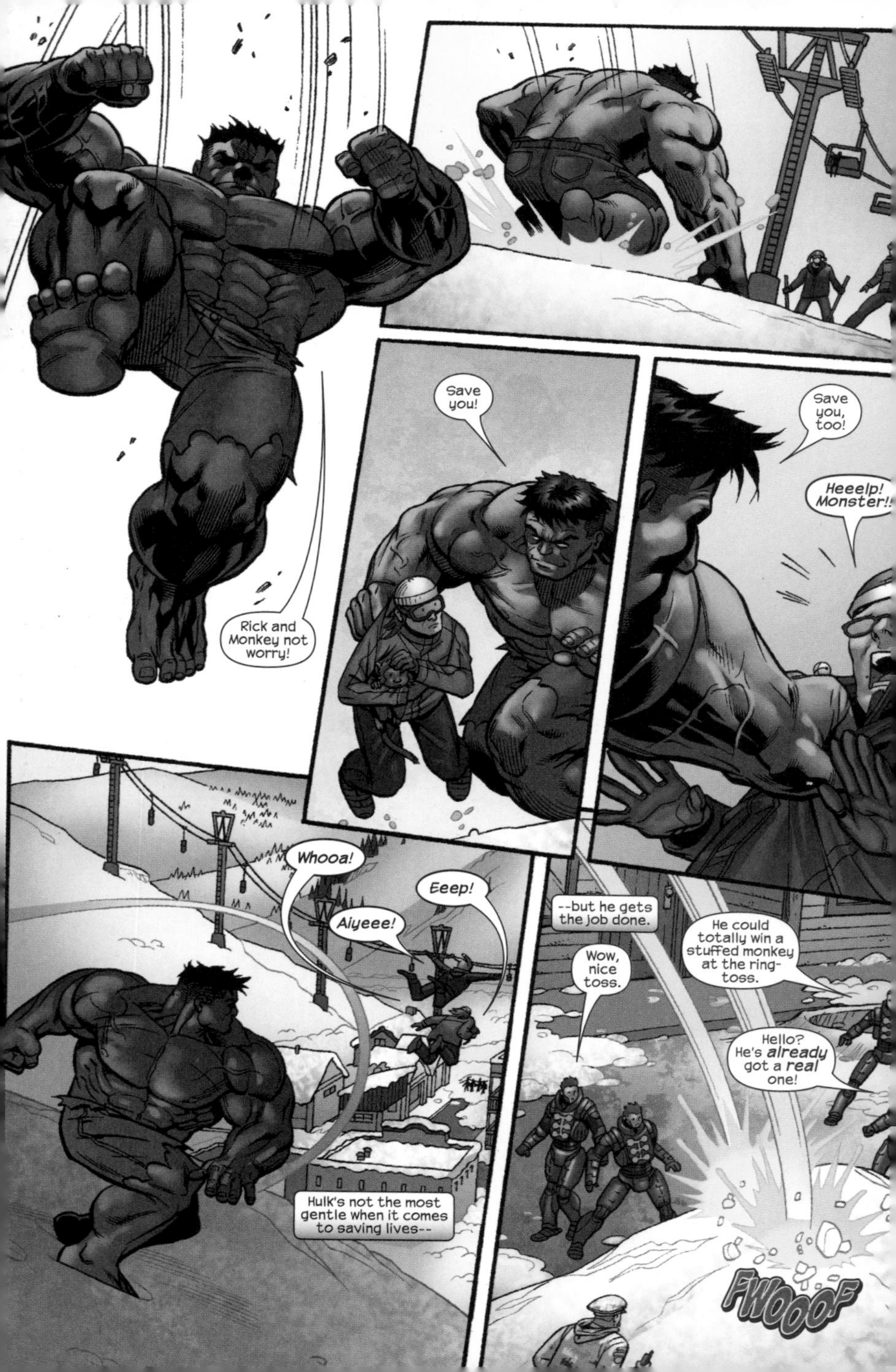

Rick and Monkey not worry!
Save you!
Save you, too!
Heeelp! Monster!!
Whooa!
Eeep!
Aiyeee!
Hulk's not the most gentle when it comes to saving lives--
--but he gets the job done.
Wow, nice toss.
He could totally win a stuffed monkey at the ring-toss.
Hello? He's already got a real one!
FWOOOF

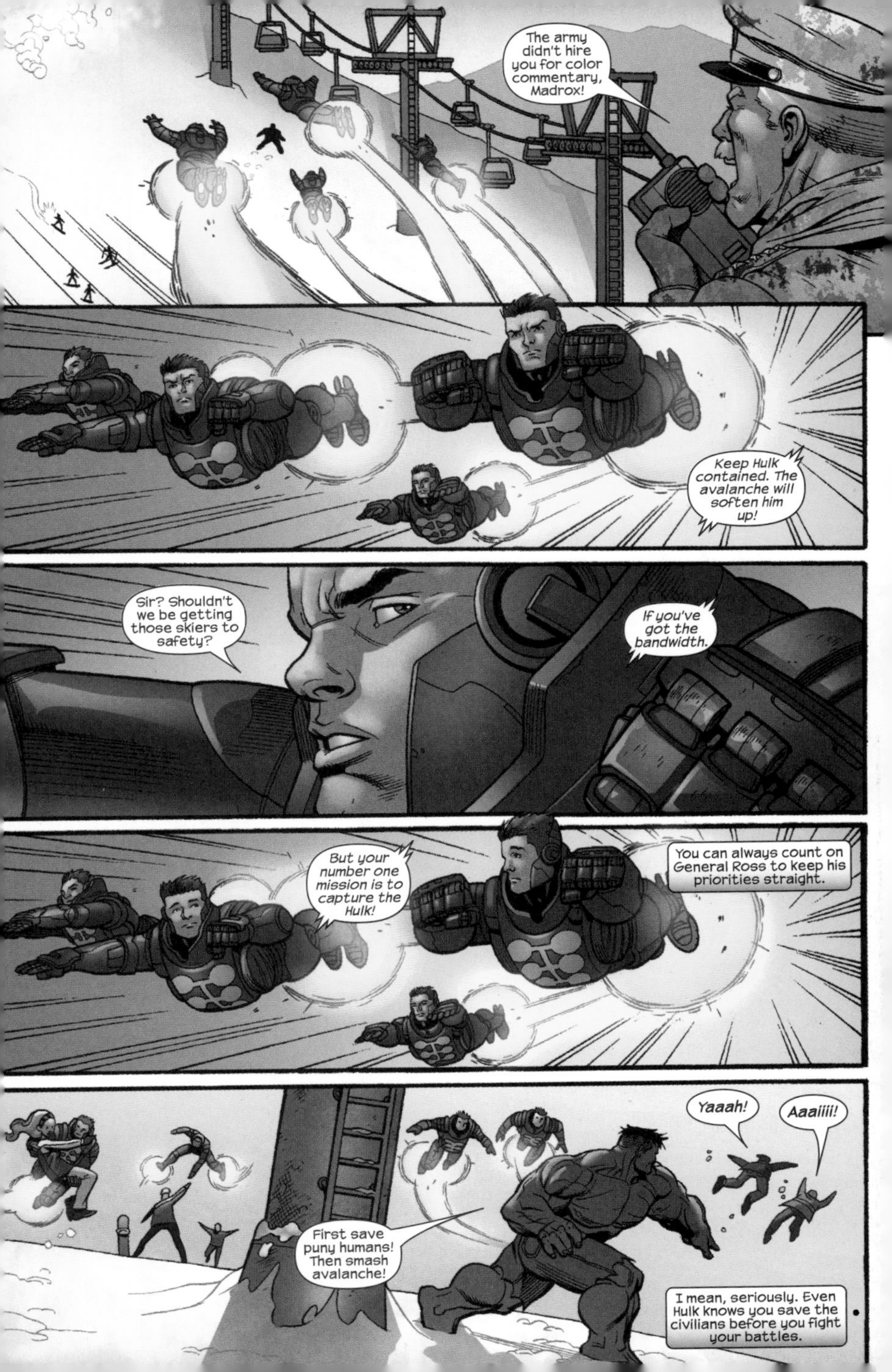
The army didn't hire you for color commentary, Madrox!
Keep Hulk contained. The avalanche will soften him up!
Sir? Shouldn't we be getting those skiers to safety?
If you've got the bandwidth.
But your number one mission is to capture the Hulk!
You can always count on General Ross to keep his priorities straight.
Yaaah!
Aaaiiii!
First save puny humans! Then smash avalanche!
I mean, seriously. Even Hulk knows you save the civilians before you fight your battles.

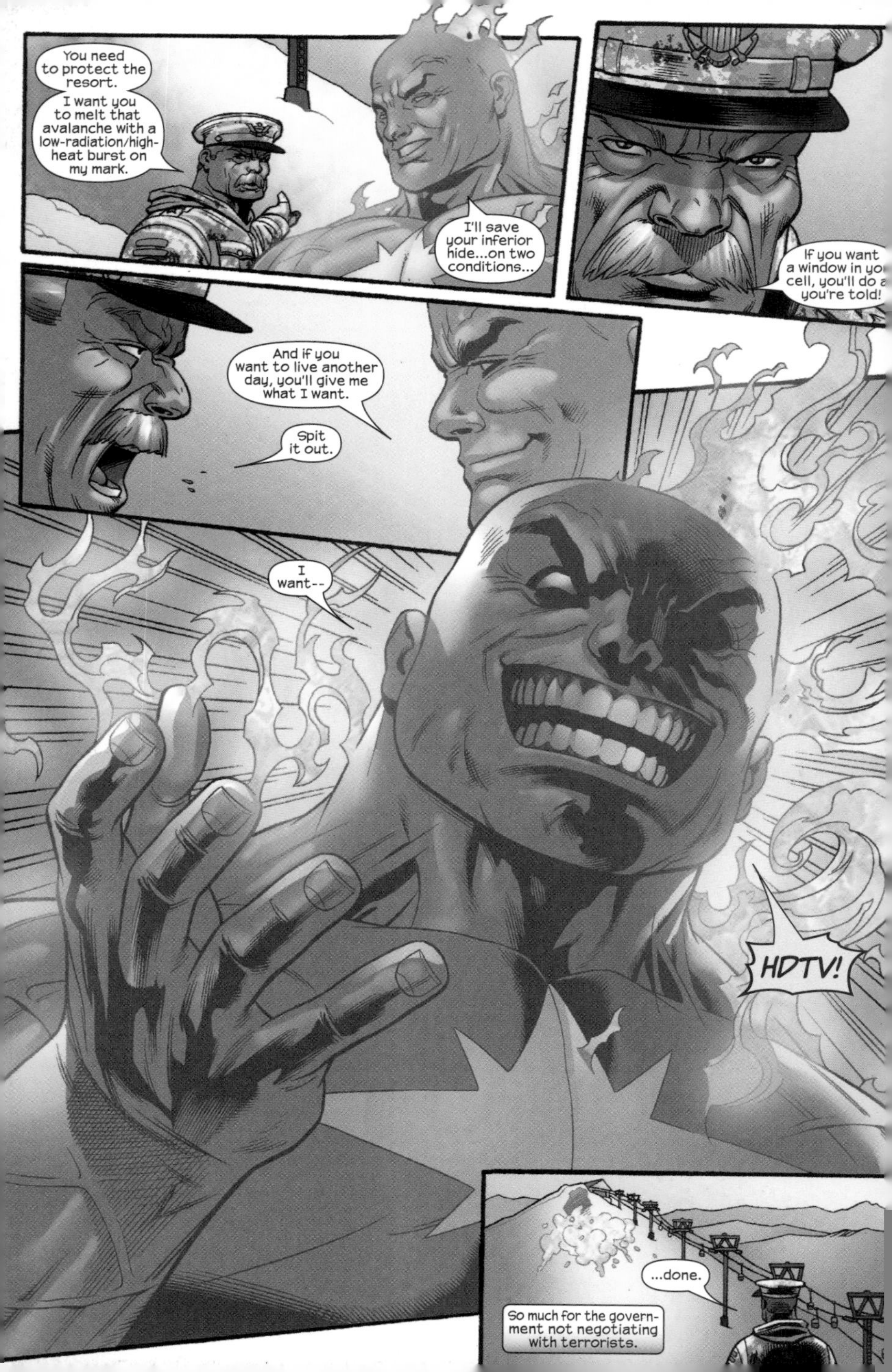
You need to protect the resort.
I want you to melt that avalanche with a low-radiation/high-heat burst on my mark.
I'll save your inferior hide...on two conditions...
If you want a window in yo cell, you'll do a you're told!
And if you want to live another day, you'll give me what I want.
Spit it out.
I want--
HDTV!
...done.
So much for the government not negotiating with terrorists.

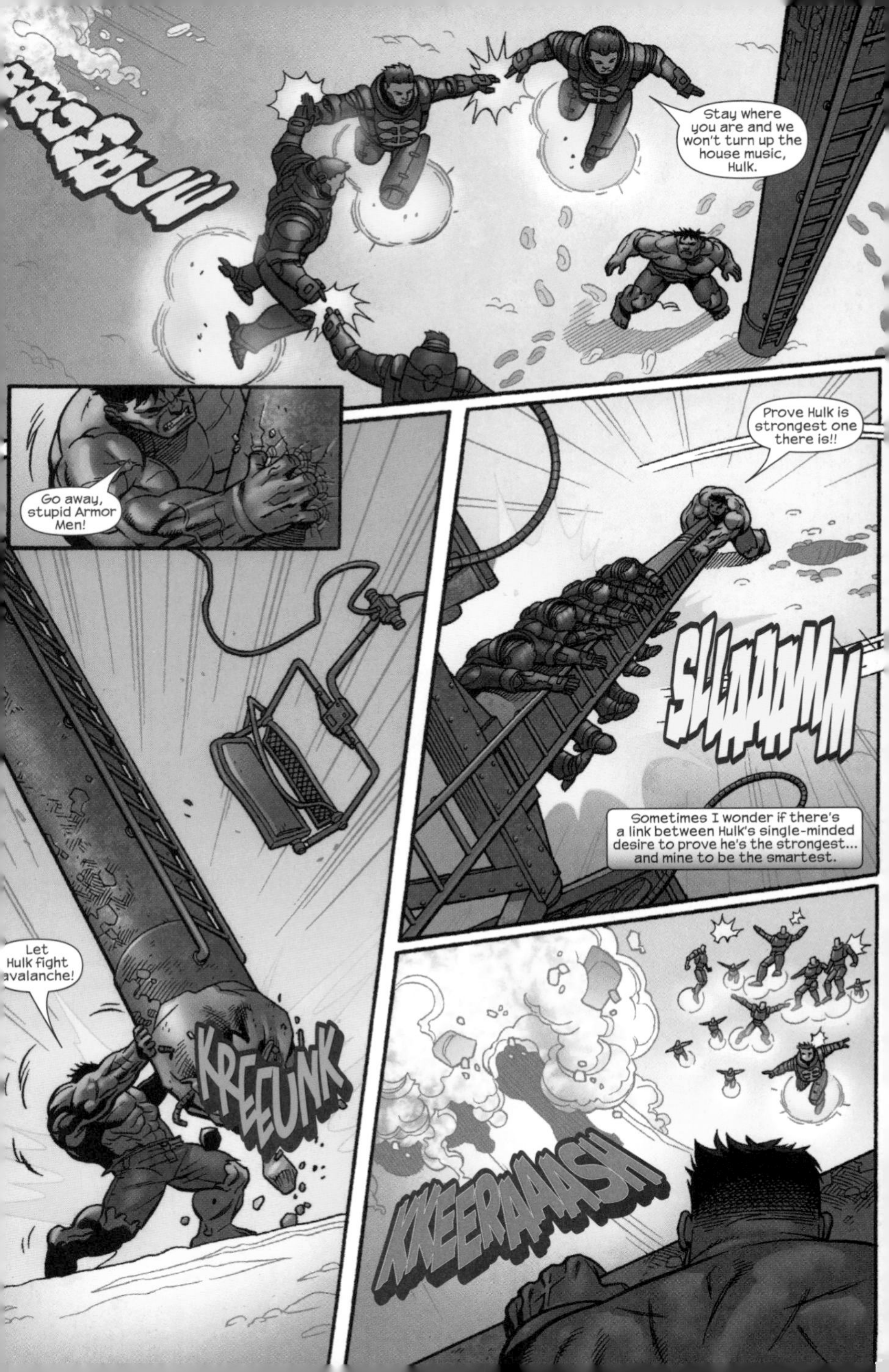
Stay where you are and we won't turn up the house music, Hulk.
Go away, stupid Armor Men!
Prove Hulk is strongest one there is!!
SLLAAMMM
Sometimes I wonder if there's a link between Hulk's single-minded desire to prove he's the strongest... and mine to be the smartest.
Let Hulk fight avalanche!
KREEUNK
KKEERAAASH

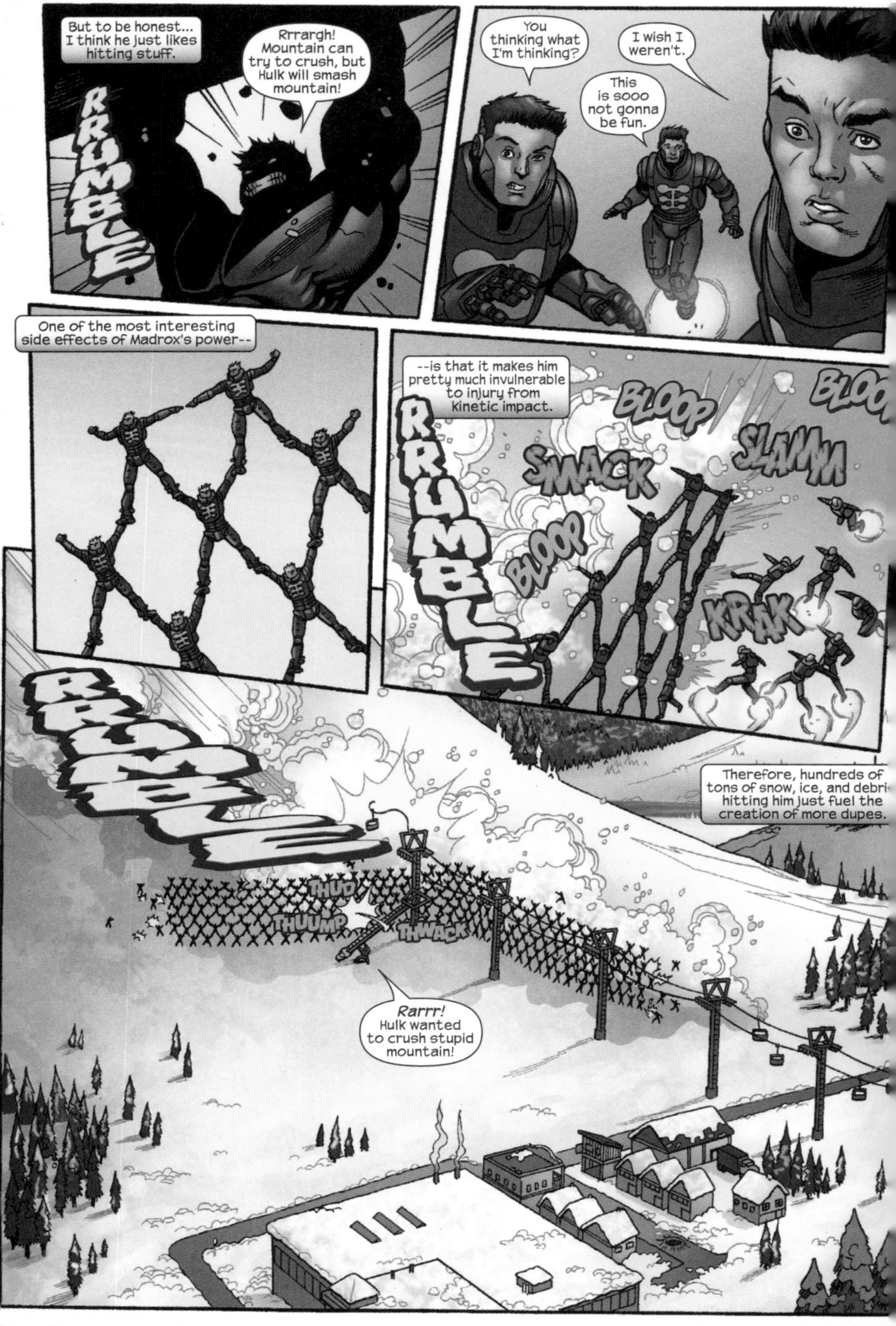
But to be honest... I think he just likes hitting stuff.
Rrrargh! Mountain can try to crush, but Hulk will smash mountain!
RRUMBLE
You thinking what I'm thinking?
I wish I weren't.
This is sooo not gonna be fun.
One of the most interesting side effects of Madrox's power--
--is that it makes him pretty much invulnerable to injury from kinetic impact.
RRUMBLE
BLOOP
BLOOP
SMACK
SLAMM
BLOOP
KRAK
RRUMBLE
Therefore, hundreds of tons of snow, ice, and debri hitting him just fuel the creation of more dupes.
THUD
THUUMP
THWACK
Rarrr! Hulk wanted to crush stupid mountain!

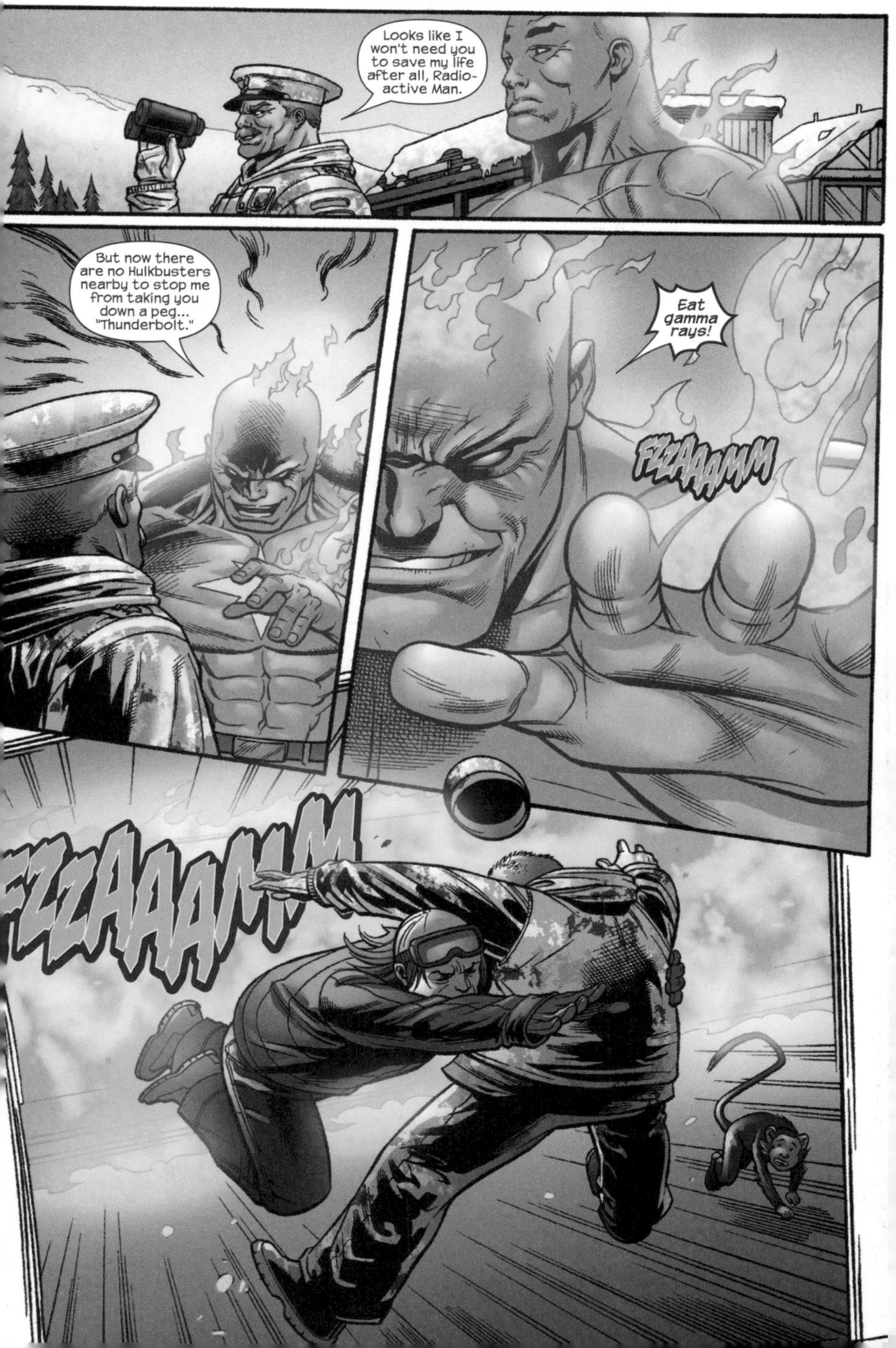
Looks like I won't need you to save my life after all, Radio-active Man.
But now there are no Hulkbusters nearby to stop me from taking you down a peg... "Thunderbolt."
Eat gamma rays!
FZZAAAMM
FZZAAAMM

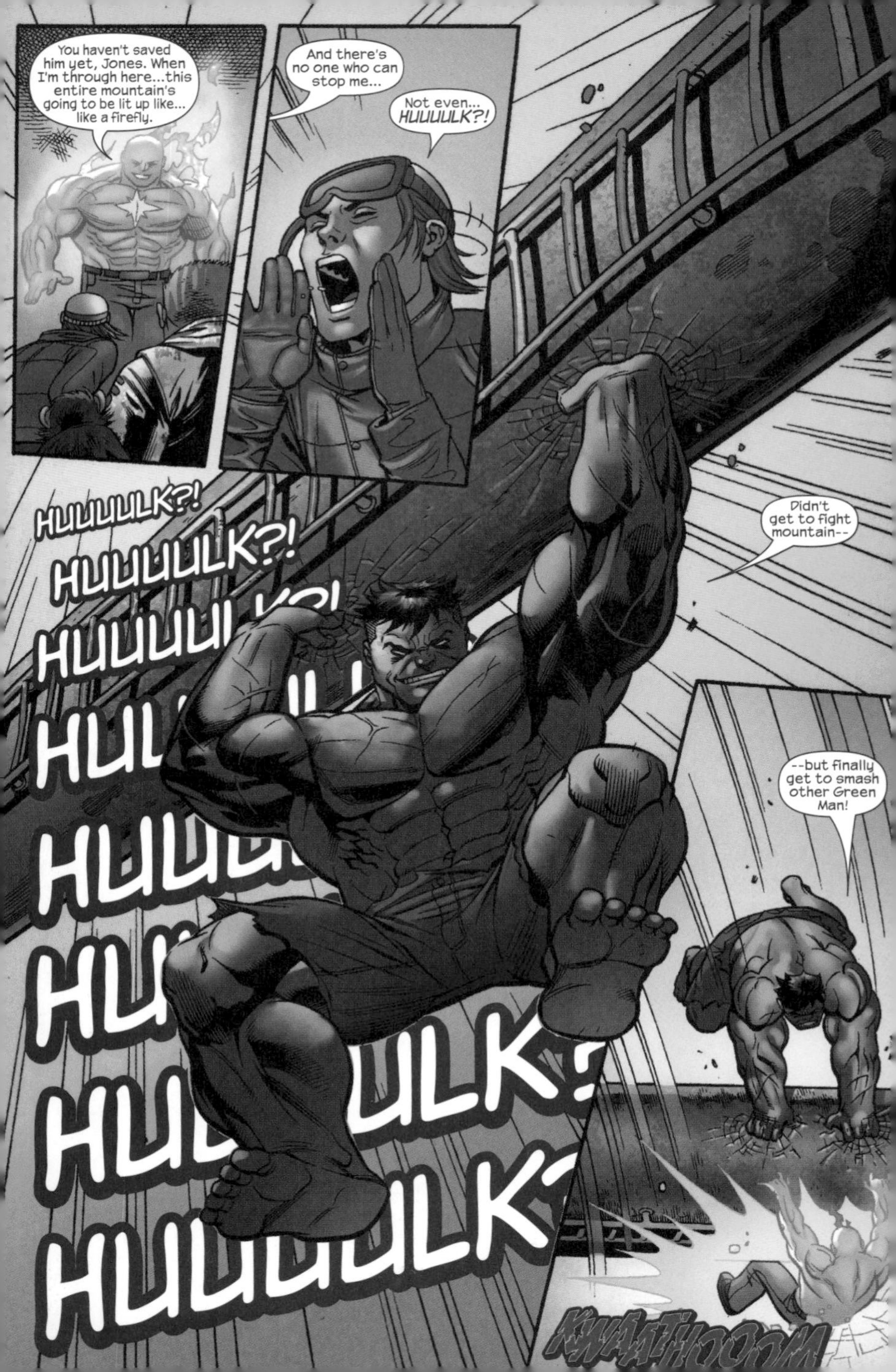
You haven't saved him yet, Jones. When I'm through here...this entire mountain's going to be lit up like... like a firefly.
And there's no one who can stop me...
Not even... HUUUULK?!
HUUUULK?!
HUUUULK?!
Didn't get to fight mountain--
--but finally get to smash other Green Man!
KWAATHOOOM

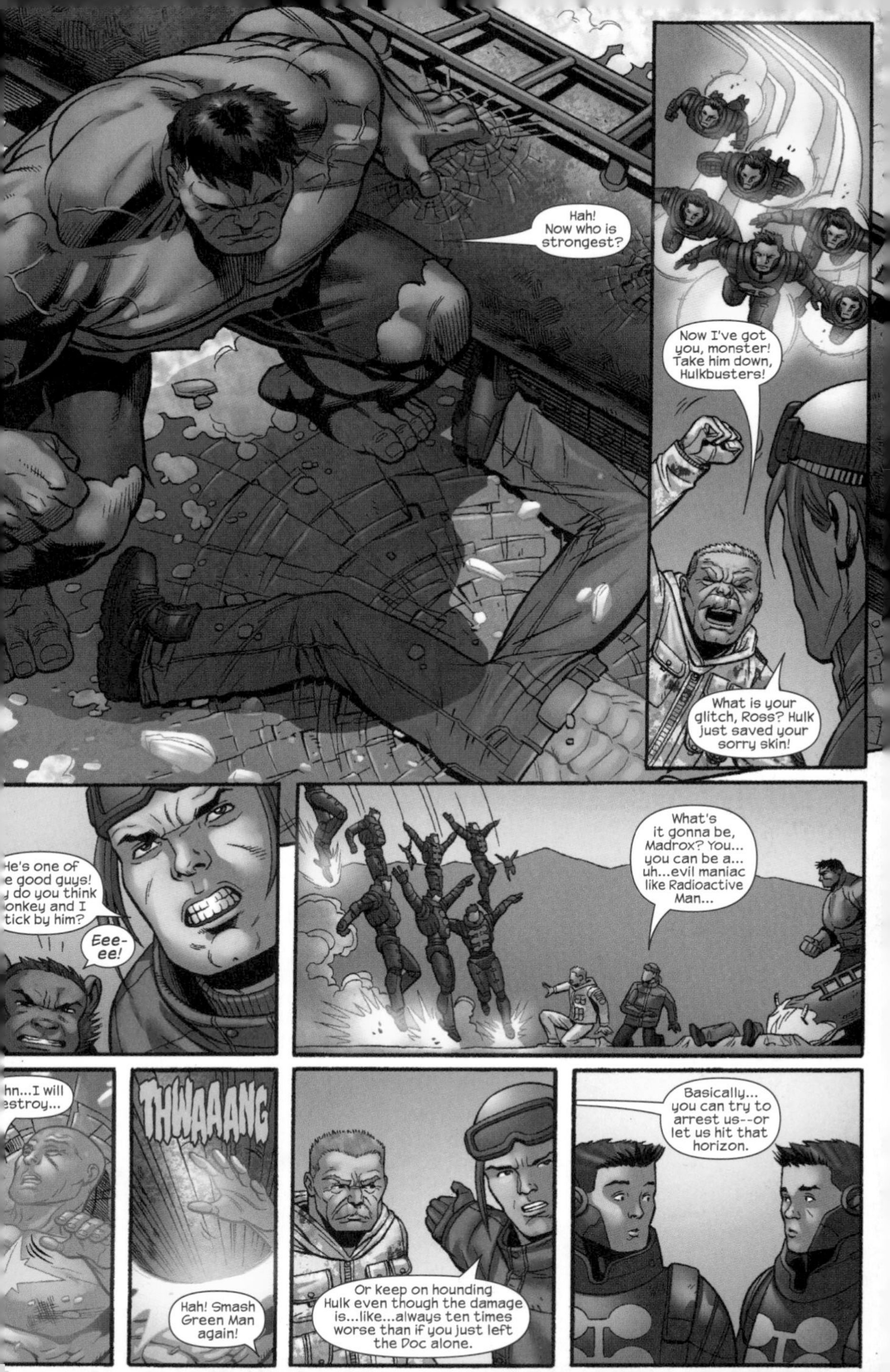
Hah! Now who is strongest?
Now I've got you, monster! Take him down, Hulkbusters!
What is your glitch, Ross? Hulk just saved your sorry skin!
He's one of e good guys! y do you think onkey and I tick by him?
Eee-ee!
What's it gonna be, Madrox? You... you can be a... uh...evil maniac like Radioactive Man...
hn...I will estroy...
THWAAANG
Hah! Smash Green Man again!
Or keep on hounding Hulk even though the damage is...like...always ten times worse than if you just left the Doc alone.
Basically... you can try to arrest us--or let us hit that horizon.

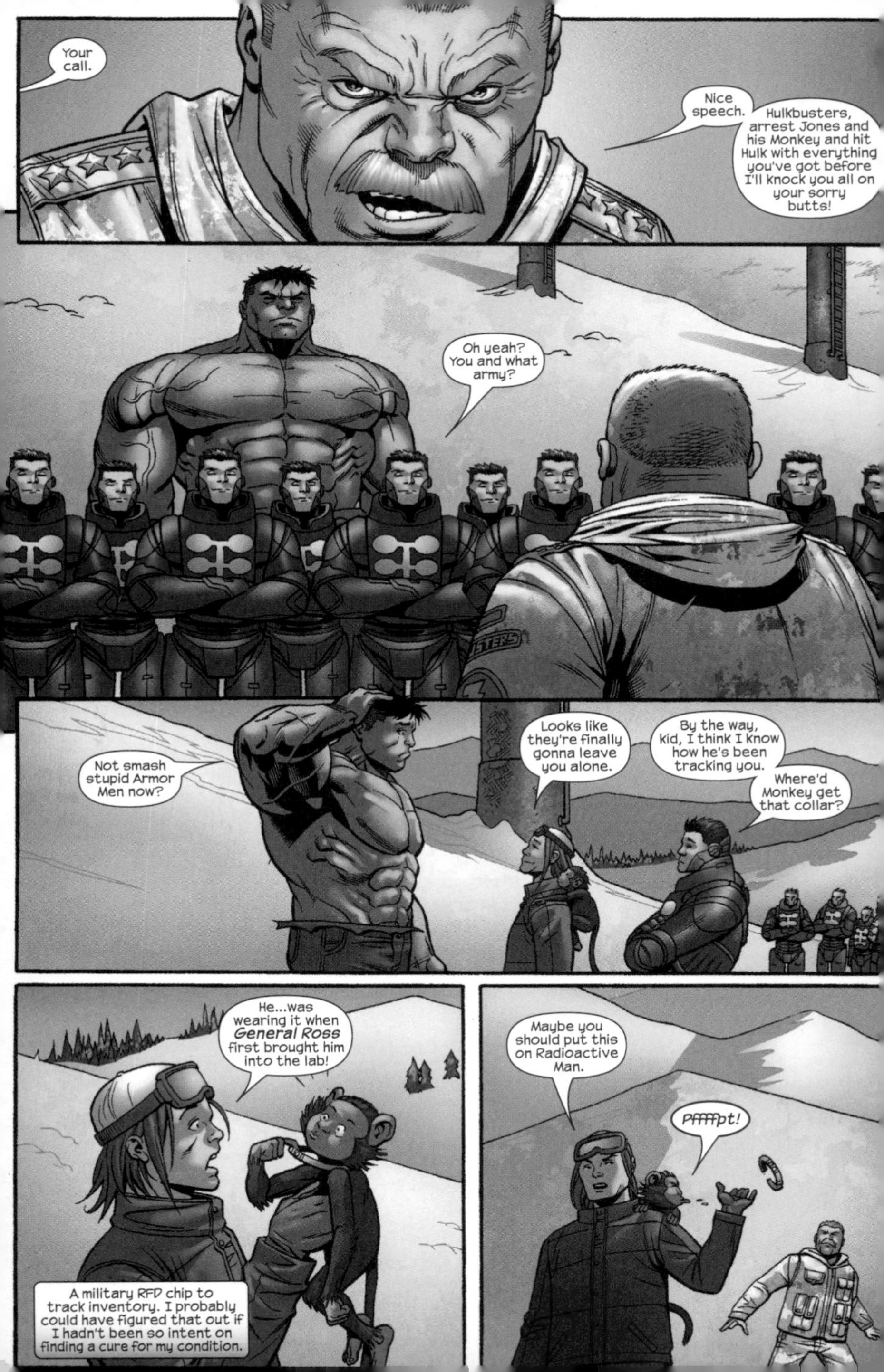
Your call.
Nice speech.
Hulkbusters, arrest Jones and his Monkey and hit Hulk with everything you've got before I'll knock you all on your sorry butts!
Oh yeah? You and what army?
Not smash stupid Armor Men now?
Looks like they're finally gonna leave you alone.
By the way, kid, I think I know how he's been tracking you.
Where'd Monkey get that collar?
He...was wearing it when *General Ross* first brought him into the lab!
A military RFD chip to track inventory. I probably could have figured that out if I hadn't been so intent on finding a cure for my condition.
Maybe you should put this on Radioactive Man.
Pffffpt!